Three Hunters

Random House New York

THREE HUNTERS

William Harrison

Library of Congress Cataloging-in-Publication Data
Harrison, William.
Three hunters.
I. Title.
PS3558.A672T47   1989   813'.54   88-43199
ISBN 0-394-57001-4

Manufactured in the United States of America
First American Edition

Cartography copyright © 1989 by Anita Karl / Jim Kemp
Book design by Lilly Langotsky

This book is dedicated to

WINONA CHESSMAN

*and my thanks also to Petal and David Allen,
Peter Beard, George Adamson, and other Kenyan hosts.
And to Merlee, again, who still travels with me.*

Although the places are real,
this is a work of fiction and all the characters
and events are imaginary.

Three Hunters

N

THE
SUDAN

ETHIOPIA

Miles
0   150
0   150
Kms.

AFRICA

Area
of Map

Trey's
Refugee
Camp

Lake
Turkana
(L. Rudolf)

Loiyangalani

Telekis
(Volcano)

UGANDA

Mt.
Elgon

Maralal

KENYA

SOMALIA

RIFT ESCARPMENT

Nakuru

Mt.
Kenya

Tree
Tops

Lake
Naivasha

Lake
Victoria

The
Mara

NAIROBI

LAMU

THE
SERENGETI

Mt.
Kilimanjaro

Tsavo

Mt.
Meru

Arusha

Mombassa

Indian
Ocean

TANZANIA

© A.Karl/J.Kemp, 1989

SAFARI:
Doctor Trey

She usually wore tight blue jeans low on her hips, frayed tennis shoes, and a stethoscope around her neck, its listening end tucked into a pocket of her loose khaki shirt. She was another American, a Californian with unruly amber hair and glowing skin, and she was trained and tough and always in control, except for that first time, when Lucien met her in Nairobi.

She was screaming at a small black lieutenant, who had promised her a lorry so that she could haul a ton of supplies to her refugees at the lake. "There's *no* food, *no* medicine, *no* supervisors at my camp!" She was near tears. "You told me everything would be ready!"

"One week," the little army officer told her. "Wait in Nairobi one week. Stay in very nice hotel and take nice baths, then our lorry will come back from Mombasa. Or, madam, you could hire a lorry from Hertz."

"There's no damn money for hired lorries!"

Lucien strolled over and stood beside them. The Red Cross depot was another of those tin-roofed warehouses near the market at the end of Biashara Street. Outside its doors hundreds of beggars and wayfarers strolled around aimlessly and, beyond, the litter of market stalls looked like a major catastrophe: flies swarming over the meat and vegetables, the poor vendors crying out as if they were in pain, gaunt children playing in the rubble. A stranger might imagine that the Red Cross had rightfully set itself down in a disaster zone. The army officer and his cousin, the dispatcher, were the indifferent guardians of all the depot's bandages, bottles, tins, and crates.

Lucien felt mildly sorry for the officer, who had to bear another white woman's complaints with the usual lack of authority. But then, she was the sort of woman for whom men usually did elaborate favors.

"Can I help?" he asked twice, but she was busy shouting and didn't hear him. "I've got an old lorry you can use," he finally offered, and she turned to acknowledge him at last.

She had deep green eyes.

"Lucien Cavenaugh," he said. "Where exactly do you want to go?"

"Lake Turkana." That was like saying the far side of the moon, because the old Cavenaugh lorry wasn't up to much. But, god, that voice. The look of her.

"South end of the lake?"

"No, up north."

He admitted that the lorry did need a bit of work. "A fan belt. Couple of new tires. Maybe some tuning up." It was even worse than that: the family lorry was perched on cement blocks behind the safari store, rusted out, with a motor that sounded like gravel turning in a metal bucket.

She stared at him, saying nothing.

"I can have it ready to go by, say, tomorrow afternoon," he

went on, figuring wildly. "We could be on our way after that, if it suited you."

"I'm Dr. Trey Nichols," she said with an official smile, extending her hand. They touched for the first time.

Lucien took her home that evening. For several hours they were alone in the old house, in the Muthiaga district of Nairobi: the den filled with mounted heads, guns, and hunting gear—stories in each item and trophy. The piano in the sitting room: a story. The rugs in the foyer: more stories. He felt amazed to see her among the family things, strangely excited and unbelievably aroused.

He had gone to the depot, he told her, to pay for a delivery of supplies to his mother's beloved charity, an orphanage out in Barton Valley. His mother was spending several days there as a volunteer worker, and his father was off somewhere, and his brother didn't live here anymore, and, yes, it certainly was a big house, out of repair, a bit musty, and they had it all to themselves, glad to be of help, no trouble at all.

While she took a bath, he rattled around the kitchen preparing supper: baked chicken, salad, rice, a bottle of wine. Later, as they ate, he asked about her work. She said she had come to the refugee camp through a British agency and one by one all the Kenyan supervisors had abandoned the project, so that she had inherited sole responsibility.

"And you?"

He explained that these days he was a merchant, the owner and operator of a safari outfitting store. But in the old days, in *zamani*, he told her, he had been a professional hunter with his father and brother.

"Now there's no more big-game hunting," he sighed. "It was banned in Kenya, so that's all long ago."

"I suppose I'm having dinner with a famous white hunter," she said, smiling, and he thought he detected a flirtation in her voice.

"My father's Chili Cavenaugh," he said, as if she might have known the name. "In his day, he was the best. He's the famous one."

"Sorry," she said, "but I don't know much about anything here except for the lake." She ate the chicken with her fingers, turning a drumstick and taking a bite off it with that wonderful mouth.

"He was the first American who had a professional license in these parts," Lucien told her, but he wanted to skip over this polite history. He felt like saying, look, you're in the infamous Cavenaugh house, you may not know it or understand, but the game's on, it's every man for himself around here, and every woman. But instead he said, "When my brother and I hunted with my father, we made good money. After the hunting ended, I stayed with the store. My brother flies his plane, taking tourists around. Mostly photographic safaris. In the old days they called him Mfifo—which, loosely interpreted, means Crazy Brave."

He knew he was talking on and on. She smiled and lifted an eyebrow ever so slightly, and he tried to read the signal, wanting it to mean, yes, there's something between us, I like you, we're all predators here.

"And what did they call you?"

"Just Lucien. No nicknames."

"I'll have to meet your father and brother someday."

"Someday maybe you will. We've all fallen out now."

"Oh? What went wrong?"

"Maybe the times. When the hunting ended, all the old hunters got out of sorts. I'm sure that's it."

She looked at him over the rim of her wineglass. He studied her green eyes as she yawned.

"You're tired," he said.

"It's the wine and the altitude in Nairobi," she offered.

"C'mon, I'll show you where you sleep."

As he led her upstairs, he was aware of his shortness of breath, of the blood pulsing around the ends of his fingers. He was a bachelor, over forty, experienced, and this was ridiculous: he fumbled for words, trying to think of something halfway intelligent to say, some overture. Something.

"Mind if I borrow one of these old shirts?" she asked, peering into his brother's closet of discarded clothes beside the bed.

"Take anything you want. And I suppose I'll turn in, too." Awkward beyond hope, he found himself backing out of the room. "I'll get the lorry repaired and we'll be on our way."

"Sure, sounds fine."

"If we reach Maralal by nightfall, we'll stay in the lodge."

"Good, that's fine."

"Or if I can't get the lorry repaired, we'll leave day after tomorrow. Or soon, anyway."

"Whatever," she agreed, and he was still backing away.

"Anything you need, just call me."

"Thanks again," she said, returning his weak smile with a bright one of her own. "You've been wonderful."

He bumped lightly into the door frame, feeling idiotic with every word and movement.

Then he lay in bed, unable to sleep as the hours ticked away toward midnight. The moon came up, filling the room with its aching glow. In the middle of the night he got out of bed, went softly into the hallway, and listened, but heard only the faraway barking of a dog. He returned and paced back and forth across a shaft of moonlight on the carpet. He felt low and common and wonderful, like an animal in heat. It was the old, giddy, whimsical Cavenaugh lust.

Exhausted, he finally moved down the corridor toward her door. It was slightly open. He edged forward, crazily, stupidly, in spite of himself, just wanting a glimpse of her.

Lucien had never done anything like this, not ever: he was the gentleman of the family, the one who read books and played piano, the clearheaded one, the businessman. Yet he closed his eyes and slipped inside her room. Addled, he tried to stay rational, inventing things he could say to her if she woke up.

The moonglow created a creamy shadow over by the bed, outlining the white sheets in the darkness of the room. Sure, he knew it: standing there, his body sweating in the old delirium, he was no better than his rutting father and brother. He took another step, closing and opening his eyes slowly so they'd adjust to the darkness. He wanted to sit down on the bed and lift her in his arms. But in his panic an irony grew: his stupidity amused him, he became his own ridiculous image, and he moved silently and quickly back to the hallway.

The next day Lucien spent hundreds of pounds on the lorry and gave the clerks at the store a series of instructions he knew they'd never obey. In the afternoon—with the lorry patched and primed and only half ready for such a safari—he loaded Trey's supplies, made room for her in the front seat beside him, and drove north toward the lake.

She distracted him, making him a poor driver. The gears announced their arrival at every hill and turn.

On the rim of the Rift Escarpment in the monsoon seasons the wind blows up wet and cold, so the drive that day was dark and rainy and a chilled dampness seeped into their clothes and skin. Along the cliffside road where the mists parted they could look out over hundreds of miles of primeval distance, one of the great vistas of Africa: this enormous valley slashed through the eastern continent. Then the mists would come back, obscuring the road ahead of them at times, and they would shiver in the open lorry and ration out the hot coffee from the thermos Lucien had brought along.

The lorry was so noisy that they didn't talk as much as he wanted to.

These were bleak parts up here on the escarpment: nature turned men into solitary wanderers in this high, unfriendly landscape. The monsoon rains made the feeling worse: the traveler often folded in on himself, burrowing down into his own skin for psychic warmth. Lucien had felt this grim, cold solitude quite a few times.

He occasionally glanced at Trey and began thinking ahead to the lodge: maybe they'd get drunk, say the magic phrases, and bed each other down. Sex was the great solace here: the old sensuality of the highlands. From the very first, Western repressions fell away and the lonely land with its immense horizons invited white men into release. In the old days, in *zamani*, the white men—like all the other nomads who had come before them—found their consolation between the legs of the native girls, and the old excitement—maybe it was the high, thin air here at the equator—still lurked around.

Lucien's own loneliness tugged at him, too. A bewildering, nameless thing, lately. His usual solution, like his father's and his brother's, had always been to fuck himself out of the doldrums, but that hadn't worked for some time now. And women, after all, had been the problem and seldom part of anybody's solution. Their women had come between them—his mother, wives, girlfriends, and the whole female array.

He could go off on some wild-haired safari, of course: the more risk, the better. He could stay out on the savannahs until his supplies were gone. Unarmed, he could move in too close to the rhino. He could drink the waters from strange rivers. He could open himself recklessly to the elements, turning his recklessness back into melancholy as if to say, here, shit, kill me; death is the final loneliness. I give up. Death, after all, was an intoxicant that got into a man's bloodstream. All the old hunters knew it.

But risk was just another diversion. Lucien knew that, too.

Again, he glanced over at Trey and found her watching him.

Forty miles from Maralal the lorry's right rear tire went out. Lucien sat in the red mud of the road and changed it as she watched from under an old poncho. Her eyes were green, like the rain.

"I see you lashed the spare tires to the outside, so you could get to them," she observed as he worked.

He turned the lug wrench and answered with a grunt.

"I like a man who thinks ahead."

"I like someone who appreciates it," he told her.

Two hours later they were lost. He climbed an outcropping of rock, shielded his eyes from the drizzle, and looked for a road in the desolate distance.

"Our road just ended," she said.

"Happens all the time up here. But we'll find it again. I know Maralal's over that way."

They doubled back, bumping along nullahs and rocky paths until they found the road again and went another direction.

She tried to discuss her problems at the camp. Although the lorry was noisier than ever, he was happy to have her raised voice. She couldn't convice the refugees, she said, to dig sanitation ditches. "When I tell them about cholera, they won't listen. They pay me no attention lately."

"When we get there, we'll bribe them," he replied. "We have all the food and medicine. I'll see that they start digging."

She gave him a spectacular smile.

After a few more minutes she said, "I watched you come into my room last night."

He pretended he didn't quite hear.

"You came to my bed in the middle of the night. You just stood there. I thought you were going to do or say something."

He gripped the wheel, grateful for the rattles and bumps.

"I couldn't sleep either," she went on. "So I was lying there awake when you came in. Then I *really* couldn't sleep. Later—it must have been an hour or more—I got up and went into your room. But you were sound asleep."

"You did that?"

"Your mouth falls open a bit when you're sleeping."

"Why'd you come into my room?" he asked, more loudly than he meant to.

"The same reason you came into mine," she answered.

The Maralal Lodge, perched on the north rim of the Escarpment, consisted of a main building and a few rough cottages spread out over several highland acres. The dining-room windows overlooked a waterhole where buffalo, gazelle, zebra, warthogs, and assorted birds came to drink. This was the last tourist stop for thousands of miles, for beyond Maralal the land fell off into the flats where Lake Turkana, once part of the Nile system, spread itself out against the harsh lowland deserts of

Ethiopia, the Sudan, and Egypt, all the way to Cairo. So this was the last cool monsoon evening; tomorrow there would be only the mystic heat.

They took a single cottage—with a small amount of shuffling and looking the other way at the registration desk while Lucien signed in. The dining room was about to close for the evening, so they hurried in for a meal, but neither of them ate much. They shared a bottle of wine and he thought of placing his hand over hers, but didn't. A warm delirium filled him, and he knew he was probably giving her the old, dumb, cow-eyed, romantic stare. That particular gaze was familiar enough: he had seen it on his father's face, on his brother's and he probably wore it, too. The lover's gawk. The Cavenaugh drool. He hated it, but there it was.

"Say what you would most like to have happened last night," she prompted him.

"When I came into your room?"

"That's right."

"I would've liked—hm, for you to say something dirty."

"A nice vulgar invitation, you mean?"

"Exactly."

"Like, oh, get in this bed and get between my legs?"

"Something worse than that," he said, and they looked at each other over the empty bottle.

"I like you," she said, laughing. "What do you want me to wear to bed tonight?"

"Wear to bed?"

"It's going to be a cold night. I have to sleep in something warm. I still have that shirt I took out of the closet at your house."

"No, that's my brother's shirt. Just wear your stethoscope."

"You *are* a dirty boy," she said.

The next morning, exhausted and satisfied, they started out toward the lake again. He was in love, but the day's heat drove the gentleness out of him. A kind of desperation came over them as they sweated through their clothes. Their bodies ached both from lovemaking and the heaving lorry ride. Soon the roadbeds filled up with reddish volcanic stones the size of footballs—or, worse, boulders they had to steer around as the lorry's load shifted dangerously.

She asked him to talk about his family, about the old days, anything to occupy their thoughts during this ordeal.

ZAMANI:
Point-Blank

When his two sons hunted with him, Chili Cavenaugh taught them to wait until the last possible moment before pulling the trigger.

"Wait," Lucien remembered him telling them. "Wait until the cat makes its final leap. Or until the buffalo lowers its head in the final charge. Until there's nothing in front of you except your quarry and until, by god, you just can't miss!"

It was their style and their brave private system.

With clients on safari or in the bars with Chili's cronies the brothers learned to laugh about it and say, well, see, we're cowards, that's the thing, and we don't want to miss a shot at fifty yards or more, do we? No, hell no, we don't want to be standing there with empty guns, we'd get mauled or trampled for sure, so we just do what Chili says, we wait, we hold our aim, and shoot point-blank.

"Saves ammunition, too," Coke always added.

There was a lot of laughter in the bars about how the Cavenaughs hunted, about who they were and what they did, and about their women. As Lucien would finally come to think of it, the women always seemed to matter most.

Women were always their real quarry. It was something Lucien could have told Trey during the hot journey along the eastern shore of the lake, but for the time being he said something else.

Chili, his father, came to East Africa just after World War I, a farm boy from Arkansas, armed and eager, handsome, full of drawl and laughter. The British settlers were just then devising a system for licensing professional hunters, and Chili contrived to join them: a misfit, a dirtwater country boy, never dressed properly whether out in the bush or at afternoon tea, but brave as any of them. He took clients on safaris for fifty years, until big-game hunting was finished. When the hunting closed, after Chili had officially retired, when his son Coke had become just another pilot flying tourists here and there, when Lucien was just a merchant, when *zamani* was gone for good, then Lucien would be left to know and understand what nobody else would: that the lovers, wives and girlfriends were the real Cavenaugh legacy, and that their history of marriages, buffoonery and petty lust somehow counted for more than all their trophies and raw bravery.

Trey heard some of this on the lorry ride, but not all.

When Lucien and Coke were very young they became their father's safari team. He was already renowned with women and famous for getting his clients big trophies; Coke was quickly known as Mfifo; Lucien was respected by everyone who knew them, as competent in the bush as either his father or older brother, if not as flashy, and the one who provided the real camp for clients because Chili and Coke seldom thought about food, liquor, pillows, rainwear, tools, cooking pots, or any other amenity of the evening. They were all energy and ammunition. So

Lucien became the unofficial outfitter, and their business thrived because their clients loved the thrill of the hunt and also cups of warm tea, real mattresses, and afterward a nip of brandy. In time, the family opened the best outfitting store in Nairobi; in further time, Lucien evolved into citizen, reader of books, investor, and, with Audrey, a patron of the arts and charities. Coke referred to him as the civilized one, meaning it as an insult.

Yet Lucien always hunted well. He could stand before a charge, he could wait, he could keep his finger steady on the trigger as long as anyone else. It was his pride, the same as theirs, and he never missed, never once, and never blinked.

But as he became the keeper of the safari camp and, later, the storekeeper, there came a deep change in that division of labor: he was no longer quite one of them. The knowledge of this burrowed into him at times, and Chili and Coke tended to forget how brave and efficient Lucien had been. He often sensed that they regarded him—and he felt this keenly in the later years— as someone who never quite held his ground.

There was a moment he remembered well. He was fifteen years old. He took a lion charge, waiting, Chili out of range and useless, the client frozen with fear and unable to raise his rifle, and Lucien waited forever, then fired. The shot ripped out the lion's heart and lungs in the final leap, but its momentum carried it forward so that it knocked Lucien down.

They pulled the dead lion off him.

"Look at you," Coke said. "Your hands are shaking! It's a wonder you hit the damn thing with your hands doing that!"

He said it in front of the client and Chili. And giving him no credit, they laughed. Chili, too. He felt they ought to be pounding his back and congratulating him, but there was just this hearty, nervous, male laughter—the sort that often comes after a close call, yet he was somehow the butt of it.

All right, he was afraid. His breath came short as the lion loped forward out of its cover. But wasn't Coke afraid, too? And wasn't the great Chili himself? And wasn't that the point of it all: one entered into peril, one went on the dangerous hunt, one went to the edge of oneself—all those soft and witless clients included—in order to feel this. Nothing unnatural or wrong in fear. That's what you went for: the blood rising, the singing nerves, the pulse going crazy.

"My hands weren't shaking before I shot him," Lucien had argued. "You saw what happened."

"You lucked out," Coke accused him. "Look at you!"

Later, it seemed, his father and brother wanted him to be the coward of the family. Was it part of their vanity? It seemed to be, plainly. They wanted him different and set apart. They wanted him to be Audrey's boy, the camp attendant, the store-keeper, the family accountant, the other half, and they spoke of him in this way, often kidding him to his face and talking about him, he knew, behind his back.

He thought at times, come on, it isn't as if the three of us live in constant peril like mythical adventurers. We live mundane lives on the whole—city lives. For years Chili existed in a fixed domestic pattern around the house and downtown: coffee and newspapers on the back porch with Audrey in the mornings, then his daily rounds. He usually went to New Stanley for morning tea, to the Norfolk or some seedy bar for beer and lunch, to the store in the afternoons to see if some client or crony wanted to swap stories, then home again. He took extended afternoon naps, then after supper went off to his concocted appointments—

in the late years, odysseys that weren't even occasions for comment between Audrey and himself. Her love for him had become a kind of matrimonial pity: she knew he had to find somebody new who would listen to his stories. All hunters, she once said, were mostly just storytellers. And if the gypsies got her husband—drink, other women, some new fancy—then so they did.

Coke wasn't special, either. In recent years he crawled out of bed around noon, met Chili for lunch, stopped at the house to visit his mother while Lucien was occupied at the store, then hurried off to his current girlfriend. In the evenings he made the rounds of restaurants, bars, and the apartments of friends before ending his nighthawk travels in the lounge of the Blue Hotel.

Normal, all this. No peril in any of it with the possible exception of a drunken fall. But the uneasy times came again and again, and Lucien came to hate those times and yet to regard them as inevitable.

He couldn't tell Trey any of this. So he talked instead about the old days at Ambrose School. The first cheetah hunt. A little about the famous boxing match. All the old stuff.

SAFARI: Rendezvous

The camp was desert squalor along the mud flats at the lake. To the east were craggy mountains and the wind blew day and night: swirling heat that obliterated the senses. The refugees huddled under their canopies and lean-to huts, searching for whatever shade they could find, lying there listless and helpless while Lucien took charge.

He bribed nine men to dig sanitation ditches from the middle of camp down to the shoreline: eighteen beers, some old clothing, and ownership of the tools they worked with. He bribed mothers to bring their babies to Dr. Trey: powdered milk, more used clothing, and a large tin of Campbell's soup for each family. Others were bribed to sweep out the clinic, to return stolen items, to boil their water properly for drinking, and to put medication on their own sores. He settled disputes. He shot waterbirds and donated them to community cooking pots. He shamed the fishermen for being afraid of the crocodiles. He attempted to transform various refugees into cooks, interns, houseboys, and spies.

For all this, Trey rewarded him at night—and sometimes in

the early mornings, too—in the clinic. And he found himself
thinking, there, this can heal me, this is medicinal, oh nurse, I'm
cured, this it it.

The clinic: a honeycomb of wattle, thatch, and corrugated tin.
His shelter and paradise. Its main room served as dispensary,
dining room, and office. The smaller rooms—including the one
where they fashioned a double bed for themselves—were used
as wards or staff quarters. An outdoor washroom and kitchen
completed the compound. A wreck, all of it.

He soon sorted out some of the refugee groups and rivalries:
Ethiopian familes who had fled the drought, a few rebels from
the ongoing wars over in Uganda, a dozen Somalis, some long-
time lake inhabitants including the reluctant fishermen, and a
few Turkana—although most of this local tribe remained herdsmen and wanted little to do with such camp rabble. Since Lucien
spoke bits of their languages and had better Swahili then Trey,
the food was soon fairly distributed and the sanitation ditches
dug. Trey had been asking Turkana men to dig ditches meant
to convey the shit of aliens; Lucien worked it all out with an
intertribal committee and payments of beer.

She applied cream to his sunburned nose. He watched the sway
of her walk, her gentle touch with the children, the firelight on
her hair.

After eleven days he decided that the old lorry wouldn't do
anymore, and radioed for a plane. He went back to Nairobi,
tended to his store for two miserable days, bought a used Land
Rover, and came back with supplies. Hic cycle began: a few days
at the store, then back to the lake, then back to a lonely time in
Nairobi again. It became a tiring schedule, and everyone in the
city heard about this woman.

"I think you're losing weight," his mother told him.

"Oh no, I'm fine," he insisted, but Audrey raised her chin, studied him, and jabbed an exploring finger between his ribs.

"There's a gleam in your eye," she went on. "But you definitely have the haggard look of love."

It was during his fourth trip to the lake that the leopard came.

A child was taken out of its blanket during the night. The mother and two others saw it happen. Never mind the everyday terrors—possible cholera, vipers, crocodiles, malnutrition, insects, thorns, shit and madness. Now the whole settlement was being stalked.

"It's a damned big one," Lucien admitted to Trey, studying the tracks.

"So what do we do?"

"We have to find it and kill it. But let me think about it."

He went up the path toward those craggy hills, cursing the fact that he didn't even have his weapons with him. Clearly he needed help, and he had to think fast. Time was against him; the leopard would probably feed on its kill for two days, maybe three, before going on the hunt again.

From his vantage point the camp looked small, sad and vulnerable. He could have the refugees dig pits or rig snares, but that left too much to chance and sooner or later the marauder would have to be flushed out. Lucien would have to radio Nairobi for at least one other hunter.

But who? Chili, of course, and that was complicated. Lucien had called him a prick and a liar—which he was—and ever since that night in the Blue Hotel he and his father had lived out an uneasy truce. Yet Chili was the best and perhaps this was what they needed together. Another hunt. Neither had been allowed to shoot a big cat for years. Sure, he'd like this, Lucien decided, and maybe it could patch things up between them.

At noon Lucien radioed the operator at Wilson Airport, giving him a series of instructions for Chili: get permission from the authorities to shoot a man-eater, bring my guns, bring lots of groceries and ammo, and get somebody to fly you up here—but not Coke.

That afternoon he built two wire snares up on the hillside, baiting them with a couple of rotted fish he found along the shore. Trey came up the hill to talk and to watch him work.

"Think that thing'll hold a leopard?"

"Probably not," he admitted.

"There's a big rumor about the leopard," she told him.

"About it being blind? Yeah, I heard it."

"Could that be true?"

"Sounds improbable."

"The child's mother said it had milky-white eyes."

"Well, maybe."

"They think it's the devil," she said, staring at the sweat on his naked back. He turned his gaze on her: those low-slung jeans, her fingers on the shiny stethoscope, her lips in a half smile.

"You're the devil," he told her, grinning.

"And you're not bad yourself," she answered. They enjoyed another little wanton moment. And he kept inventing that perfect thing to say to her.

The next afternoon they heard the plane and stepped outside the clinic to watch it circle in. It came in low, dipped its wings, and Lucien saw the familiar stripes and numbers. "Damn," he said, watching its flyover.

"What's wrong?" she asked.

"It's my brother's plane."

They stood on the mud flats with two dozen refugees watching the plane's wheels retract into the pontoons as his brother made the final approach. The plane landed and taxied in, steadying itself in less than two feet of water before the props died, then Lucien saw his father's arm go up in greeting.

Chili was a big man, smiling, with a thick mane of white hair, and oversized hands. He did his trick—walking to shore on those hands, his boots wobbling overhead, his chin up, still grinning. An old man, sure, but he showed off his vigor and Trey laughed out loud, already charmed, as he made his way slowly toward them.

Lucien had seen his father do these handstands and walk upside down out of dozens of rivers and streams—always to get that same laughing response from scores of impressionable girls and women. He was seventy now, but still scoring, still proving himself, as if to say, look, I'm damn strong, see, still acrobatic. Watch me.

Trey pulled back a strand of hair. As Chili scrambled to his feet beside her, she touched his arm. Women always touched him first.

"I do it that way 'cause it's practical," he assured her, and her open smile encouraged him to go on. "Because it's easier to wash my hands than my feet! See, my boots aren't even muddy!"

"Too much," she said, touching his arm again and laughing.

Out at the plane Coke waved and happily unloaded gear. Two scrawny refugees awaited the items he pulled from behind the seats: cartons of beer, rolls of bedding, bottles of Worcestershire sauce, and the bright rifles and pistols of the old trade.

Buster, the family dog, splashed around beneath the struts.

Coke held up a rifle, the big Armsport 4010, and called out, "Hey, Lucy, look what I brought you!"

"I suppose you're staying for the hunt?" Lucien called back.

Their voices echoed across the shallows.

"Had to fly the old man up here, didn't I? So, sure, I might as well stay!"

Coke was uninvited and unwanted, but at least they would know what to do and how to work together, so the job would get done.

As Chili and Trey started walking up through the loud shale toward the clinic, Coke jumped out of the plane and splashed ashore. Buster barked and followed. Shirtless, Coke looked paunchy as a lion. He needed a haircut and his mustache was unevenly trimmed so that it drooped on one side and rose on the other, hanging between a sneer and a grin. He carried an armload of weapons and beer. His eyes gleamed, as if he had arrived at another party.

"Damn me, you're disappointed I came along!"

"Not at all," Lucien managed. "We can use the extra gun."

"Why should I stay home and miss a real hunt?"

"Right. Why deprive yourself?"

"Lucy, you look good. Got yourself some rose in your cheek."

"Don't call me that, okay?"

"Lucy? Don't call you Lucy?"

At the clinic Lucien led them through introductions as Chili and Coke went through their old routine: yes, that's what we're called, we don't have regular names, only Lucien has himself a regular name, we wanted to call him Hot Dog but he wouldn't go for it.

Coke opened the warm beers and gave one in payment to the two scrawny refugees, who began arguing over sharing it.

Then Trey, who acted oddly nervous, began talking about the flagpole. She laughed an uneasy laughter through the monologue, saying, well, there had been a flagpole here at the clinic flying the colors of the Red Cross, but both flag and pole had been stolen. Everything up here gets swiped, she said: medicines, mattresses, radio parts, silverware, clothing, even flagpoles. She understood why a refugee might want a kitchen knife or a mattress, she told them, laughing, but what did they want with a piece of radio or a flagpole? And where *was* the flagpole? It wasn't as if they could hide it easily.

As she finished all this, she showed them where to stack their supplies. They propped their expensive weapons against the thatched wall of the main room—each gun engraved with the same floral pattern of gold filigree. The Cavenaugh arsenal.

She kept fidgeting with her hair all the time, talking and acting like a hostess, and although Coke and Chili addressed Lucien or each other they looked only at the curve of her jeans.

Soon it was evening, and they sat around the small fire at the outdoor kitchen. They had a meal of fish, potatoes, beer, and tea with sugared biscuits. Chili dumped Worcestershire sauce over his potatoes and made his customary noises sipping tea. Occasionally some dark figure appeared at the edge of their circle whispering *mbaya sana*, very bad, Dr. Trey, you come now, and their hostess would slip off into the surrounding camp for a few minutes, attend to the complaint, then rejoin the dinner. Two old women served food and beer, grunting and nodding as they moved around the fire.

After dinner and a round of beer, Chili started his stories. Trey listened, her hair tinted red by the firelight, as he told how he used to bring clients to the lake in the old days. As Chili talked, Coke got up, cupped his hands against the stiff evening breeze, lit a cigarette, and paced around. Unlike Lucien, he could still listen to his father's stories and digressions for hours without interrupting, but he tended to pace.

"So how'd you come to be here alone?" Chili finally drawled.

"Oh, it's a long story," she said. "But it's much better with Lucien here."

"Lucien's a dear," Coke said, to nobody in particular.

"He really is," she agreed, ignoring the sarcasm.

As she talked on, Lucien remembered how they used to make camp near the volcano at the south end of the lake—150 miles from this northern shore. The windblown straw huts of the Molo fishermen were like sad birds' nests thrown to the ground. That was in the days when their clients came from all over the world and the Cavenaugh family lived off Chili's reputation.

He listened to Trey's explanations. Although humanitarian motives were officially cited for establishing the refugee camp, she was saying, it was really here to keep refugees at the border and to give them bread and bandages so they didn't trickle down to Nairobi. For a few months the Red Cross helped with the enterprise, then withdrew. Then government aid ended. And the camp director ran off. Yet the flow of refugees and wanderers continued.

"And you stayed on?" Chili asked.

"I'm paid by an independent British fund and my contract is for two years. I'm sticking to it."

"Good for you, honey," Chili drawled.

"I want her to quit and come to Nairobi with me," Lucien added.

"Be a hell of a deal for you, son, if she did," Chili said. He leaned forward, giving Trey elaborate and courtly attention.

"Up at this end of the lake the waters are shallow and infested with crocs," she went on. "Only a few fishermen venture out, so the daily food supply is short. With more than two hundred refugees in camp, sanitation has been awful. The factions bicker among themselves. Lucien's helped with that. But the stealing goes on."

She tried a smile, but sighed heavily instead.

"And now you got a leopard," Coke added.

"There's lots of crazy superstition about it," she said.

"So Lucien asked Pop to come shoot it," Coke went on.

"Not exactly," Lucien said. "I asked for help. When you see the hills above camp, you'll understand why."

"I'd've come up here just to meet this fantastic lady," Chili drawled.

"She is fantastic," Lucien agreed.

He and Trey exchanged a smile.

"Lucy, you've done all right this time," Coke put in.

Trey asked the old women to fetch more beer. "Now about the leopard," she said. "Did Lucien tell you about the rumor that it's blind?"

"Blind?" Chili repeated, grinning and looking up.

"Probably the local exaggeration," Lucien offered.

"Mind you, I'd like it to be blind," Chili said. "That'd help a lot."

"We could always hunt it on moonless nights if we wanted to make things even," Coke suggested.

"One or two of the refugees claimed they saw it," Trey said. "They said it's got milky-white eyes—and behaved as though it's really blind, too."

"Love this," Chili said, rubbing his hands together.

"Of course, everyone thinks it's an evil spirit."

"Any tribesman thinks it he eats something, that's good," Coke observed, grinning. "And if anything wants to eat him, that's evil."

More beer.

"Blind or not, he's up in those hills east of camp," Lucien said. "He probably comes to the lake every night to drink. And now he's got a taste for human flesh."

"This camp must look like a supermarket to him," Coke said.

"We'll get him, don't worry," Chili promised, and there were notes of happy anticipation in their voices.

"The hills are trouble," Trey told them, sipping her beer. "Between the boulders are lots of sharp stones and volcanic ash—a dust as fine as face powder. Gets hot there when the stones heat up at midday. You'll find it tough going."

"We'll manage," Coke said confidently.

"Good, then I'm off to bed. I'll leave you men to concoct your strategy."

"No strategy to it," Coke informed her. "We just track the bugger and shoot him." He flicked a cigarette butt out into the darkness beyond their circle. There, quickly, it was picked up and inhaled upon, and for a moment glowed red in the mouth of an unseen refugee, who had finally been rewarded for his vigil.

"You coming to bed, too, Lucien?" she asked.

"I'll just check the snares first," he answered, and Trey's offhand invitation in the presence of his father and brother pleased him more than he could say.

But Chili interrupted. "Trey, listen," he said. "Have one more nightcap with me while Lucien makes his rounds. Just one, okay?" In his voice was so much: an overture, the old authority, a promise of private business.

"I've got to get some sleep, but, sure, one drink? I guess so," she replied, glancing at Lucien.

"G'wan, Coke, you too," Chili said. "Let me have this little lady to myself."

"He's going to tell you long, long stories," Lucien warned her.

"I'm tired, sure, I'll go," Coke said obediently, shuffling off toward the plane.

"Both of you, get on. I wanta sit here and gaze at her."

"I'll just finish this one beer," Trey promised.

Lucien made his rounds. On the hillside the snares were intact and empty, but he couldn't think about this feeble security anymore. He walked back through camp, urging those refugees who were still awake to build up their fires. Where he couldn't get them to respond, he occasionally tossed a few twigs into their glowing embers.

He tried to get his mind clear during these chores, but old resentments and arguments nagged at him. He thought of that night, long ago, when he and Coke came to blows. And thinking of it, everything came back: the wrongs done to his mother, the condescensions, the Blue Hotel, the Fourth of July, the grand piano, bolts of cloth, their old friends Terence and Emilene, Ambrose School, and all those endless competitions.

As the wind died away for the night, he heard the immense lake murmuring to itself.

When he came back to the clinic, Chili and Trey were talking, their canvas chairs pulled close together.

"Let's turn in," he suggested brightly.

"A few more minutes," she answered, and he was committed to retiring without her. When he paused, she added, "I'll be along."

In the empty back room of the clinic, cut off from the remaining breeze, Lucien took off his clothes and stretched out on the double cot. As their muffled voices penetrated the thatched walls, he thought, stupid, so stupid, how did I let this happen? Why let Chili have his way?

The beer swam inside him; exhausted, he closed his eyes. The leopard hunt was already botched.

He had wanted to get Chili up here so they could make one more start together, but with Coke around he feared the worst.

Trey's laughter drifted across the darkness.

He thought of going back outside and joining them, but stayed where he was. Lying there soaked with perspiration, he thought of the gypsies, the old safaris, and this dark inland sea. Then he was asleep, everything calm.

Later—far into the middle of the night—he was awakened by Buster's faraway barking.

Outside, he zipped his shorts and fastened a single button on his shirt. A moonless blue: the stars giving a pale radiance to the landscape. With the breeze almost at rest, voices echoed from the lake—voices accompanied by the soft lapping of the surf. Drowsy, he moved toward the shore.

As he reached the mud flats, he saw Buster come panting and wagging his tail in greeting, circling, and leading him to the edge of the shallows.

"I've got to get out of here!" he heard Trey insisting loudly.

"Get on, so we can get some sleep!" Chili urged her, and Coke's drunken laughter became a descant.

Lucien's father and brother were stretched out on the wings of the plane. Their clothes dangled from separate propellers as their naked bodies, faintly silver in the starglow, posed like statues.

"Trey!" Lucien called, and her name rushed out of him like a command. She was somewhere around the plane, lurking beside a pontoon or under the wing, paying him no attention.

"Trey?" he called again, and this time it was an appeal. "Hey, come on! The crocs are in the shallows at night! Where are you?"

"We plan to sleep on the wings of the plane," Chili explained, unnecessarily. "S'cool out here, right pleasant."

"Don't fret about crocs, Lucy, don't worry," Coke said. "Have a beer and a dip in the lake."

"Trey?" he called again, his voice calm.

"Be right with you," she finally answered. She was in the shadow beneath the wing, holding onto a strut, hiding behind Chili's dangling shirt.

"Wade right in," Coke offered. "If a croc gets you, Lucy, by damn I'll shoot it for you!"

The three inebriates laughed as Buster, splashing around, barked a raucous note of his own.

"Don't be afraid, son! Wade on out!"

Coke struggled to his knees on the wing of the plane, tilting everything with his sudden movement.

Trey's laughter was a drunken gasp and she hovered beneath the wing, lost in shadow, hiding from him, not thinking about the night's danger or tomorrow's duty. Lucien took a deep breath and waded toward them.

"Here he comes! It's a party now!" Coke yelled, and he stood on the wing, rocking the plane wildly so the Chili had to hang on. For Lucien, the sight of them blended with dozens of memories; they had slept on the wings of planes—the three of them, sometimes with clients—in half the lakes and rivers of East Africa.

"Trey, where are you?" he called.

She moved into the open, holding a hand over her mouth to stifle her laughter.

"Whoa! Whoa there!" Chili drawled at the rocking plane.

Buster splashed around Trey as Lucien took her arm.

"C'mon," he said gently.

But she pulled him toward her, wrapping him in her wet arms, pressing her breasts flat against him, and burying her nose in his neck. "Gotcha," she said. "I gotcha."

"Let's turn in," he said.

Coke stood on the wing and rocked back and forth, raising his arms to those thousands of pale stars. Illumined, he presented himself: white body, shadowed muscles, slant of mustache, an insolent stub of penis, hands out, fingers splayed open.

Chili began singing, his voice badly off-key, as usual, as he kept rhythm with the rocking wing. "*Hold* that ti-*ger*! *Hold* that ti-*ger*! *Don't* let him get away!"

Lucien implored her, urging her to come with him, trying not to sound irritated or possessive, but she pulled against him. As Buster barked and splashed around them, she actually pulled him toward deeper water. Her laughter beckoned and he had to take her arm roughly to pull her back toward shore.

ZAMANI:
Bolts of Cloth

Coke had enjoyed dozens of girlfriends, assorted romances with female clients on safari, one nasty adultery, hundreds of nights in the Blue Hotel, and six marriages. Of all his wives, Lucien had probably given more thought to Colly over the years—he had been accused of taking her away from Coke—but it was over Kira, the black wife, the most beautiful of all, that the brothers had come to their deepest trouble.

She had arrived in Nairobi with her father, a Somali cloth trader. Within a week she had become the lover of a stunt man who was there with an American movie company. Everyone desired her that season, but the stunt man was formidable: possessive, thick in the neck and arms, and quick-tempered.

As soon as the movie shoot ended and its crew, including the stunt man, had left Africa, Coke made his move. To compensate Kira for the loss of her lover, he took her to dinner at all of the city's best cafés, induced her to go on holiday at Lamu, and then took her off on safari with a couple of German clients. Then he came to see Chili about marrying her.

"Marry? Again?" Chili complained.

Coke accused his father of being racially prejudiced.

"By damn, now, this will be your fourth wife!"

"Technically, my fifth," Coke corrected him.

They sat on the wide porch of their family house in the Muthiaga district. The front of the old house was plain enough, but the backside had a peculiar seedy splendor: white columns, chipped concrete steps, ceiling fans over the wicker furniture of the porch, and, beyond, out on the lawn, a swimming pool filled with green scum. Chili called it a Southern mansion turned around backward.

The jacaranda tree was in bloom. Buster farted in his sleep. Audrey sat through this new discussion of the marriage of her eldest son without raising her eyes from her magazine.

"Coke, see here," Chili explained, "give the girl a history lesson. Tell her there's fornication in our tribe, same as in hers. Tell her it's an acceptable thing. I mean, the two of you should copulate, but, damn, son, don't marry again!"

"Can we not discuss the sex act right now?" Lucien suggested, glancing toward his mother. He didn't want his father's notorious behavior to become the next topic, but Audrey's mouth showed nothing as she idly turned another page.

"I won't stand for racial prejudice against Kira," Coke went on, poking his finger at both Chili and Lucien. "I'm proud to be seen with this lady! I want to be seen with her, by god, and I plan for us to spend our honeymoon right down there at the Norfolk, right here in town, everybody looking! Right there in the bar every evening with our pals! I'm far from being ashamed! Just the opposite!"

He talked loudly to no one in particular.

"You know, you should try your best to marry for money," Chili advised.

Coke pointed out that he had done that, twice, with no particular advantage gained either time.

"Now come on, Mama, you'll like this one," Coke told Audrey, but she wouldn't even acknowledge him.

"Long legs and full breasts," Lucien added. "She's your sort of gal, Mother, you'll love having her around."

"Shut up," Coke said, glowering at his brother.

They were married for nine weeks. Both wedding ceremony and divorce hearing were conducted by a dapper official in the same cramped musty office on Kuanda Street, an official who wore a bow tie at the ceremony and who removed it for the divorce hearing, which was attended only by Lucien and the family solicitor. Coke's attire for the wedding was his usual starched khaki shirt with matching trousers. After a month of parties with his bride and cronies, he went off on a long safari in Zaire.

Weeks later, when he came back from the hunt, Coke visited Lucien. "You wouldn't believe the country over there," he said, excited. "We're just too damn tame here in East Africa now! There's jungle over there so you can't see an elephant at thirty feet! Our camp was just this tiny clearing in thousands of square miles of greenery! You could hear the monkeys screaming as they ran from the snakes! You stalk one species and another species stalks you! And, damn, we had good times. Old Tom had malaria again and kept us awake all night with hallucinations! Better than telly! And there were official government whores. And remember the gunbearer we called Old Spic and Span? He was there! And so were Bernard and the duke!"

"Kira's gone into business," Lucien informed him.

"What sort of business?"

"Her father's cloth. She has hundreds of bolts of cloth in your apartment."

"Well, no matter," Coke said. "I'm not going back there anyway. It just hasn't worked out between Kira and me."

"But it's a little more complicated that that," Lucien explained. "She's using the family name. Trying to get export permits as a Cavenaugh. Also trying to sell cloth right out of the apartment, as an illegal retail outlet. Look, I want to help her out, but Chili's dead set against her and wants to bring charges. We don't want a family squabble over this, do we?"

"Well, see, I'm divorcing her," Coke said with a sigh, as if that were a perfect solution. Lucien could make no reply.

Kira turned to Lucien after the divorce because he was the logical one, the businessman. But his explanations meant little, and each time he saw her things were worse. He found her in the store one morning, standing beside a stack of camouflage jackets and looking like one of those dark, lovely, misplaced apparitions out of *Vogue*. Lucien saw those distressed eyes, those beautiful and pained eyes, and found himself unable to speak before she began telling him her troubles.

"We must bribe someone," she said. "You must tell me who."

"Kira, that won't do any good. You can't ship your cloth out of the country. And it has nothing to do with our laws or regulations here, but with laws in America and Europe. I explained it to you."

"I know if we bribe some official," she insisted, "we can do anything we want! I know how this country works! Ivory is shipped out! And sisal!"

Her voice broke.

"You had a fine idea," Lucien went on. "You thought you could get your cloth into stores in London and Dallas, but there are tariffs. They don't want foreign cloth. They have their own textile mills. So they charge too much for you to ship it there— twice the cost of your cloth. So you can't do this, you just can't."

"It's all I have," she said, her voice breaking sharply, and she covered her face with her long fingers and painted nails.

"No one here can change the tariff laws in Europe or America," he said quietly.

"Oh god," she muttered.

Lucien looked around the store to see if any customers were watching. He wanted to touch her shoulder.

"I have only my father's cloth, nothing else."

"Kira, believe me, I don't know how to help you."

"Coke won't help me."

"That's right, he won't," Lucien agreed.

"You know what I have to offer as a bribe, don't you?" she asked, wiping away her tears. "I was going to offer my body. They all want me. That's why I go into the cloth business, you see, because after my father died and left me the cloth, I think, good, I do not have to be the whore."

She was crying steadily, her voice unchanged.

"You never have to do that," he assured her.

"You don't see. What else? Tell me what else?"

"You can marry again. Or you can find work."

"Say to me who I can marry. Or what job."

"Kira, we can't stand in the store like this. Here, wipe your face. Please." He gave her his handkerchief.

"Lucien, I ask you, come talk with me about what I am to do. Come to the apartment."

"Soon," he said. "I'll come sometime soon."

"Think about me. You will see what to do with me."

"Yes, I promise I'll come see you. But now you should go."

It was a promise he shouldn't have made, he realized, because things between him and Coke had been uneasy for a long time. Yet there she stood, struggling for control, her sobs making no sound at all.

A customer entered the store as she departed. Lucien sold him one of the straw safari hats.

Audrey was busy at this time with the symphony orchestra that made its annual visit to the city. She always enlisted Lucien to bargain with government representatives about arrangements and he often accompanied her to meetings, to luncheons at the club, and to the annual performance.

The club wasn't Audrey's place any more than it was Chili's. (After proving that he could be admitted to membership, Chili quickly exiled himself back to the bars of the city.) With its white walls and columns and terraces, its stuffy young men who were far more pretentious than the old boys—all of them hemming and hawing with fake aristocratic drawls—the club could hardly be taken seriously by anyone, least of all Audrey. But she worked for its occasional charities and for the arrival of the symphony each year.

"I'm just always happy to see the musicians again," she explained to Lucien after the performance. They were sitting on the back porch where Buster had settled himself, his head resting on the tops of Lucien's black dress shoes.

"I was watching you with that conductor tonight at the reception," Lucien said. "It occurred to me that you really like him."

"Gorman? He's a dear friend. They lose money on this stop in their tour, you know, and the flight always exhausts them."

"He was paying you awfully close attention."

"Is that what you think?"

His mother was a woman of almost seventy, her beauty faded now into a tough refinement. Her eyes saw everything and she had a proud way of holding her chin.

It amused him to think of her with the orchestra conductor. Did she still have some of the old fire she had years ago with Chili? And maybe they were much the same, the two men, both with their secret crafts and strengths: the music in one, and, in Chili, the hidden natural rhythms. Lucien studied his mother as she sipped her nightcap and as they listened to the locusts.

Then she began talking about money. The store business was booming. Chili and Coke were taking out lots of rich clients. Prices were climbing, she said, and they might never see such solid times again.

"Put aside some money for yourself," she advised him.

"We're all doing fine. And it's family money and belongs to all of us," he replied.

"No, do as I say," she said quietly. "Times like these don't last. And you deserve the success of the store. And you've made decent investments. Your father and brother will never see a good investment in their lives."

"They're too emotional," Lucien agreed.

"They're shallow. And they're spenders, just spenders. So I want you independent of them. And do the same for me."

"You want a separate account?" he asked, making sure. They sat in the darkness in silence before she responded.

"Yes, my own account."

"I can arrange it, but both Chili and Coke will know if we start to split things up."

"Tell them exactly what you're doing," she instructed him.

"Tell them I want it. They won't fuss. For one thing, there's plenty of money and they believe there always will be. For another, they trust you to make all the sane decisions. And they don't care about money, not really, they just don't care."

"Except if there isn't any."

"Later there won't be," his mother told him. "But when that time comes, they'll adjust."

They sat in the darkness with their drinks, both of them clearly realizing what had been agreed on. The separation of the family had been made formal.

Lucien finished his whiskey. "I'll turn in now," he said. He shook Buster off his shoes, went to Audrey, breathed in her lavender cologne, and kissed her cheek. "You want me to turn off the downstairs lights before I go up?"

"No," she said, touching his face. "I'll just stay here a bit, before your father comes home."

In his bed upstairs he kept thinking about how few women had been in his life, how many there had been in Coke's and Chili's, and about Kira. He could see her again as she had been that morning in the store, her painted nails over her face. Her hands were like the rest of her—instruments of beauty.

A week later he went to see her. He knew better, but there she was, trapped between the tribes and the times, another nowhere person like so many in the city, and his family had made its cruel little contribution to her fate. Never mind how beautiful she was; beauty had only brought her into a momentary limbo of hope. The white world had held a bent mirror up to that delicate face of hers, and she had moved inside the mirror to live in its distortion.

Her flat was in one of those grim compounds off the Uhuru

Highway. He climbed two flights of bare cement stairs to her door.

The rooms bulged with all those bolts of gaily patterned cloth. A warehouse of false promise, all of it: bolts up to the ceiling, blocking the windows and burying the furniture. He sat on a stack near the bathroom door, while Kira, dressed in a long white *kekoi*, told him that her rent was only paid for another three weeks.

"Coke says he will give me money, but he doesn't," she said.

"Why can't you sell all this locally?" Lucien asked, knowing the answer.

"The merchants expect to get it cheap later—when I'm even more desperate than now," she said. "They want to hate me, to take me to bed, and to buy my father's cloth for nothing."

She placed those long fingers on her forehead and tried to smile. Lucien could think of nothing remotely sensible to say.

"Yes, I should marry," she went on. "Someone even richer than your brother. Maybe a Moslem businessman."

Her English was good. If she practiced under the right circumstances, Lucien found himself thinking, she would have this beautiful voice with a charming accent. And those hands and eyes.

"But how can I marry again here and be happy? I will be the married whore."

"Don't say that about yourself."

"It's true. Silly, but in my head I was becoming very free. Making my own way like the girls in the American magazines. Coke wanted this for me. Liberated. He said so. We talked about my cloth business."

"Would you like dinner?" Lucien asked. "We can go out to a good restaurant."

"I can't go anywhere without trouble. Someone will make a remark. Let me make coffee and sandwiches here."

"That will be fine, too," Lucien said, and he followed her to the kitchen. Bolts of cloth cluttered the top of the refrigerator and protruded from open cabinets.

They talked about small matters, then she asked, directly, "Could you give me some money? You could possibly get it back from your brother later on."

Lucien thought for a moment. "How much, Kira, and what will you do with it?"

"If I have money, I will go to Europe and never come back."

This hurt, for in one corner of himself Lucien wanted her in the city, yet he knew she had to get away. She stirred his coffee and gave it to him.

"How much do you think you need?"

"If I have one thousand pounds, I can go to Europe and live while I find work. If I have only five hundred, I can still leave— and I will accept anything. I would take one airline ticket to Cairo. To anywhere. Think of this, please. You don't have to answer tonight."

"No, I can do it now," he said. "I'll give you the thousand."

It was impulsive, he knew, but worth it. They were standing close together in the narrow kitchen; the smells of cloth and coffee were sharp in his nostrils, and his senses intensified as she turned those wide Somali eyes on him.

"Why are you such a friend?" she asked. "Because of what your brother has done or because of yourself?"

"My father and brother wreck lives," he admitted. "Sometimes I try to pick up the pieces."

"Why do you?" she asked, moving a step closer to him. "Is it because you are a good man? Like a priest?"

"No, not at all like that," he assured her.

She gave him a direct look. "I think you are not at all like the priest," she said, almost whispering, and as she moved ever so slightly closer their coffee cups clinked together. And Lucien told himself, yes, all right, this will happen, and he thought about those soft mounds of cloth in the front room. But regret mixed with whatever desire he felt; Kira would now make payment, the same payment she understood so well, the little favor, the *baksheesh* for goods received.

Then they heard Coke's drunken voice. Kira's eyes widened again, but this time as if she knew what was about to happen.

" 'Lo, where are you?" Coke shouted. " 'S me!"

He found his way into the kitchen, and seeing them only a step apart managed a tilted smile. "Well," he said. "Look here."

"Coke," Lucien said, acknowledging him calmly.

"He is going to help me," Kira blurted out.

" 'S only natural," Coke replied, trying to set his feet apart in a firm stance, but failing. Nothing after that moment sounded right or went well.

"He's going to give me money."

"I'll bet he is."

"The money you won't give me!"

"It's all the same damn money, dearie," Coke said, and he tried another grin, but it didn't work.

Lucien wanted to say, no, it isn't all the same, the accounts are all separate now, you'll soon understand what that means, the little family pot of gold isn't there anymore.

"I'm leaving," she went on. "He is giving me one thousand pounds and I am leaving this place!"

Something in her voice made Lucien understand that Coke had been dropping by on a regular basis since the divorce.

"Hey, one thousand?" Coke asked.

"Yes, and I am flying away from here!"

Coke moved toward Lucien, the odor of bad gin coming with him, and Kira screamed as he threw a punch.

Lucien raised his cup to protect himself, and Coke smashed it with the blow, cutting his hand so that shards of porcelain and a spray of blood went everywhere.

After this, confusion and surprise. Lucien grabbed Coke and began hitting him. With a hammerlock on him, Lucien led him back into the front room, bumping from side to side against the bolts of fabric as they struggled. Lucien drove his fist once, twice, three times into his brother's face as he dragged him along. Kira screamed out instructions that nobody heard. Coke reached for Lucien's hair, but failed to get a grip on it as Lucien pulled him along almost effortlessly, hitting him every time he resisted. By the time they reached the front door of the flat, Lucien's fist was swollen and Coke's face had turned to gore. A smear of blood left a new pattern on a yellow bolt.

Lucien fumbled with the door, got it open, and tossed Coke into the concrete stairwell.

Coke turned and faced him with a snarl.

But he faced Lucien's own boyhood rage. Since the time of their youngest manhood, when they had roughly equaled each other in size and strength, they had never fought. But before that—in the years when Coke had been older and stronger—the fights had always been uneven and Coke had been master and leader. In boyhood, Coke had teased and beaten Lucien without mercy, and now a debt was owed. Lucien was pleased that Coke stumbled forward for another assault.

As Kira screamed, neighbors opened doors and filled the stairwell. "This be government housing!" an old black woman shouted. She repeated this over and over, but her protest became lost in the confusion.

Lucien slipped Coke's charge, cuffed him on the ear, and threw him backward so that he stumbled and went down again.

"He's with my bloody wife!" Coke told the neighbors, waving the cut on his hand so all could see. As he tossed his arm about, a little signature of blood sprayed the wall. "My wife!"

Kira stepped out to protest this.

"We are divorced! This is not my husband!" she screamed at the attentive audience, and Coke was about to muster another accusation when Lucien stepped forward and silenced him with a heavy blow. Coke slumped against the concrete wall, looking up with a bleary half smile. But Lucien was on him. He grabbed Coke's collar and this time heaved him headlong down the stairs. The fall could have easily killed him, but he tumbled into the arms of the gawking neighbors.

Raging, Lucien went after him, but Coke raised an arm.

"Lucien," he managed.

Coke's wrist was clearly broken, a splinter of bone trying to angle through the skin. Kira saw it and sent up a howl.

Lucien sighed heavily and gained control. Then he pushed his way through the crowd, walked past his brother, and reached the street. His fist ached and he felt sick, yet he loved himself. The cries of the neighbors and Kira's shrill denials blended with a police siren. Someone must have phoned the police, he told himself dully, and he got to his car and drove away before they arrived.

Lucien remembered that night in strange ways. His most vivid recollection was of Kira moving so close to him in the kitchen that their coffee cups clinked, then moments later Coke shattering the cup with a wayward punch. The cup motif: its odd little pieces continued to play in Lucien's consciousness for a long time.

The bank accounts were separated and arranged, with Audrey doing most of the transactions herself. It was about that time that the family's most lucrative period came to an end, and not long afterward the Kenyan government stopped all big-game hunting. Chili Cavenaugh's long career as a licensed hunter was over. Coke started flying tourists around—camera safaris, camping trips in the Mara or across to Lake Victoria, all that. Audrey had her house and investments. Lucien had the store.

Lucien and Coke didn't see each other for six months, then one evening they both came to Audrey's dinner table as if nothing had happened. After supper Lucien played the piano while Coke sang twenty verses of "The Good Ship Venus" as Chili led the laughter.

Kira got the money she was promised and left for London. A few months later Lucien sold her father's cloth at a tenth of its value and sent the money to an address in Highgate. She wrote a postcard thanking him for his trouble. Later there was another card, a picture of the Savoy Grill, where she'd had a meal. Then nothing. She had gone, Lucien decided, where beauty goes: to a cold place far away, beyond the glass and quicksilver, to the other side of the mirror.

SAFARI:
At The Darkness

The next day passed, and the hunt still failed to get organized.

Because she had stayed up so late and had been so drunk, Trey took some pep pills and became unlike herself: humming tunes, full of jerky movements and overdone laughter. The refugees who came by the clinic regarded her with fascination.

Lucien wanted to say something, but didn't. Coke slept all day in the plane. Chili, sitting outside the clinic on a stool, following the shade as it moved around the compound, gazed off toward the lake and told as many croc stories as he could remember to all who would listen. Buster went where the stool went, putting his wet nose on Chili's leg now and then. As Trey fought her hangover, she watched Chili through the thatched walls, listening to him and laughing occasionally, making him aware of her.

An old man named Abba also became a listener. At the first pause in Chili's storytelling, Abba reminded him that they had once hunted together.

"Abba?" Chili repeated, trying to recall. "Abba?"

"Far away on the lake! The volcano! You have a safari for this rich man!"

Chili couldn't remember.

Abba wore a pair of human ears dangling from his own: grotesque earrings of human flesh and cartilage that spun on brass wires. These were his cousin's ears, he explained. Years ago when he hunted with Chili he didn't have them, he said, so this was why Chili didn't remember.

Chili reached out and touched one of the ears.

"Are these things decorative or magic?" he asked.

"Oh, much magic!" Abba grinned a mostly toothless grin— and tilted his head to one side as if listening to something. "With my cousin's ears I listen to the underworld voices!"

Chili was impressed. He always fancied the supernatural: blind leopards, any medicine man's trickery, or such human antenna as these. He gave one of the ears a spin, smiled, and complimented the old man.

"That safari you put airplane pieces in a big white bowl," Abba reminded him. "You have two such white bowls, very large. You put the machine pieces in one of them!"

Chili still didn't remember, but Lucien overheard and did.

"We were with the DuPonts," Lucien reminded him. "We had an air-conditioned mess tent, that Swiss chef, and those two enameled bathtubs. You put airplane parts in one of the tubs so the ants wouldn't eat the grease."

"Yes, all right," Chili allowed, though perhaps he recalled this and perhaps he didn't. "But what did you do, Abba?"

"Oh, sir, please! I was gunbearer for Mfifo!"

"Coke's gunbearer?"

"Oh, very much yes!"

Chili grunted a short acknowledgment.

Inside the clinic Trey removed bottles from a carton. Her cassette player gave them a background of classical music, but she hummed something else, tuneless and unidentifiable.

"Okay, sure, you can kill a croc with a twenty-two, but anything in the seven-millimeter range is best," Chili began again, talking mostly to Abba. The old man, sitting cross-legged beside the stool, had become a perfect one-man audience. "And you know where you shoot a croc? Always shoot at the top of its smile."

"Top of its smile?" Trey repeated, overhearing him from inside the clinic.

"Absolutely," Chili called to her. "Severs the spine or blows out the brains or both. Otherwise the brute flails around and gets back in the water, don't you see? If you don't make a proper shot, you lose him for sure."

Trey moved so that she could address Chili through the thatch. "The poor refugees keep trying to get themselves a croc to eat," she said. "But they never manage it."

Abba nodded severely, confirming this.

"Back in the fifties, crocodile shoes became fashionable," Chili went on, looking out toward that distant sheen of water. "I was up here on dozens of croc safaris. Hunters everywhere. We shot hundreds. And the wardens, hell, they shot thousands more. So the crocs thinned out considerably."

The sad look in Chili's eyes suggested that he was about to suffer an attack of nostalgia. Lucien wished he had a camera. It would be the perfect late-afternoon shot: a sunset over the lake, Abba with his double set of ears, and the possibility of real feeling in Chili's face.

"In those days, see, our licenses allowed us to shoot only two crocs, but nobody paid that any attention," Chili told Abba. "We should've paid attention, but we just didn't."

Lucien watched and smiled. If Chili suffered one of his nostalgia attacks, he knew there was no hope unless the gypsies came to get him. Sometimes the gypsies were old cronies, sometimes the girls at the Blue Hotel, sometimes new acquaintances who hadn't heard any of the old stories. Chili would be gone for days, even weeks, then come home recovered. Audrey had long ago stopped asking about his whereabouts or wondering who the gypsies might be.

Watching him like this, Lucien saw him as a man apart, not so much a father or a legend anymore, but just one more of the displaced hunters who had been forced to find other things to do. Seven years had passed since big-game hunting had been banned. For some, like Coke and Chili, the ban was a sad affair; for Lucien, his exile from the profession had begun much earlier, with the beginning of the store.

The hot afternoon had faded. Abba still sat there listening, regarding Chili as anyone might regard a god perched on a stool beside a lake.

"Sure, the wardens shot croc. And there were poachers, lots of 'em," Chili continued. "There was a damn black market in croc skins—the same as in ivory."

Lucien stood around listening. He's bringing on an attack, he told himself, and I might have one myself.

The hunters had scattered, going off to Zaire or South Africa or Tanzania or wherever a professional might find work. Percy Spence married a Greek woman and lived in Alexandria. Dooley went to live with his daughter in Florida. Jambo Tiner drove a tourist bus for a while, then disappeared. Dilly and Capstone died of their liver ailments. Teddy Wickham, who had been mauled by a lion on the last day before the ban, had also finally died. Montagu simply shot himself.

He had known them all, same as Chili.

The long twilight was beginning as Coke came toward them from the plane, shirt in hand.

Trey stood outside the clinic and watched him coming. A rivulet of perspiration fastened a strand of hair to her forehead. Tiny whirlwinds of yellow dust formed in the hills above them as Coke approached and called out.

"He's alive and walking," Trey answered.

Coke was all smiles, and made elaborate jokes and apologies for the previous night. This was his familiar way: heavy scenes, drunken confrontations, foolish nights, followed by expansive apologies, followed by a resumption of happy offenses.

"Guess who this is?" Chili asked Coke. "It's old Abba!"

Everyone moved to a wobbly card table. Trey went into the clinic, then came back with a bottle and glasses. The balance of the day, Lucien assumed, would turn to gin.

Abba insisted that he knew Mfifo well, but like Chili, Coke teased him and denied it.

"They called you Mfifo!"

"Who would call me such a name? What an insult!"

"Everyone call you this! You called yourself this!"

Coke just shook his head.

Exasperated, Abba screwed up his face and tried another proof. "The father of your wife called you this!" he argued. "You tell this story yourself! He made the curse at you and made you to fly through a glass window! He called you Mfifo and other bad words!"

Trey laughed and poured drinks.

Lucien remembered very well. Colly's father did toss Coke through a window once, toward the end of the marriage. Or maybe it was French doors. It hadn't been all that amusing at the time, but later Coke told the story everywhere.

As twilight deepened, the two old women arrived for the night's kitchen duties. For an hour or so, everyone sat around the card table talking about the wind, the crocs, the flies, the schools of tilapia and giant Nile perch out there in the lake, and finally Trey's music.

"My mother likes that sort of music," Coke said. "Music without words. But not me."

"You're a cultural moron," Chili told him. "You never learned a damn thing up at Ambrose School."

"Maybe I am," Coke admitted with a grin. "But later on I'll fetch us some real songs out of my kit."

Lucien decided to take a stroll. Abba, who now seemed to be a fixture in their hunting party, joined him. Night was comimg on quickly: another moonless dark.

Spread out between the lake and hills, the refugees made sweet-smelling sagebrush fires. Their meal tonight would be a nameless mush with pan bread. They were already hunched around their fires, the children curling themselves into sleeping positions. *"Jambo!"* someone called, as Lucien and Abba shuffled near, and Lucien raised a hand to return the greeting. If he sat down among them, he'd have to listen as they told him all their news: a storm over the lake a week ago, poor fishing, only a few bags of grain left from the relief agencies, complaining children, a bad time.

There were no sentries around camp, Lucien noticed, although he had called for volunteers. Gathering what little wood he could find, he stopped at each pit and started the fires. Didn't they know they had to take precautions against the leopard? Later, from the hillside where he had set the first blaze, he watched them hovering around their fires with weary fatalism.

The lake had a deep echo like a voice.

Abba became mildly helpful, gathering a few twigs for kindling, and they slowly made their rounds. But the fires remained small, so Lucien decided to go down to the shore and break up a rotted boat in order to build fires that would last.

Abba kept pace. The first stars came out.

The name of the lake was now, officially, Turkana—after the sullen tribe of herdsmen who wandered its shores. For years it was Lake Rudolf, called that by a partially demented Hungarian nobleman, Count Teleki, who strayed into the wilderness and gave the lake the name of his beloved emperor. But names in Africa come and go. The natives around these shores for thousands of years—Turkana, Molo, and all the others—had always called the lake *Ngiza*, or, simply, The Darkness. At its center, they said, the bottomless hole went down to the underworld. The crocodiles were its guardians. Its waters gave both life and death.

All this reminded Lucien of Abba's second set of ears.

As they pulled loose planks off the rotted fishing boat down at the water's edge, Lucien approached the subject gently.

"Feeling all right tonight, Abba?"

"Ah, *mzuri*, fine."

"And, uh, you hear anything on your cousin's ears?"

"Chanting and music," the old man replied, struggling to keep pace with Lucien's efforts. "But not my cousin's chanting, no, I think somebody else is chanting very much. Far away beneath the water."

"And is it happy music and chanting?"

"Not so much happy," Abba reluctantly admitted.

"So, sadness in paradise," Lucien commented, gathering an armload of wood.

Abba, probably wary of another melancholy white man, said nothing.

They struggled uphill with their loads and built up the fires. The camp had fallen silent except for the low murmurs of voices over at the clinic, and, once, Trey's laughter drifted out over the night.

Coke and Trey were dancing when they got back. The little cassette player wheezed American pop: something soft by either Chicago or Styx or Barbieri that Lucien didn't know. The curse of the electric guitar, as Audrey said. Coke's thumping rhythms.

Their dance was a swaying embrace. Chili, inside the clinic, clanged around in search of another bottle, so only Buster, wagging and slobbering, welcomed Lucien. Five or six male refugees had gathered to watch the evening's entertainment at Dr. Trey's.

"Lucien," Chili said, as his son stepped inside the thatched walls with him, "tell me. What's the biggest croc you've ever actually seen?"

"We're still talking crocs?"

"We are, yes. Years of shooting the brutes and I never saw one much longer than fifteen feet. How about you?"

"Fifteen feet, yeah, that's about it."

"Now I hear stories of larger ones," he said, pouring out two glasses of beer from a newfound bottle. "Met a chap once who said he saw an eighteen footer on North Island in the middle of this very lake. But never me. Fifteen feet—sometimes a fat brute—but I never saw one longer than that in my whole damn experience."

"Did that eighteen footer wear any jewelry?" Lucien asked.

"Jewelry on a croc?"

"The Egyptians decorated their gods with precious stones. Maybe that was an old Egyptian god."

Chili drew closer, waiting for more of this.

"Crocs go back millions of years as a species," Lucien went on. "And some say crocs live for centuries. Scientific nonsense, but that's the legend. Lots of exaggeration about them."

"Jewelry on a damn croc," Chili said with appreciation. He loved drunken tall tales in the late evenings—and the more mysterious the better.

"And, let's see, I'm trying to remember the name of that god, that Egyptian crocodile god, but I can't think of it. Anyway, Pop, maybe you know about Caesar's army. When the army crossed the Nile at ancient Memphis, the crocs attacked and devoured more than a thousand Roman soldiers."

Chili moved closer and squinted into his son's face.

"Damn," he drawled, and for a moment Lucien thought he was pondering that famous military catastrophe, but then Chili added, "You know a bunch. You really do. You know stuff." His tone was both complimentary and disapproving.

Lucien went outside. The twang of guitars.

Touching Coke's shoulder, he moved between the dancers and took Trey in his arms. Coke shuffled off without a word.

Trey put her nose against Lucien's neck as they danced. Her body was warm and damp with perspiration.

"I didn't know you could dance," she whispered.

"Defend yourself or I'll step on you," he warned her softly.

When the song ended, she moved her lips against his ear, whispering, "Let's go in. I'll get a cool washcloth and do us."

They were laughing as they retired. It was still hours before the hunt.

ZAMANI:
The Early Years

After the deaths of his parents, Chili sold the Arkansas farm—
four rough acres of ground, he once said, and a house that was
all porch—and bought himself a Winchester rifle, a case of five
hundred-grain bullets, a few traveling clothes, and a steamer
ticket that took him from New Orleans to Panama to Mombasa.

In the photographs of him from those times his clothes are all
wrinkles: canvas trousers, an old dress shirt perhaps a size too
large for him, a pinstriped gray vest, a bandanna knotted around
his thick neck, and a western-style straw hat. He had no money
when he reached Nairobi, but his plan was simple: he would
somehow get one of those professional hunter's licenses, then
stand his ground against man or beast and become the first
American to enter the insular society of big-game hunters.

The country in those days was already a haven for cads, dream-
ers, adventurers, failed aristrocrats, loners, egotists, and entre-
preneurs. The early settlers, like Lord Delamere, were rough
eccentrics. And there were deals to be made, investments to

pursue, careers to think about, but before all that there was a prevalent and rough male adolescence. Physical presence mattered, and Chili had size. Stamina, good humor, a taste for mischief, loyalty, and quick pride: it was this boyish innocence that was valued most.

The men at the famous Long Bar liked Chili, everything from his name to the look of him in those ill-fitting clothes, and as soon as they observed his marksmanship and his bold safari manner they saw to it that he got his license.

It was British Kenya and a knock-you-down time.

Most of the white men in those years were busy selling off the land as if it had never belonged to the tribes who lived on it. But Chili wasn't interested in business, just in hunting—which gave him his charm. He was no man's competitor; he was more like everyone's son, the one who grew up biggest, who didn't do well in school, and who went out for sports.

He had a way of striding into the tall grass, kicking up the lions and shooting them point-blank. He was reckless and lucky and everyone wanted to hunt with him. Later on his charm would become a complication, but in those early years before all the women he gave his youth and vitality to the profession like a raw gift.

Old Sam Dilly loaned him his dinner jacket and his best dress shirt with the brass studs, and took him to the Muthiaga Club for the annual charity dance. The jacket was too small, yet somehow Chili looked better than most as he stood near the buffet and sampled the dishes. Then he saw Audrey Winston.

She had come down from the Highlands with a group of young people including her lanky escort, whose father was a partner of Audrey's father in coffee plantations. Chili went over and tapped her on the elbow.

"I don't dance," he said in his most pronounced drawl. "But will you consider walking outdoors with me?"

"Is it a little walk out you want?" she asked, turning to him and smiling.

"Sure, that's what I said."

Audrey and her friends had a long laugh. The phrase—a little walk out—had sexual connotations Chili didn't know about. So he stood there without expression, braving their laughter and derision, without a trace of comprehension in his face. Audrey kept toying with him.

"I don't go walking out with just anyone," she said.

More laughter. Her lanky escort said something aside to a companion.

"Why be rude to me?" Chili asked her.

"Am I being rude?"

"I can't think that a girl pretty as you would ever have to be rude to anyone," Chili told her.

"I say, is that old Sam Dilly's dinner jacket?" the lanky one suddenly put in.

Chili gave the escort a hard glance. "I don't like fancy Brits who say 'I say,' " Chili said.

Sensing that the worst might quickly happen, Audrey took Chili's arm and turned him toward the terrace.

They crossed the dance floor. She had a way of tilting her chin that he decided he liked.

On the terrace they sat down on a stone bench and listened to the orchestra play another foxtrot. He offered her a bicep.

"Here, feel this," he commanded, flexing.

"Muscle," she said, touching his sleeve.

He took off his jacket and shirt.

"Put your hand there," he told her. "See? I'm hard as brick."

With her fingers resting on his bare chest, she couldn't fully get her breath, and in a hoarse effort she asked, "Who are you?"

"Chili Cavenaugh," he said proudly.

"Ah, yes. I've heard of you." It was the most flattering thing she could have uttered, never mind *what* she had heard.

He put on his shirt, tossed the dinner jacket over his shoulder, and led her back inside to the buffet. They ordered gin fizzes. Then they went into a parlor and she drew a map on club stationery of where she lived, making Lake Naivasha quite small and the X that marked her father's plantation unduly large. When they strolled back toward the dance floor, some of her group tried to talk to Chili, but he paid Audrey elaborate attention and failed to respond. With his jacket flung over his shoulder he looked supremely confident, while the others had to console themselves with being merely fashionable.

The orchestra played "Good Night, Ladies" as everyone swayed to the last dance. Chili pulled Audrey into a cloakroom and kissed her throughout the whole song, one long, wet, crushing kiss with his hands sliding down her body. She felt violated and stunned. When he let her go, at last, a short burst of laughter came out of her; she looked at him with amazement, an open wonder that she felt even more completely for herself.

Years later she told all this to Lucien. She wore a gardenia that night, she recalled, that turned brown with the crush of Chili's body in the cloakroom.

And she told the rest of it, too: how Chili came courting with a garish yellowed trophy more than ten feet long, an elephant tusk he had collected on one of his safaris. Shreds of rotting meat still clung to one end, and before he knocked on the door of her house up at Lake Naivasha he tossed it on her father's neatly trimmed lawn. Since her mother's death, her father had continued his wife's gardening: the lawn, the iron gate, gazebo, fountain, and all those little islands of flowers were a tidy tribute to her memory. Yet Chili came up the front walkway with the tusk on his shoulder, and tossed it carelessly onto the grass.

"Sir, a small gift for you," he drawled at Mr. Winston.

Audrey's father sniffed it. "Stinks," he remarked.

"It's my present especially for you," Chili said.

Mr. Winston regarded this brute specimen. Did the boy possibly intend any insolence in that last reply? What had happened at the charity dance? But before her father could think or say anything more Audrey came through the front door and moved between them. She wore a sleeveless white dress with an orchid pinned to the belt.

"Daddy," she said, "this is the famous Chili."

Her voice and manner gave it all away, and her father's shoulders sagged in resolution.

The tusk remained on the lawn until the grass beneath it died. In time, her father gave them the big empty house in the Muthiaga district of Nairobi, their wedding present. He had no more need for a house in town, he told his daughter, and he intended to die on his plantation beside the lake—which soon he did.

Stories. Even the parts Audrey felt reluctant to tell Lucien he eventually asked about until he knew them all. She told him the best and worst of it with that same elegant tilt of her chin—a bemused teacher reciting a history of folly.

She learned that there were other women in the first year of their marriage. "What women?" Chili had demanded at the time. "Name just one!"

"Hannah, that whore at the Blue Hotel!"

"Her? Hannah?" he shouted, his consternation somehow

weaker than his voice. "I don't know her at all! I just go round to the bar at that damn place!"

"For all I know you're servicing half the black girls there."

"You're listening to rumors!"

"I saw you myself Tuesday night! Coming out of her door with her hand in yours! And she's bug-eyed like Bette Davis, too!"

Chili sat down hard in a chair.

"There's just one thing I want from you now," she told him. "Give me a baby before you disease yourself."

"Look, I can explain Tuesday night," he lied.

"Get me pregnant," she said. "Go to a doctor and make sure you're safe. And kindly stay away from the Masai women. And the Blue Hotel if you can manage it—at least until you've accomplished your duty at home."

He paced in anguish through the dark house after she had gone to bed that night, as if he were the offended party. He thought of running back to the States, but the big four of Arkansas were only bear, razorback hog, deer, and coon—hardly worth the effort. He concocted a series of appropriate names for her: iceberg, hanging judge, sneaky spy. He hammered a downstairs wall with his fist. Then he stalked into her bedroom and switched on a light.

"If you want to get pregnant, when do we do it? Tonight or when? Let me know."

"Not tonight," she said. "Beginning next Sunday, three nights in a row." He wandered outside, curled up on the lawn beside the empty pool, and went to sleep. She watched from her bedroom window, aching for him.

They would make love again, but would never share the same

bed. His newly acquired sleeping habit she had put down as a form of self-punishment, yet as the years went by she came to dozens of conclusions, sometimes wondering if he listened to the earth out there in the yard, pressing its murmurs into his dreams. She knew he was what the natives called *dume*, the Kiswahili word meaning "very much male." He liked discomfort and danger, yet he also liked to be groomed and well dressed in the city: his male plumage, as he once said himself about his brightly colored silk shirts. He seemed cunning, yet wildly stupid. His vanity was childish without threat to anyone. It was as if she kept a big cat as an unleashed pet and always waited, breath held, until it either moved in some sleek and powerfully graceful manner or came at her to maul her. Was this sexuality? This spellbinding, dumb, irresistible, awesome crush?

After seeing him with that woman, she told Lucien years later, she had only one certainty: she wanted to transform these crude, naked feelings of excitement with all their ambiguities into a love she knew she might eventually get from children.

When I have my child—or perhaps two children—I'll most certainly divorce him, she decided. But, by god, I'll breed with him first. Those shoulders, those arms, that narrow waist, those dark blue eyes: I do want this particular stallion, there's no one like him physically, he has this instinct, this energy, this raw life, and let some of it flow through me.

Later, when Coke was three years old and Lucien had just turned two, Audrey and Chili had their big fight about his rough play with the boys. They wrestled and swatted at each other, Chili always saying, "There, that's how the lion cubs play!" as he gave them loud pops with his open hand. He kept his face close to theirs, so they could swat him back. But eventually one of them, usually Lucien, would end up crying.

"You're simply mean to them!" she screamed one day.

"It's how the lion cubs—"

"Here, pick on someone your own size!" she bawled at him, and she picked up the flyswatter—the one kept in the magazine rack in the sitting room—and struck him with it. The blow raised a welt on his neck.

The boys sat bawling as Chili grinned at her. But she hit him again, drawing blood from his forehead.

"You always keep it up until one of them cries!"

"I'm a good father!" he protested.

She hit him again: another welt and blood. "See how you like it! There! How is it?"

And he began to cry, too, a pair of large wet tears forming in his eyes, not so much from the pain but from his embarrassment and frustration. "Sorry," he told her, and she grabbed up the boys and hurried out of the room.

Years later Lucien asked his mother about those roughhouse sessions with Chili. "You think he held it against me because I got hurt and cried?"

"Nonsense," she said. "You were two years old!"

"But possibly a father just doesn't like one of his children. Just for instance, I mean. Maybe it goes back to the crib: the baby cries too much to suit him. Something like that."

"I'll tell you why that's nonsense," Audrey said. "Because Coke bawled more than you did. He was a big, spoiled crybaby and you know that as well as I do."

Lucien did remember Coke that way—or wanted to—but, even so, he was relieved to hear his mother say it.

SAFARI: Disturbance

In that hot little room they peeled away their clothes and moved together. "You're slippery," Lucien told her.

"Lucky you," she whispered. But their lovemaking seemed oddly changed, more desperate than usual. Then they lay apart, sweating until they fell asleep.

Sometime before daybreak Buster began barking: the low, quick, raspy bark he had for intruders. Lucien got up quickly and pulled on his shorts. When he got outside the clinic, Chili was already striding around with his big Korth pistol.

"The leopard, isn't it?" Lucien asked.

"Ah sure, he's here," Chili replied drunkenly.

He fired off a round from the pistol and it sounded like a cannon, so shapes jumped up everywhere. They were soon surrounded by drowsy, frightened refugees. Buster continued to bark. Coke staggered out of his sleeping spot beneath the wobbly card table and tried to wake himself by putting together a string of obscenities.

For the smallest moment in all this confusion Lucien thought he heard the leopard's deep cough. It had been a dry, hoarse, rattling expanse of breath—unmistakable, when he thought about it. Leopards might look slightly different from place to place, but they had the same terrifying sound, not nearly as loud as a lion's roar, yet somehow a more menacing, subtle, deadly noise.

Now Abba arrived, giving everyone an extravagant toothless grin. A real event was taking place, confirmed by the pistol's discharge, as all around the clinic fires were rekindled.

Trey emerged, wrapped in a sheet.

"I know I just heard it," Lucien told his father.

"You heard what?" Coke wanted to know.

"The leopard," Chili said. "He thinks he heard it."

"Then, damn, we'd've heard it, too!"

"Now that I think about it, I'm certain," Lucien added.

"You heard nothing of the damn sort. You haven't hunted in years and you wouldn't know a leopard cough from a titmouse fart."

Chili, pistol in hand, turned in slow circles. The refugees watched him with stunned awe. "By god, he knows I'm here," he told the darkness.

Others of the refugees drew close to Lucien and Coke so they could listen to the bickering.

"You didn't hear anything, did you, Pop?" Coke asked.

Chili continued to walk in circles. Buster kept up his barking while Trey stood primly in her sheet.

"By god, he knows," Chili said again.

Matters remained unsettled until daylight. Then it was discovered that an old woman had been taken, soundlessly, from the midst of her sleeping family.

ZAMANI:
Leaving School

Ambrose School was in the highlands near Nakuru: a main build-ing where classes were conducted, nine small dormitories made of the same grim brick with dining tables on their screened-in verandas, a dusty playing field, a bath and laundry house, and the principal's bungalow. Almost one hundred boys were en-rolled, including both Coke and Lucien for a number of years.

The staff of nine teachers, imported annually from England, solid at their subjects, if not inspired, and dour in their person-alities, lived one each to a dormitory—each man forced as part of his two-year contract to serve as warden and keeper. Lectures were in mathematics, Latin, science, history, literature, the arts; the brutalities of the playing field were of a more informal nature. Each year some student would set a cobra loose in a dormitory, someone else would take a terrible fever and almost die, and one instructor or another would be accused of sexual misconduct. There were also regularly scheduled and formal atrocities: each morning the principal would cane some unfortunate lad with a bamboo rod, each Sunday some visiting clergyman would drone for an hour as the guest sermon would be delivered in the hot little auditorium of the main building, and each term there would be a Parent's Day picnic.

The meals were the ongoing daily misery.

"What exactly *is* this plate of food?" Coke demanded one noonday of a black dorm waiter on the veranda.

"Ah, master, sir, please, that be yams, chips, mash, and very tiny little boiled ones!"

"Do you mean to say four kinds of potatoes?"

"Ah, sir, yes, thank you very much please!"

Coke and Lucien were the runaways at Ambrose, averaging almost one flight a month. In their first years they hitched rides down to Nairobi and their mother's kitchen, but as they grew older they went off in all directions. They were constantly expelled from school for these infractions, then reinstated. Chili threatened them—he was secretly proud of them, they knew—and paid out sums of money to purchase the tolerance of the principal. Audrey lectured them on the vital necessity of education and gave them muffins.

When Coke was thirteen and Lucien had just turned twelve they ran off to the racecourse over at Lake Nukuru, where they slept in the grandstand for a week and met Sir Archibald. All the wayward highland landowners had gathered for the racing season. The jockeys wore bright silks. Soda, bangers, candy, popcorn, beer and ice cream were sold by black vendors who wore white aprons and straw boaters. The white women had a low, sluttish laughter. Lucien got a job selling programs while Coke ran bets for some of the swells, including Lord Archibald. Coke always laid a few bets of his own with the black stableboys.

They slept in the high, dark reaches of the grandstand—stretched out in the warm Ambrose blankets they always carried with them. Beyond the grandstand were the parked cars, cara-vans, and pitched tents occupied by the highlanders. All night long ukeleles plunked and girls squealed. Glasses clinked and thick British voices uttered things like, "But, ah, my sweet, you *must!*" which fired Coke's imagination so much that he couldn't sleep.

After midnight during the second night of the session, Coke nudged Lucien awake and brought his attention to Sir Archie leading a plump black woman in a wide-brimmed straw hat into the benches nearby. Coke knew Sir Archie well enough by this time. The old man energized the much younger men and women in his party. Money flew from his fingers. He wore a bowler and bossed the stewards around, and for all purposes seemed as though he ran matters at Nakuru.

As the boys watched, the black woman was arranged on a bench very much as if she were a pillow, then mounted. Although they paid extremely close attention to the activity just below them, it was dark in the grandstand so they could only discern the bobbing movements of the giant straw hat and the equally white buttocks of Sir Archibald. The old man pumped, never altering his pace, until he and his partner finished in a crescendo of short gasps. Then there was a long pause. Lucien speculated that the pair might be asleep, stacked male atop female, bowler against straw hat, but then they began to rise and straighten themselves.

As the old man stood up in those deep shadows, he stared up into the darkness directly at Coke and Lucien.

"Now then, who's there?" he asked sharply.

They held their breaths and tried not to be there.

"Down here, both of you, or do I have to fetch you?" Lucien stirred, but Coke burrowed deeper into the Ambrose flannel. The woman made her way down an aisle between the benches and out of the grandstand. After considerable stalling and shuffling about, the boys presented themselves.

"Ho, I say, didn't you run bets to my punter?" Sir Archie asked of Coke. "Didn't you?"

"Yessir," Coke answered, and introduced his younger brother.

"And tell me again, who's your daddy? Don't you have a rather well-known daddy?"

Coke bravely stated Chili's name and occupation.

"Ho, good, it's him, eh? Well, see here, I can't be taking my midnight pleasure down in the middle of camp, can I? Because my wife's there, isn't she? You two can see the indelicacy, right?" He spoke in questions—which had the effect of putting Lucien at ease, as if there was some uncertainty about this odd little man. "So you just had yourself a show? Well, what of it? You liked it, I fancy? And now, see here, what shall I do with you? You can both work for me, what say? Do you two sleep here every night?"

"Yessir," they both replied.

"What say? You'll work for me?"

Lucien seized the chance to do business. "We do sleep in the grandstand," he put in. "We're poor runaways, making our way as best we can. And if you employ us, we'll be loyal."

"So you will, eh? Then you can stand guard here, so the girls can do me proper favors?"

"All night long?" Coke asked, wanting clarification.

"You think I'm that spry, do you?" the old man asked, laughing. "No, not me, who could go all night at my age? Just around this time every evening, how about it? For two shillings each?"

"That's two shillings every night?" Lucien inquired.

"Wouldn't give you less, would I?"

"And do I still run bets for you during the races?" Coke asked.

"You like that, do you?"

"Yessir, very exciting."

"Ho, you lads will work hard, won't you? You'll never tell on me or cheat me?"

"We're loyal, that's sure," Lucien told him again.

"Then you're adventurers and sports like your daddy, are you? I fancy you are, am I right?"

The deal was struck. They entered the employ of Sir Archie, the unofficial patriarch of the picnic, and soon they moved among those caravans and tents with ease. They met a drunken earl, some famous lady horse trainer, an even more famous footballer who had gone fat, and dozens of drifters and amusing liars. The adults played bridge, gin rummy, or bezique as the vendors in aprons and straw boaters hurried around with trays of drinks. Occasionally groups of highlanders strolled out to the paddock and back again under the protection of bright parasols, or pitched horseshoes under the trees, or took lengthy naps. Everyone stood against the cars talking racing odds. But none of them talked hunting, Lucien noted, and their skin was less ruddy and their laughter was a lot less convincing than the hunters he knew. The highlanders seemed at times—and he strained with all his labored reasoning to comprehend this—desperately jolly.

Yet Coke relished their every word and gesture. When Lady Berta, Sir Archie's wife, carried on about jockeys, Coke listened in and hid his laughter under his hand.

"I take it they have small, very hard, perfectly formed male appendages," she remarked to those who were at her table beneath the shade of the poinsettia tree. "They can't have much, I mean, but I suppose they're so terribly *frisky*, wouldn't you agree?" Riding britches covered her ample bottomside and her metallic voice echoed across the nearby exercise track, where everyone watched the thoroughbreds at gallop. She sipped spiked lemonade and ate wafers.

In two days the boys made so much money that Coke decided to purchase himself the favors of a fifteen-year-old black girl named Tamu.

"You can watch," he told Lucien.

"I don't think I really want to, but thanks."

"Why not? You watch Sir Archie every night?"

"It's in a dark grandstand."

"Lucien, believe me, it won't bother me for you to watch, and you very much need to observe the mechanics," Coke advised him.

"Do you know how?"

"Better than you. And, besides, one learns by doing."

The liaison took place one afternoon between races in an empty stable. Bars of sunlight slanted across the new straw as Tamu presented herself for inspection. She was a slender reed of a girl with enormous ebony breasts and a glistening slit. They moved her into one of the bright patches of sun for a closer and better look and for a while they both behaved like doctors. She became bored. Lucien was keen to observe, but far less inclined to touch her or to get into any real calisthenics, but Coke suddenly let his short trousers fall, presented himself to Tamu's indifferent gaze, then jumped on her and began to wrestle. For several anguished minutes he failed to make any essential contact, pumping the air with the same determined rhythm Sir Archie had been demonstrating in the night shadows of the grandstand. Tamu and Lucien exchanged weak smiles during these unattached moments. She occasionally tried to guide her attacker and to make suggestions, but Coke was too busy to take much notice or instruction. At last she fought him off, held him, calmed him, and guided him home. After that the bout lasted no more than another thirty seconds.

Coke had to pull up his trousers and hurry to Sir Archie for the next round of bets.

"Touch her, go ahead," Coke called to Lucien as he departed. "She's paid for."

Lucien remained, gazing at her. Then he fumbled a coin out of his pocket, paying her a bonus to let him touch her. She allowed him to stroke her for only a moment before she stood up, brushed the straw off her body, and tied the *kekoi* over her nakedness.

The boys made good money throughout the remainder of the week. Coke spent his on sweets, beer, a souvenir riding crop, bets with the stableboys, and two more bouts with Tamu. Lucien saved all his and wore britches that drooped with the weight of his shillings.

Meanwhile, the boys observed the highlanders at play. The intrigues fascinated them: meetings in canoes out on the little lake, trysts under the favorite baobab tree, engagements between this husband or that wife in neutral caravans or automobiles, and Sir Archie in the grandstand. When it was over the boys were exhausted and worldly.

Back at Ambrose, Coke told extravagant stories about his prowess—safely away from comments that might have been added by the stableboys or Tamu herself. And Lucien, surrounded by eager listeners in his own dormitory, spoke, in general, of life on the outside and, in particular, of female anatomy. On this last topic he brought back to his classmates the information that the orifice of their constant speculation was located further below the belly button than any of them had previously contended. "Actually, she sits on it," Lucien divulged, speaking like an authoritative geographer who had just come back from a nether region. Several dorm residents insisted that his findings were wrong. But everyone had comments, both lewd and scientific.

The days stretched on: bright, crystalline mornings that called them outdoors, but now, because of their frolic at the races, they were confined to dormitories and were watched. Audrey wrote a long letter of apology to the faculty. Chili donated two sides of beef to the kitchen at school, claiming it was good meat, but when cooked it had the texture of rhino.

The boys endured, suffering classes, schedules, and the Ambrose odor that none could bear: a musty, mildewed, bookish smell that wafted out of the skimpy library and seeped into the instructors' clothes, into the food, into the very pores. At night Lucien buried his nose in his beloved blanket—the one he carried on his escapes—and tried to breathe from it the free spices of the savannah.

Since the term continued from September into June—the same as in the English school system—this put the boys indoors at their desks throughout the best weather. Their holidays in July and August were often spent in the misery of the monsoon rains and chilly African winters. It seemed unfair, and they told their parents so in a letter of petition signed Your Only Sons, Coke and Lucien, so their precise relationship might be remembered at home. In reply, Audrey wrote how sorry she was and told various bits of family news. Chili, she also revealed, was soon off to the old camp near Mount Meru, where he would be on a cheetah hunt. The boys remembered the camp well. They had gone down there on a long weekend picnic with their parents and others—including somebody's female cousin who had pigtails and the beginnings of breasts.

They began to calculate. Their father would be at the camp on the first of the month. They decided to run away and join him, allowing themselves four days for travel. It gave them little concern that the camp on the slopes of Mount Meru was nearly three hundred miles away. After all, they were white boys, experienced hitchhikers, sassy, with Lucien's shillings in their pockets.

For days they smuggled their possessions out of their dorms, stowing everything in the stump of a eucalyptus tree beyond the playing field: clothing, the blankets, Coke's souvenir riding crop, Lucien's precious lion's tooth on a silver chain, candies, and the money.

"I say we don't come back to Ambrose, no matter what," Lucien said, surprising himself with his certainty.

"Good," Coke said. "Agreed."

"This should get us expelled, in any case, but I worry about what Audrey and Chili might do. I think Mama might ship us off to England, so we'd never get home."

"She wouldn't do that, would she?" Coke asked. "We're not bloody Brits, are we? We're Americans!"

"Are there schools in Arkansas?"

"Lucy, quit thinking all the dark thoughts. This is it. We won't go to school anymore. They can't make us. And as for me, damn, I'm going to hunt with Pop. It's time for it."

That settled, they fled at morning light and were picked up by a lorry driver on his way down to Nairobi. In the city they decided against phoning Audrey. Instead, they went to warehouse row and found a transport driver who accepted a pound in cash to take them toward Namanga. The wide boulevards of Nairobi became narrow streets, then dirt roads, then rutted paths winding toward the horizon.

In the western sky they eventually caught sight of the looming silhouettes of Kilimanjaro and its sister peak Meru. The sky about them whirled with vultures and kites. A pack of dogs ran beside them on the road, keeping pace, their muzzles caked red, fierce glints in their eyes. Giraffes moved in the twilight like awkward puppets that might come loose and fall apart in their angular strides.

Columns of smoke rose up from the windless savannah as if to announce here is a man, here, and here is another one.

The boys sat on the splintery wooden bed of the lorry, smiled at each other, and felt drunk with their destiny.

The driver let them off at a village crossroad where dozens of black travelers from several tribes huddled in ditches to wait out the night. Nearby was a tiny duka, its kerosene lamp still burning, children playing beneath its oversized Coca-Cola sign. They bought strips of dried beef, bananas, and more candy, then stood outside eating as fast as they could so the children wouldn't beg away their suppers. In the ditch with the others, they wrapped in their blankets, glanced up at the canopy of stars, and closed their eyes.

Chili was cutting leather thongs for his hunt when he looked into a distant valley and saw two figures moving toward him. He put the binoculars on them: Coke and Lucien, walking un-armed across a land of low bushes where both lion and cheetah hunted. He picked up his rifle and hurried toward them.

When he was within shouting distance, he began cursing.

Coke waved and smiled, but under his breath cursed back.

"Stupid, silly, bloody little shits!" he called to them in greeting.

He wore a soiled cotton vest without a shirt. The muscles in his arms were like thick coils of rope and he had a manly stench. The big Winchester in his hands glinted in the sun. Both sons felt a keen sense of awe, yet a curious distance; they were paralyzed with fear, yet delighted to see him. "What the hell do you think you're doing? How far have you walked? Why're you here?"

"The thought of a lion seeing us did cross my mind," Coke admitted. "But, Pop, if one had attacked I would've given him Lucien."

The joke failed. Chili shouted and cursed some more.

"You ran off again, didn't you?"

"We finished exams at school," Lucien said, offering only a partial lie.

"Got firsts, both of us!" Coke put in, lying with more enthusiasm. "We made the honor roll, so they gave us a holiday!"

Chili, believing none of this, gave them a mirthless laugh.

"We hitched rides down to Nairobi, then over to Namanga," Coke went on, trying to fill the moment with as much chattiness as possible. "We slept in ditches. Then we walked. Maybe we walked a hundred miles. We remembered how to get here, as you can see."

Lucien cringed. His father regarded them in fierce silence, then turned and started walking toward camp. The boys looked at one another, then followed.

"You'll mind everything I say out here," he told them. "You'll do exactly what you're told."

"Yessir," Lucien managed, and Coke broke out in relieved laughter.

Lucien woke up cold the next morning, wrapped himself in his blanket, and left the tent to poke up the ashes of the fire. He stood looking across the plain toward the mountains: scrub brush, low thorn trees and sandy earth. Meru had become a pavilion of clouds. The spike grass had beaded with droplets of heavy dew and the breeze was fresh.

His father's two favorite workers—Watu and Bubba—saddled the horses and gathered gear: burlap bags, leather thongs, and pistols. Chili had left camp before first light to scout the low hills and now Lucien wished that he hadn't slept so late, that he had mounted up and gone along, and that he and his father might be sitting together on a rock out there, scanning the horizon and telling each other personal things. He wished he could say something—anything—to Chili that came out right. He wished he could be either Watu or Bubba, with real skills.

Chili returned for breakfast. Coke eventually struggled out of his tent, drowsy and silent, and they all stood around the fire eating hotcakes as the sun came up.

"There are two cheetahs," Chili revealed quietly. "A mother and her big cub. They're out there chewing on a jack zebra they probably killed late yesterday. Just over there, maybe a mile off."

Watu and Bubba looked expectant. Lucien and Coke stuffed their mouths with hotcakes.

"Now that's real money at the London Zoo, boys, so pay close attention," Chili went on. Lucien waited, hoping to get precise instructions. But Chili just sipped his coffee.

"Go on," Lucien urged.

"When we ride out, stay single file. When we get there, do exactly as I do and say."

Lucien's hands tingled. Clearly, they would get their training on the job.

They rode out quietly. The boys shared the oldest nag, while Chili, Watu, and Bubba sat on lively mounts. The horses had been borrowed from Archer, another crony of Chili's, who, of course, didn't know what dangerous work was planned.

"Pop, I should have a *pistol*," Coke complained.

"Me, too," Lucien added, feeling like a fool for not making this obvious suggestion himself.

"You won't need 'em," Chili said.

They clomped over parched ground, unarmed. Lucien hated the old horse, its flanks jolting him with each step, its flesh smelly, everything fat and slow. He also hated sitting in the rear, holding onto his brother's belt. Yet a tiny tremor of fear—a pleasant, nervous quake—pulsed in his blood.

They arrived at a low hill that gave them a view of the cheetahs. There lay the zebra, torn open. The cats were beside it with their bellies full.

Again, Lucien expected detailed instructions and waited, but something was happening to Chili now: a look had come into his eyes.

"You two follow your daddy," Bubba told the boys. "Never mind where we go. We all very busy. So you follow Daddy."

Fascinated, Lucien watched his father. He had never seen this expression before, not even when Chili was angriest with them for their mischief. An altogether new look, hideous and funny and entertaining.

Chili turned his mount and kicked its sides.

"Yah!" His horse went straight for the two cheetahs. Lucien saw the cats raise their heads to see what foolish thing came at them.

Watu and Bubba, waving those burlap bags around their heads, kicked their horses into a gallop and followed.

Digging their heels into their nag, Lucien and Coke strained to go forward.

The two cheetahs broke in separate directions, so the chase was on. Lucien held on to Coke's belt and struggled to see the action, worrying that they'd be left behind and worrying that they'd get there without pistols.

For a thousand yards the cheetahs easily outran their pursuers; then the gaps began to close. Suddenly the big mother cat took cover in a clump of thorny weed—a poor place for her to hide, but she was too weary to go on. Chili and Watu arrived beside her, pulling up their mounts in a cloud of dust. She tried to burrow out of sight, the horses circled that clump of weeds and Chili brought his horse forward to paw at the ground beside her snarling face. Then she broke cover again, but her strength was gone and the horses easily kept up.

Coke and Lucien gained on them during this pause and saw everything that happened afterward.

She took refuge beside a lone boulder, her back arched, unable to hide or run. Again, Chili and Watu rode up, but this time they dropped off their mounts and confronted her. Hurriedly, Chili took off his vest and wrapped it thick around his forearm. Watu separated those leather strands.

As she clawed at them, Chili feinted one way, then another, and Watu darted in. Lucien's mouth went dry as he watched his father fall directly on the cat's back, driving her to earth. There was no question who was strongest. If the cat's blood was up, Chili's was up higher.

Watu entangled her hind legs with the leather strands. Chili stuffed his wrapped arm right into her mouth and as the dust flew the horses reared away, trotting off at a safe distance.

As Lucien and Coke arrived, the cheetah struggled to bring up her hind legs so she could rake or gut their father, but Watu was in charge. In another ten seconds her forelegs were tied, too.

Then she was poked into the burlap bag and the package was tied off with more rawhide.

Chili was grinning and running. His vest was torn and he had a few scratches while Watu had only a single wound: a bright bubble of blood adorned his shoulder.

Chili got to his horse, mounted again, reined up, and yelled, "Lucien! Get down from there and sit on that cat!"

Watu gave off a loud, happy cry.

Then Chili was gone, turning his horse toward Bubba and the big cub. Terrified, Lucien slid off the nag to do his duty.

Coke rode off to watch the next catch, but Lucien could see that the big cub had taken refuge in a pig hole not far away. Again, Chili rode up and dismounted in a cloud of dust, then pulled the cub out by its tail while Bubba bound its deadly hind legs. The cat was too exhausted and afraid to put up much of an argument, Coke said later, and didn't even try to bite the men as they stuffed it into the second burlap bag.

It was scary sitting there on the cheetah. Lucien could feel the creature's heavy breathing underneath him and could hear its deep moaning purr. He worried that at any moment it might get its strength back and roar out to take its revenge on its tormentors.

But soon Chili galloped toward him again, so he relaxed. His father rode up, dismounted again, and started pacing in circles. That strange look was still in his face: a crazed and innocent excitement.

"Good!" his father said, breathing wildly. "Good work! Very good, son!" His vest was in tatters, his scratches bled, his hat was gone, and the sheer idiotic brutality of it all had hold of him.

Lucien sat proudly on the prize, turning so he could watch his father circling around him.

And Lucien had no words for what he felt, but later, years later, he would think more clearly about it. At that moment he was in the true and deep wildness of things, in the blood and marrow of the dirty earth, and eventually he would remember knowing one thing out of it all: that he never wanted to go into rooms again, certainly not into schoolrooms, that life was free and in the open, untamed, and that among the beasts his father was by far the greater beast.

SAFARI:
Tracking

In the late morning they followed the obvious trail the leopard had made when it dragged the old woman out of camp.

They climbed into the rocky hills above the clinic, Chili in his cowboy hat, Lucien in mirrored sunglasses, Coke with a blue bandanna tied across his brow, Abba with his double set of ears, all of them followed by Buster.

The leopard was serious business, but they felt some of the old pleasant anticipation of sport.

"When we get to the rocks up there, don't lose sight of each other," Chili warned them needlessly. "C'mere, Buster!"

The big retriever fell into step.

Father and sons were a deadly little platoon. Their movements were often slow and deliberate, but when they spotted their quarry they had a way of swinging quickly and silently into line to back up the man nearest the target. Buster worked well between them, sniffing out of his low crouch, pacing hard, and he never missed when the quarry got near, raising his nose, going on point, and lifting his foreleg. They had hunted together for so long that the Cavenaughs and their dog, by turns, scanned the horizon, observed the middle distance, and studied the various prints beneath their feet.

Higher up, they left the spike grass behind and found themselves walking through a powdery, dark, volcanic ash. All around were boulders the size of tents. The call of the hyrax accompanied their steep walk.

Then the leopard's tracks ended in a field where the powdery ash looked as though it had been combed. Thousands of tiny lines crossed it—the tracks of insects that had moved with the morning wind across the top of the ridge.

"I'll be goddamned," Chili drawled.

Lucien crouched down for a clearer look. "What did this?" he asked Abba.

"Centipedes," the old man said.

The leopard had dragged its victim all the way up here, making an obvious trough through grass, sand, and ash, then suddenly this: it was as if another part of nature had conspired to let the marauder get away.

They walked across the barren, combed stretch—perhaps fifty yards wide along the top of the ridge—until Coke climbed a boulder at the far side. He could see the lake to the west, now, and the desert to the east. A vast nothingness.

Lucien kept inspecting those insect tracks.

"Centipedes?" he asked Abba. "I can't believe that."

"Then ants or scorpions," the old man said with a shrug.

"And where did they go? There would be thousands of them!"

"They are very much into the stones," Abba explained.

Chili called them together and they decided to spread out on the ridge, make a slow circle, try to pick up the leopard's trail again, and meet in fifteen minutes. Coke grunted and went off. Abba joined Lucien and Buster fell in with Chili.

"Don't go too far and keep an eye on each other!" Chili called, but Coke, impulsive as ever, was already out of sight.

The hunt—at least for this fifteen-minute period—had become risky. As Lucien advanced toward a cluster of boulders to the north, he gave his pistol to Abba. The old man held it with both hands like a true burden.

The boulders formed avenues of rock filled with crevices and alcoves where anything could happen. Lucien felt the first tinge of fear. Fear like cold water: it splashed you awake. Out here, once more, he was elemental, and the old wariness arrived quickly.

A bird's cry jerked Abba around.

Further on, they passed a crudely made windbreak of thatch. A shepherd's isolated spot, Lucien speculated. Or some crazed and lonely tribesman, who had come up here to avoid even the simple commerce of his kinsmen. Inside the windbreak there was a broken gourd filled with spiderweb.

Fifteen minutes passed.

The boulders seemed to go on and on. There were dozens of places where the leopard could hide his kills, so Lucien turned back.

Chili had somehow lost Buster.

"Okay, we wait for him," Coke said when they were all standing together again.

Chili broke the silence of the ridge, bellowing out Buster's name and whistling, but he didn't come even then.

Lucien told them about the boulders to the north. Chili had

gone east, where the ash turned into rough gravel before spilling over a barren cliff. Coke had seen nothing to the south.

They turned back toward the boulders in hopes that Buster had chased a hyrax or a ground squirrel into the maze. Chili became silent, his eyes darting everywhere, as the rocks surrounded and enclosed them. It was like a stone cathedral. Coke committed the sacrilege of pissing on some wildflowers.

Further on they entered a wide path filled with sparkling cinders and lava shards.

"There must have been a volcano here, but where?" Lucien asked. "There's no crater." He wondered if long ago the ground in this loathsome stretch of land might have opened up: a fissure of hot lava, a crack that led into the land of the lost.

"It's bloody noisy enough," Coke said as their footfalls snapped and popped.

There were places where they could see the lake: an immense sheen. Chili stood mesmerized, once, and had to gather himself together before joining them again.

Under an overhanging ledge of rock Lucien imagined that he saw some crude lettering and drawings, but dismissed the idea. Yet there it was: dim pastel that might have been the marks of some Stone-Age artist and the shape of some creature, perhaps a kudu. The hunters stood in the shade of the overhang, discussing their next move, and as they talked Lucien decided that the rock's minerals had simply bled, faded into the odd shapes and figures. Yet this was a curious place. The hills seemed to be waiting for them.

"He's right here, he's close," Chili said. "I can feel how damn close he is."

"All I feel is thirsty and hungry," Coke said. "What time is it?"

"Just past four," Lucien answered, and passed him a canteen—the only water anyone had bothered to bring along. Coke drank out of it until Chili took it away from him and drank, too.

Abba had a drink, then Lucien, as they went on discussing their problem. On a usual hunt, they agreed, they would be on open ground and proceed as a unit, everyone keeping silent and watching while Chili directed them with hand signals. But here the terrain favored the leopard. The boulders kept them from seeing one another, so they were forced to call out and give away their positions. The leopard had probably abandoned the ridge by now, but if he was still nearby—as Chili claimed—he could hide, outflank them, and study them while they stumbled after him.

The proper tactic, they agreed, was to hang a bait on the outskirts of the camp, post a man with a rifle, keep careful watch, and wait. But this simple and obvious plan was no good now. The leopard had acquired a taste for humans and probably wouldn't respond to anything less than one of the refugees. And, besides, family pride was at stake. They had announced to Trey and the whole refugee population that they would track and kill the devil.

There was a very good reason why men didn't hunt leopards and they saw it clearly here: unlike the lion or cheetah, both of whom hunted on open savannahs, running down their prey, the leopard was a solitary raider, living on high ground, coming down from his hiding places for nocturnal kills or waiting in ambush in his own domain. He was a secretive cat, seldom seen, and often lived in a situation like this for years without attracting attention. And more than any other creature of the continent he often became a man-eater. He might live on monkeys, rodents, birds, antelope, or jackal until he tasted man, but after devouring human flesh, they knew, the leopard always preferred more of it.

"Dammit, I want to find Buster," Chili finally said.

They all exchanged a glance and feared the worst.

Lucien tried to calculate Buster's age. He had given the family some brave moments, but he was old and slower now. And they hadn't even heard him barking.

"Hell, maybe he's on point," Coke offered.

"Maybe," Chili said, hopefully.

They moved out of the shade of the ledge and started walking again. In spite of himself, Lucien could see Trey dancing with Coke. Their swaying embrace. It was romantic paranoia, he realized, and he felt idiotic, but he couldn't stop thinking about it. My love in the arms of Mfifo.

They headed for the highest point among the boulders, climbing at such a steep angle that they often had to lean forward and grope with their weapons rattled on the stones. Old Abba kept up very well. For a few minutes after they reached the top Lucien could hear only the sound of his own breath.

Up high, they could view the whole situation. The outcropping of boulders covered perhaps a half-mile square along the north of the ridge. It was like a little stone city set on a hill, and somewhere in its alleyways the leopard had its lair.

"This is a bitch," Chili admitted. He took out his field glasses and studied certain formations.

Abba's second set of ears rotated in the wind.

"I don't think we've got a blind leopard," Coke said. "Maybe an albino. You know how an albino's eyes get? I figure that's what the locals saw."

"Might be a good guess," Chili allowed.

"Up here near the desert the leopards bleach out, you know," Coke went on. "Their rosettes get pale. They get blond."

"If that's so, our leopard is about the color of these rocks," Chili said, still peering through his binoculars.

"I've seen jungle leopards that were damn near green in their pelts," Coke said, keeping up the dissertation.

"What's the biggest leopard you ever saw?" Chili asked Lucien.

"They're all about a hundred pounds, aren't they?"

"That's what I'd say: all about the same. You might see a fat croc, but there aren't any giant leopards, right?"

Their discussions always had about the same tone, and echoes of hundreds of other discussions were in this one. They had talked about every creature on the continent, then repeated their observations over and over to one another by way of confirming them. Lucien knew he had heard Coke talk about leopards before—probably imitating Chili's views—and he knew what was going to be said next.

"No two leopards alike." Coke sighed. "Their rosettes never have the same pattern. And they have different colorations."

That ended their ritual conversation on the species, a conversation Lucien had anticipated since the plane landed.

Slowly, they made their way back down.

One day, Lucien told himself, we should have a conversation about women. We're all interested in the species. That's our very most special subject—and we know it and we don't.

They walked a difficult quarter of a mile back toward that field of volcanic ash and isolated boulders. Chili, Abba, and Lucien shared the last contents of the canteen, and Coke said he didn't want any, then changed his mind and complained that the water was gone.

At one of the large boulders near the east cliff of the ridge they found what was left of Buster.

"Goddammit!" Chili called out, walking in circles around the bloody remains. Coke bent down and touched a mat of sticky hair where the leopard had bitten through Buster's spine.

"Look at this," Lucien said, showing them the tracks.

The leopard might have dropped out of nowhere. Buster was killed beside a boulder and all of the cat's tracks led away from it.

"Maybe it was just sitting up here on this boulder and Buster didn't see it," Lucien speculated.

Chili and Lucien walked around the perimeter of the rock looking at prints, blood, hair, and signs of a struggle. Large prints: a big male, for sure.

"Think the leopard could've jumped from one of those boulders to another to this one?" Lucien asked, and he and Chili paced off the distance to a boulder close by. The big rocks were set twenty to thirty feet apart. Chili studied them and nodded.

"Yeah, look at this," he said, showing Lucien where the leopard took a running start and in a series of leaps from the top of one boulder to another landed on Buster.

"That settles it," Lucien said. "Our cat's not blind."

"Doesn't look like it," Chili agreed with a measure of disappointment. "Unless the leopard can feel the warmth of these boulders and knows exactly where everything is around here." The old man somehow wanted this mysterious, blind foe, and Lucien could only give him a smirk. Meanwhile, Coke gathered up Buster in his arms.

"No, son, leave him here," Chili said. "If the refugees see him like that, they'll go crazy. Besides, the leopard will maybe decide to eat him—and that may spare somebody's life down in camp."

Coke set Buster down gently. "Dammit, he'll want something to eat better than dog."

"Well," Chili said, "he's got himself an old woman tucked away somewhere. And now Buster. A leopard will eat on a kill until it's putrid, so let's just buy a little time. We're gonna have to find this cat and shoot it, so we need a little time, right?"

Both Coke and Lucien agreed. Reluctantly they turned and started back downhill as the sun began to set beyond the lake. They knew what this meant: the shadows falling across the boulders and the pale light of sundown made further hunting impossible.

Abba said he remembered this same fine dog from the time they hunted together at the south end of the lake. "This was a very true dog," he told them.

Coke asked Chili if he remembered that big Fourth of July celebration, when Buster got shot and the big family argument erupted because of it, but Chili went on downhill without responding to any of this. He wasn't thinking of times past or of losing Buster or of anything except the strategy at hand. This was a dangerous hunt in these little hills, far more dangerous than he wanted to admit or than any of them wanted to talk about.

ZAMANI:
A Boxing Match

During World War II, just before Lucien and Coke attended Ambrose School, their father served as a sergeant in the Kenya Regiment. His first duty occurred in Tanganyika, where he helped round up German civilians, all of whom Chili later said he rather liked and one of whom, a widow who owned a plantation near Iringa, Lucien later found out became Chili's mistress.

When Coke first used the word *mistress* Lucien understood this to mean a fancy female client, one who paid his father for special attention on hunting safaris. Years later he would come to have a better understanding of the word and a clearer picture of Chili's services. He would also meet this German woman in person: a thin creature who smoked cigarettes with all her soul, inhaling down that narrow tube of her body and blowing out streamers of ice-blue smoke. Of course, Lucien promptly compared the woman with Audrey, finding her far less attractive than his mother and feeling that Chili had lowered himself terribly in the affair. The woman was so skinny that she seemed transparent, bones and veins showing through her pale skin. A ghastly trade, Lucien felt, but he failed to understand that his father had traded nothing, for even when he met the mistress he was too young to fully comprehend sexual foolishness.

After Tanganyika, Chili served at the Ethiopian border where an Italian division had massed itself for an attack. But weeks at the border came to nothing because the Italians preferred not to fight, so Chili's regiment was eventually moved to the Nanyuki Sports Club, where the officers played polo. In this tour of duty, Chili was twice offered commissions, but he chose to remain a sergeant. Rumor was that he was once offered a lieutenant's rank for drinking a quart of Irish whiskey at a party, then managing to make reveille the next morning.

He visited Nairobi only rarely. On such occasions the boys would be warmly greeted, hugged, then offered a few shillings to spend away from the house. Their mother was always required for long talks upstairs. Sometimes the boys returned from the local *duka*, where they bought candy and colas, to find their parents still unavailable, so they made thick jam sandwiches and played in the yard. Jam and marmalade were scarce items during the war, but the boys were never scolded.

Often the house filled with soldiers and women, most of whom Audrey didn't like. But Chili was popular, and during his leaves he always served as host. Audrey locked the family food in the pantry and for a while Coke was entrusted with the extra key, but he abused this privilege with Lucien, so Audrey took it away from him.

There were nights when the boys watched from their bedroom window as couples strolled outdoors, stopping to fondle and kiss. An old gramophone played "Elmer's Tune" and everyone danced around the pool—which was always in embarrassing disrepair. Late at night the sounds of breaking glass could occasionally be heard. Sometimes Teddy Wickham or another drunken corporal slept on the couch in the downstairs hallway.

Toward the end of the war Chili was assigned to a special unit to hunt lions. Quite a few lions on the northern frontier got a taste for human flesh—especially those poor Italians who lay around after ambushes, according to the boys' sources—so Chili rode around in an armored lorry looking for man-eaters with Percy Spence, Teddy Wickham, and a young British major. They shot thirty-odd lions, and all the men in the squad got medals except for the major, who met a grisly fate. Audrey forbade the boys to keep repeating the story of the major, but they couldn't help it. He was caught out in the open by two large cubs after his rifle jammed. They had already fed, but they swatted and mauled him, then finally tore him open and left him there. After they were gone, the major crawled back to his weapon, got it unjammed, loaded it, and put himself out of his misery.

In those last days there weren't many Germans in East Africa, so the regiment traveled here and there for parties. Audrey accused Chili of roaming the countryside looking for drink and women.

"I simply follow orders!" he complained in his defense. This was an April evening the boys remembered well.

"You follow that pointer in your pants!" she screamed at him, and he tried to put an arm around her. "Don't you dare touch me! You've probably fouled yourself!"

"Audrey, please, c'mere, I have not!" he kept saying, and he followed her around the house while the boys listened. They quickly withdrew from sight up the stairwell, but paid close attention to the ongoing confrontation.

That night Chili went to the back lawn and kicked with the heel of his boot until there was a hole in the ground beside the empty pool. Then he put his bottom in the hole, curled up, and went to sleep. It was the first time Lucien remembered seeing his father do this peculiar thing.

Then the fleet came to Mombasa.

Suddenly the house filled up with men from Chili's regiment and dozens of strangers. Two servants were hired to pick bottles off the lawn and carpets, to cook, and to do Audrey's wishes. A delegation arrived from a battleship: bright naval officers in white uniforms, who met Chili's colonel and toasted Audrey with champagne. As the boys soon understood it, their father was going to fight the heavyweight champion of the fleet, but a celebration was in progress as if he had already won. One of the new servants stole a silver dish and was dismissed. A formal dinner was announced at the Muthiaga Club for which Audrey bought a blue dress, her first new dress in years. Chili hoisted barbell weights in the side yard: a makeshift gymnasium in the red clay dust beneath the jacaranda tree. Men sat in the parlor all night telling stories and showing off various weapons. It was a time of confusion, hard sentiment, and gaiety.

Lucien watched his mother in the blue dress as she prepared her face for the formal dinner. She had no proper eye makeup, so used the tip of a burnt match.

"I only hope I marry someone as beautiful as you," he told her.

She sat on the bed beside him and took his hand in hers. Tears boiled in the corners of her eyes and he knew she'd have to use another match. She tried to speak with him.

"It has been such a long, awful war," she said, and she seemed to be crying for someone in particular, but he didn't know exactly who. Maybe the young major killed by lions, he thought, but, no, someone else, somebody more dear. He hated that he had upset her.

But as always when he interrupted her, she had a way of stopping whatever she was doing, coming to him, taking his hand, and giving him her full attention. Her cheek was wet and faintly discolored by the burnt match when she kissed him. Then she went back to her mirror, dabbing at her face and fixing her eyes once more.

A few days later they boarded the train for Mombasa. It was an impressive train, but hot: flies everywhere, porters selling gummy sugar rolls in the aisles, the stench of bodies, and Audrey and her sons looking starched and prim as they occupied facing seats. The seats were green leather, old and cracked, but the wood was polished and the handles at the corners were genuine ivory.

They passed through Tsavo, where they could see elephants lolling in distant waterholes. They also saw a vulture feeding on the back of a wildebeest that wasn't yet dead, but was docile and near the end. Audrey ordered them not to look at this sad spectacle, but they couldn't help themselves.

"I don't understand either of you," she scolded them. "Why are you so obsessed with gore? You're worse than your father!"

Lucien couldn't think of a reason, but later he remarked, "I think it's because blood is so serious."

"What's that?" Audrey asked him idly, having forgotten about the poor wildebeest.

"Bloody things. They're serious," Lucien pointed out, but her thoughts were elsewhere.

Chili had gone down to the coast earlier, so here they were: this restless, abbreviated family in sticky clothes, following Father across a wasteland. There was only one sanity: a wicker picnic basket that Audrey carefully controlled. From it she pulled out fruit, bits of toast, candy canes, muffins, trimmed sandwiches, and bottles of mineral water. She bribed the boys, one morsel at a time. Day became night. Coke slumped over in sleep, and Audrey produced a deck of cards so that she and Lucien could play slapjack.

How old was he? He wore short britches, he remembered, and they talked about the Yanks landing on the Normandy beach—wherever that was—and how proud they were to be Americans. And he remembered those ivory handles on the seats in the train, the elegant feel of them, and how important the journey seemed.

They stayed at an old hotel near the harbor in view of the Portuguese fort with its cruel walls. Dhows with bright sails glided by their window. A muezzin called from his tower atop the mosque, while vendors bellowed in the streets below.

Their room had a slow ceiling fan and two beds, one for Audrey and the other for the boys. Chili was somewhere else—in training—but on the afternoon of the event he came for a long visit. The boys were given shillings. They went to the hotel lobby and spent their money on shandy, but the streets looked forbidding so they came back upstairs and kept their exile in the corridor. The transom was open into the room, so they became interested in the argument in progress.

"You didn't have to come," Chili told their mother, and perhaps she was crying. "I mean, it's a dumb lark, after all," he went on. "Everybody'll be drunk as usual. And, hell, there's terrible wagering—that's all anyone's talking about. And, see, you'd be the only woman there. It's on the deck of the ship itself, see, and I imagine there's probably rules and regulations about women."

She whispered her insistence.

"It ain't me arguing and stalling," he insisted. "This is a navy thing. I don't know what's proper, see, that's all I'm saying."

"The boys expect to see this spectacle and so do I," she said, her whisper becoming a full forthright voice. "And I want to be on your arm. I want you to usher your family to their seats."

"How can I do that? I'll be in the damn dressing room! I'm the challenger! I'll have to make a proper entrance!"

Lucien knew his father was walking in a circle beneath that lazy ceiling fan.

"Find a way and do it," she told him.

"See, for all I know you don't even have seats! You can't expect to sit ringside along with the admirals and colonels, can you?"

"That would be fine, yes."

"I'm just a sergeant, aren't I? How do I arrange that?"

"You can do it. You're the challenger and you'll get consideration. And I want to be on your arm with the boys."

"Christ almighty, Audrey!"

"Go on. Attend to it. You have time enough to make arrangements."

"Haven't I got plenty to do today just getting my brains knocked out?"

"Win or lose, I want to be there in front of your whole regiment. And I want the boys seeing it, too."

There was a rustle, then silence. The boys assumed that an embrace was in progress, so gave each other a grin. Then Chili laughed and began talking about his opponent, a man from Bristol, a fellow the size of a rhino, undefeated. Everybody at the harbor was drunk, he said, and there was trouble coming no matter who won. Yes, yes, Audrey kept saying, but go arrange matters.

"It's not a proper sporting event, not at all," he said. "It's just a stupid lark. Men getting drunk and wild. And I'm the regimental fool for stepping into the ring."

"You'll do well," she told him.

"It'll be damned awful, don't you see that?"

"You'll be splendid like always."

There was another prolonged rustle.

"You shouldn't be here," he said with a last sigh.

"Get on your way," she said. "Arrange everything."

The door opened and Chili emerged, looking concerned. As he passed his sons, he mussed their hair.

That afternoon they saw the ship and harbor decorated for the occasion: streamers, Chinese lanterns, the Union Jack, bright *kekois*, bunting, hand-painted signs, and hundreds of spectators. Horns sounded. Arabs in flowing robes stood on the roofs of nearby houses so they could view the ring that had been set up on the foredeck of the cruiser.

"It's so big, look, god, it's a battleship," Lucien kept repeating, looking at the two large cannons whose shadows cut across the ring. It was certainly a wonderful ship: thick coats of white paint over all its bolts, coils of heavy rope, machine-gun turrets, portholes, and a little brass band perched on an upper deck.

A young naval officer with a real sword walked by, touching the brim of his cap as Audrey smiled.

One crudely painted sign read PRIDE OF THE KING'S AFRICAN RIFLES. And another: BLACK STAN FROM BRISTOL.

The crowd parted for them as they made their way toward the gangplank, a crowd made up of completely naked blacks, coffee vendors with old copper urns, Europeans in white suits, priests, beggars, punters, and finally the shining sailors who helped them aboard.

At the top of the gangplank they stood with their mother as she paused and looked about. Coke clung to her skirt on one side while Lucien's palm grew sweaty in her grip on the other. Her chin was elegantly high as she studied the hundreds of men who waited for the brawl, and they in turn studied her. This was perhaps what they fought for, this very image of womanhood: a tall woman with a plumpish figure dressed in a high collar and ruffles, a woman of bearing who looked proper and British, her strapping sons at her side. This homey tableau went on and on. A few of the sailors even applauded.

Lucien fretted that his father wouldn't come forward as Audrey had pleaded for him to do.

The band struck up an anthem and everyone stood. From those distant rooftops arms waved and dozens of dirty burnooses bobbed up and down. Lucien felt like saluting, but didn't know who he might salute to.

Then Chili came forward. He wore his full uniform with medals. Offering Audrey an elbow, he led her forward and the boys followed as if this were carefully rehearsed. An appreciative murmur arose from the men and Lucien heard a few stray words: the wife, challenger's lady, the wife and sons.

At their front-row seats, Chili continued to hold her hand as she settled herself and the boys. Then Chili turned smartly, saluted the officers down the line, and marched away. The anthem played on.

Long ago, all this. Lucien remembered some of it all his life. A sailor in the crowd had a monkey on his shoulder and Lucien thought, there, that's dangerous, sir, you're going to get yourself bitten or shit on. And the ship's flags: messages on a slanted rope, flapping against a sky as blue as Audrey's eyes.

The day was hot almost beyond endurance. As they perspired,

Coke consoled himself with a litany of hope: "He'll win, he'll beat the very hell out of Black Stan, he'll win."

Lucien daydreamed of battle: sailing off on rough seas, German U-boats, his finger on the trigger of one of those cannons.

An orderly brought lemon squashes for them.

When Chili made his next appearance he wore a pair of khaki trousers cut off just above his knees and high-topped black army boots that made him look short, stumpy, and ill-equipped. But he was muscled and impressive for all that—a thick chest matted with dark hair, a belly flat and hard as teakwood, broad sunburned shoulders. The men of the regiment called encouragement to him and as the little band sent up a flurry of peppy music, Coke reached across his mother's lap and poked Lucien's knee.

"Barbells!" he called, in all the noise. "If you don't lift weights, Lucien, you'll always have those skinny arms!"

"He doesn't have proper shoes!" Lucien called back.

"Shoes don't matter! He'll beat this dumb Brit!"

"Mind your language through this," Audrey reminded Coke.

Chili's opponent was a brute half again as large, who seemed to sweat more than anyone on deck. Rivulets of perspiration gave his body huge yellowish stripes. His forehead bulged with hard bone and below it, set deep in his face, his eyes glared out.

Chili grinned and waved at his mates.

An argument began about the gloves: Chili's, clearly, were several ounces larger than the champion's.

An officer of the regiment stood up and shouted. "Is our man supposed to hit your damn Limey with those pillows?"

Everyone screamed and called out vulgar opinions in response. At last a colonel stepped into the ring, slipping between the ropes to confront the referee and Black Stan's seconds. Soon a naval commander joined them. Pillows! Unfair! Men stood with their hands on their hips and cried foul.

Audrey bit her lower lip in distress.

But since the champion was left-handed, the matter of the gloves came to a compromise: each fighter would wear one light-weight glove and one pillow. The lighter glove would be worn on each fighter's deadlier hand. This gave both men a lopsided look, Lucien felt, but sportsmanship prevailed.

During the introductions Chili played the clown. He was announced as the finest of the King's African Rifles, for which he seemed grateful as he raised his gloves and accepted the regiment's cheers. But then the announcer recited the champion's credentials: Champion of the Southern Command, Champion of all Indian Ocean Garrisons, Champion of the Fleet, and so on. As this continued, Chili ducked under the ropes as if to get away. Laughter went up all around and the sailors yelled good-natured insults as the brigadier and the colonel howled and clapped the shoulders of the men around them.

Then Chili was back on his stool, waiting. He wore a nervous smile, but glanced toward Audrey and tried to fix it right again.

The first round.

Black Stan was large and quick. He jabbed hard, popping Chili's head back with each blow, and circled well. Then a combination. Chili tried to be even quicker than his larger opponent, but was caught twice, three, four times on the ropes—each time taking brisk volleys of jabs and hooks. He made two vain attempts to hit back, but for such insolence he took a hard blow on his ear that made his legs wobble. He tried to smile and dance away, but the ropes were there again. A sudden hook in the face broke his nose. Everyone saw it clearly as he grabbed the champion and held on.

Lucien was mortified. At the end of the round his father lay back on his stool in his corner as his seconds stuffed rag up his spurting nostrils. A piece of membrane stretched from his nose to his blood-soaked khakis and his mouthpiece was tossed away so he could breathe.

Round two. Chili took a blow that turned his head and splattered blood on the trousers of the naval officers in the front row. A groan went up from the men. Audrey lowered her eyes, so Lucien held her hand with both of his.

Another blow and a piece of rag from one of Chili's nostrils sailed out of the ring. Lucien bent forward and looked up into his mother's hidden face, wondering if she might be crying, but as he did this she raised her chin proudly and resumed watching.

Coke stood on his chair, cheering. But the sailors behind him told him to get down because he blocked their view. He paid them no mind, so they had to stand, too. The monkey was howling. Members of the brass band leaned over the rail on the upper deck.

Then Chili's first real blow: toward the end of the round he dug a hard right into the champion's belly. The grunt was heard over the noise of the crowd. Furious now, the champion started chasing, but Chili spun away as the bell sounded.

More rag got stuffed into Chili's nose. When this was finished, Chili turned on his stool and attempted another smile in the direction of his family. There was nothing of confidence in the smile and his eyes were slightly glazed, but his face seemed to say, there, all right, things are fine, everything is going just as we knew it would.

The third round. Chili went forward, feinted, stepped aside, moved back, then came forward suddenly once more to land another solid blow to the champion's middle. The man gasped, then recovered himself. He went after Chili once more and the boys watched in horror as their father was made to pay. A flurry of punches. Coke was cursing furiously. Then Chili was caught with a hard uppercut and dropped both his hands. The champion measured him for a blow, but Chili turned away as it came. Arms hanging down, he was measured again. This was it: the gory end, Lucien knew, and he sucked in his breath. But Chili somehow slipped that punch, too. Then a quick right hand caught Chili flush in the face and sent him to his knees where he knelt, as if praying, as blood dripped into a little pool between his legs.

But he had gone down from a blow with the champion's big pillow and he stayed down, resting himself, as the referee counted. Chili took several deep breaths, watching his own blood and waiting, then on the count of eight he got up.

Everyone stood now. Deafening cheers and vulgarities.

The champion moved in, trying to finish the fight, but Chili seemed to have a sudden renewal of energy. He found his attacker with another of those deep body blows, a right hand hard in the midsection. The bell rang. Cries, whistles, prolonged shouting, and the monkey's screaming. Both fighters paused, staring at each other, the champion's breath gone, Chili bloody and swollen. But as the crowd roared on, Chili struck again: yet another right hand plowed into the same place. Perhaps he didn't hear the bell. Black Stan bellowed, the veins in his bulging forehead straining as if they might explode; his eyes flared out of those deep sockets and sweat rolled off his steaming frame as if he were a thundercloud.

"After the bell! Foul! Late blow!" cried hundreds of sailors.

Loud protests went up as the fighters retreated to their corners.

"Foul!" the cries went on, then the naval commander had his fist in the air.

Chairs were thrown. A band member dropped his trumpet into the throng below.

Managers and seconds worked quickly, but now both men were badly damaged. Chili's men had turned crimson with blood as the champion bent forward on his stool, his eyes trying to focus, beads of sweat thick as jelly clinging to his shoulders.

The fourth round.

The champion's speed was gone, but Chili's eyes were almost swollen shut, his nose lay grotesquely to one side, and his mouth sucked for air. Chili feinted, stepped back then forward again, and tried for another body punch, but the champion blocked it. He caught Chili, instead, with a peculiar hook: a slow, ponderous, heavy blow that took forever as it circled toward the challenger's head, that came like an iron pipe weighing too much to be delivered with any speed. But once again Chili's arms went to his sides. Black Stan came forward, brushing aside Chili's protesting elbows, shaking loose from a weary embrace, and pounding the neck, face and shoulders. He used his fists like hammers: sidelong, desperate, roundhouse blows.

The sailors screamed now as the regiment sat in silence.

The champion's arms were like clubs—without much real life or energy of their own—but he flung them at his retreating foe.

Chili's seconds were half through the ropes, ready to stop the bout, but there was yet another punch left as Chili dug a final hard right deep into the champion's stomach again. The man grunted like a buffalo, bending over so that his gloves touched his knees. His jaw was exposed, but Chili had nothing more, and as the bell rang Chili sagged to the canvas. His seconds hurried out to him.

Coke, still standing on his chair, wheeled around to address the sailors behind him, yelling, "Call that one a foul, you bastards!" Audrey plucked him out of the chair and shook him.

The naval commander, Chili's colonel, and a doctor entered the ring, consulting with each other and interviewing the fighters. Chili, it seemed, couldn't be revived, but the champion also bent forward on his stool so that his face almost touched his shoes, and no amount of encouragement or applications of smelling salts convinced him to rise. The referee wanted to lead both contestants to the center of the ring, but neither could make the trip.

Skirmishes broke out. Someone was hit with a bottle of Tusker beer. The monkey climbed from sailor to sailor, trying to escape.

Then Chili managed to stand in his corner, holding onto the ropes for support. He was battered almost beyond recognition and his mouth opened and closed several times before it was understood that he was trying to speak. Then the noise slowly settled and Chili's wheezing voice began to be heard. The band members leaned hard on the rail to listen and voices called for quiet.

His father was endeavoring to make a speech, but Lucien was perplexed by this, and strangely embarrassed. The familiar drawl began and the swollen lips struggled to get the words out. Chili's voice lacked the educated, confident accent of the officers, Lucien also found himself thinking, and his father looked oddly small: an amateur in makeshift trunks and improper sporting shoes.

There were calls for silence. Then the sailors and the men of the regiment calmed down. One could hear the flapping sounds of the ship's flags and streamers.

"We thank the Royal Navy for being in our waters," Chili began. His voice was strangely weak.

Audrey held her hands over her mouth.

"And I thank your champion for giving me the honor of this beating today."

Hear, hear, some of the sailors grunted in response.

"And we salute those who have already given their all in the greater fight and are no longer with us today."

A deep silence now, everyone listening. Chili held onto the ring ropes for support, trying a smile, his nose bent and oversized, his lips fat and raw. He was the enlisted man: beaten, not all that articulate, but having his say.

The champion tried to stand, but couldn't. Chili spat and cleared his throat.

"I say we're all champions here," he went on. Applause began. "We have all fought bravely. Our time has come and we have shown ourselves well. We're all champions, that's what I say. We're all champions, every one of us." The men clapped their hands and called out as the little brass band played. "We're all champions," he repeated, but now his voice was lost in the ovation. Audrey clasped her boys to her sides. Hats were in the air.

"Who won?" Lucien wanted to know.

Then Chili staggered across the ring to give the champion an embrace, but Black Stan couldn't straighten himself to receive it.

More rag went up Chili's nostril.

The monkey waved from a perch high on a rope.

Bottles of lager appeared everywhere. Some of the sailors sang a song, but its music blended with the cheers. And even the Arabs on the rooftops who couldn't possibly make sense of what they had witnessed applauded and sent up their weird high-pitched African lulliloo as the cheers from the deck of the cruiser went on and on.

SAFARI:
Evening Conversation

"What is it between you and me?" Lucien asked his father.

The fire burned low.

Trey had gone off after dinner to spoon out diarrhea medicine to some children and to scold a group of male refugees who had failed to dig new sanitation ditches as they had promised. Coke had wandered down to the plane. Abba had crawled underneath the wobbly card table and gone to sleep.

There was never a really good time to talk directly to Chili, but Lucien was determined. The whole trip to the lake was meant to serve that end, yet now he had spoken he wished he hadn't.

"I don't follow your question," Chili finally replied.

"Why don't the two of us get along better?"

"Hell, I thought we got along fine."

The tactic Lucien expected: immediate denial of any problem whatsoever.

Chili had his ways. Weak men often brought out the bully in him. He treated all his enemies with extreme courtesy. Women who flattered him got his full devotion and affection. Superstition was his religion and American military power was his politics. And although he felt that whiskey was a basic food, he considered that it had other useful purposes. And he would always deny that tasks were difficult, that past grievances mattered, or that life was complicated. Most of all, he considered all forms of introspection to be unmanly.

"We seldom see each other anymore," Lucien went on. "You come around to the store occasionally, but you stay maybe ten minutes."

"I stay longer sometimes. We have our chats."

"After the hunting ended, we used to go to lunch. Or you were at home more. You sat around on the back porch smoking that old pipe."

"Damn, I wonder where that old meerschaum went to?" Chili said, grateful to have a specific object to consider.

"I'm not talking about your smoking habits. I'm talking about how we just don't get together."

Chili fell silent. Lucien knew that the distance between them widened even as he tried to close it. The effort itself became the barrier, for Chili believed, if in nothing else, in reticence. In Chili's world there were only projects and duties, competitions and journeys, never the thing itself between people, never pure relationship. Not even kinship. Not even blood itself. Men came together to work or play. Women the same. Other than that there was solitude and the making of one's own way apart.

The fire crackled and Lucien took a deep breath.

He decided to take a less personal approach.

"About the leopard," he said. "I think we ought to get some drivers. They could form a line across the top of the ridge. It would be slow going in the rocks, but if they made plenty of noise and if we put a gun ahead of them and guns at each side it might work."

Chili leaned forward, much more interested in this line of discussion. "I thought of drivers, too," he said. "But we won't get many volunteers."

"We can offer to pay them."

"With what, son?"

"Maybe with beer. We have more beer than anything else."

"They think the leopard's bad magic," Chili said. "And, be-sides, we've already told 'em we'd shoot it without help."

"That was before we saw those rocks up there," Lucien argued. "It's harder than we thought it'd be."

"Maybe we can get some drivers later on," Chili conceded. "But for now I'd like to see what we can do."

"You like it this way, don't you?"

"Aw, sure, son, this is a hell of a deal. I haven't hunted a cat in years."

Lucien peered into the darkness. The night wind gave off its low, steady whistle. Around the base of the hill the fires burned down to their last glow as the refugees huddled in darkness.

"I wonder how long Trey's going to be?" Lucien said.

"Remember that countess we took on the lion hunt?" Chili asked.

"Sure, I remember. Out in the Mara."

His father opened two beers and passed one across the embers. "I shot that big male. He fell right at my feet, remember, and lifted up his paw as he died."

"In a salute," Lucien said, taking a drink.

"Like he wanted to touch me or shake hands."

"More likely he wanted to swat you, but just didn't have the strength."

"No, it wasn't a swat. He just lifted his paw. I'll never forget it."

They had probably said all this before, using the same words and phrases. Sometimes their stories seemed more real, more important and more permanent than the original events.

"You liked that contessa," Chili reminded him.

"As I remember it, I liked her in the mornings and Coke liked her at night," Lucien countered.

Chili shook his head sadly, smiling.

Silence between them again.

"You disapproved of the women. All the damn time," Chili said.

Lucien shrugged. He did disapprove and he felt like saying so. He wanted to say that his father had compromised him by making him party to constant infidelities. He wanted to invoke Audrey's name, but didn't.

"Come on, you liked working with the contessa and all the others," Chili said.

"Those days are dead and gone."

"Yeah, okay. But do you remember the twins?"

"Sure. I remember them." Lucien sipped his beer and fought to say nothing in anger. Yet it was unlike Chili to mention the women they took on safaris.

The wind was like a voice.

He sensed that the things he needed to say to Chili and the things he wanted to hear would never get said. He poked at the fire with a stick.

"All right, if you don't like my idea of getting some drivers, what's your plan with the leopard?" Lucien asked.

"Well now, I think the three of us can sweep those rocks," Chili answered. "If we keep each other in sight. If we're careful."

Lucien disagreed. "The crevices and spaces between the boulders are too deep. We'll never keep up with each other. We won't even be able to climb back into view in certain spots. And there's a square mile of terrain like that."

"You don't have to go with us if you don't want to."

The words hung between them: a clear accusation. Once more it was Coke and Chili against him.

"It's such a damn bad plan that you can't possibly do it by yourselves," Lucien said.

"Maybe we can use old Abba somehow. Maybe you could take a stand at the end of the ridge while the three of us made a sweep."

"Three men or four makes no difference," Lucien said eventually. "It would take thirty men to make a good sweep. With three or four men, the leopard can move between us and flank us. Hell, *he'll* be hunting *us*."

"We're all good snap shots," Chili insisted. "We can do it. You asked me about my plan and that's it."

"Well, I've never heard one worse. One of us is sure to get mauled."

An odd silence followed. Chili, thinking, tapped his beer bottle against his lower lip. "If it got me, I wouldn't give a fat damn," he finally said.

Stupid, but true to form, Lucien thought; there it was out in the open: the old man dearly loved short odds. He wanted danger and little else. All safaris by definition had to be painful. Life was sweetened only by jeopardy. Only by risk was anything confirmed or understood, and if possible you risked everything: fortune, family, and the blood that ached in your veins.

In the long silence they heard footsteps.

Trey came out of the darkness, walking up from the lake. Her jeans were wet and Lucien knew immediately that she had been out at the plane with Coke.

"What time is it?" she asked, stopping beside the fire.

"It's late," Lucien answered.

"I've had it for today," she said, brushing back a strand of hair. "I'm off to bed. Lots to do in the morning."

As she went inside the clinic Lucien turned and stared blankly at the embers.

"Take it easy," Chili advised. "Let nature take its course."

"Screw nature," Lucien told him.

 ZAMANI:
Colly

She came with her parents to one of Chili's annual Fourth of July picnics.

Her parents disliked Chili, but regarded Audrey as a noble charity: old man Winston's daughter brought to embarrassment and shame, a mother abandoned, a woman wronged.

Colly was only five foot three, a small blonde with ample breasts and a purring voice. She was one of those women who give men a sense of the illicit: the eternal pubescent, the little girl. Although Coke was only twenty years old at the time, he wanted to be both fatherly protector and ravager. He wanted to adopt her, dress her in ribbons and lace, and commit a lovely incest. His name for her was Pet. Chili always called her the Pocket Rocket.

From that first picnic Coke pursued her with flattery and gifts: flowers at first, then perfume, then a red leather coat, a camera, a pearl-handled pistol, and an engagement ring. He confided in Lucien that in spite of her parents' protests she had accepted the ring and had allowed the engagement to be consummated in bed.

"I don't want to hear about it," Lucien said.

"Lucien, listen to me. She doesn't make love, she ruts. It's fantastic. She's perfect for me. I should've thought of marriage a long time ago."

"No details, don't tell me."

Colly's parents soon called on Audrey, arguing against any immediate wedding plans. Coke was conducting some major safaris on his own, had plenty of money, and wanted to get married after he returned from a scheduled month in the Selous. Audrey felt he could take care of himself and, besides, she had sympathy for impetuous romance, remembering her own courtship, so defended her son. After this Mr. Prebble, Colly's father, appealed to Chili, but they fell into a bitter argument in which Chili was compared unfavorably to old man Winston. In turn, Chili called Mr. Prebble a warthog and the two of them almost came to blows.

It was Lucien who accompanied his brother to the Prebble home to make arrangements.

The house was above the city, among the coffee trees along Ambassador Row. It was air-conditioned like a fancy hotel. The boys were served tea. Everyone tried smiling. Coke constantly cleared his throat.

"While I'm off in the Selous with my very rich clients," he began, strutting around the room, "all arrangements for the wedding on my part will, ahem, be handled by Lucien."

Lucien, who was still prone to pimples, stiffened himself and attempted to look worthy.

Coke moved to the tea set, fumbled, clattered the dishes around, and emptied the contents of a cup into the large silver tray. Mrs. Prebble, a plump woman with heavy eye makeup, and Colly, who sat with her knees together primly, tried not to notice.

"I'd like to make an arrangement," Mr. Prebble said, rising and walking behind his overstuffed chair so that he could take a firm grip on it. "I'd like to send Colly to her aunt down in Cape Town!"

"Oh, Dad," Colly said with a smile that was both coy and reproving. Coke also ignored the father's remark. He strutted to the far end of the room and back again.

"We Cavenaughs have been in a very profitable business," he stated. "And I intend to become wealthy. I want a flat in town, a lodge in the mountains, and a beach house at Lamu. Colly and I will travel. I expect we'll have two or three cars. I intend to operate several hunting camps, you see, and I'm already the best at what I do—and, well, in conclusion, there are a lot of animals that need shooting."

"On that matter we disagree," Mr. Prebble said, his neck red.

"I don't suppose you'll always be a hunter, will you?" Colly asked, prompting her future husband.

"I suppose I'll always shoot for sport, but, ahem, no, not exactly. I have business plans. For after the hunting camps."

"To my mind, you're like your father and you always will be," Mr. Prebble said, and he turned to his wife. "Do you know what they call this lad? Mfifo! That means idiot."

"Actually, it's a complimentary term," Lucien tried to explain.

Coke placed his hands behind his back and walked down the length of the room again, his prepared remarks not yet finished.

"Your daughter and I might have sisal or coffee plantations," he went on. "I've been considering the hotel business. And shipping—although, ahem, I wouldn't want to live in the humidity down at the coast. I've thought—just thinking ahead, you see—that I might even run for Parliament one day."

"A distinguished career, all in all," Mr. Prebble said with a

sarcasm that only Lucien seemed to detect. Coke, clearly, had
no idea what effect he had on the room.

"But first things first," Coke conceded. "The hunting camps.
Then maybe I'll become an outfitter with my own line of guns
and shirts, things like that."

"There will come a day when big-game hunting is outlawed,"
Mr. Prebble predicted. He spoke evenly, glowering at Coke.

"Oh, beg pardon, sir, I don't think that'll ever happen."

"But it will, Mfifo," Mr. Prebble insisted. "The great herds
are already vanishing. The poor natives who haven't enough to
eat get prosecuted for poaching. They get clapped into prison
for it. And the fat Germans and Americans can shoot all the
bloody game they want to. In any case, the animals are getting
killed off."

"The tourists pay good money for licenses," Coke argued.

"But shoot more than their licenses allow! And our ridiculous
government and our wardens sometimes even help them do it!"

Coke, unable to argue on such a grand scale, glanced toward
Lucien in confusion.

"You hunters and speculators use things up!" Mr. Prebble
went on. "You plant nothing, grow nothing, manufacture nothing, give nothing back! You just spend and use up! A beach
house in Lamu—that sort of useless thing. Bloody idleness!"

"We take a certain pride in what we do," Coke said, his
argument faltering. He seemed to lose his train of thought as
Mr. Prebble took a firmer grip on the back of that chair.

"This was my paradise," Colly's father went on. "I had the
pleasure of it for just a short time in the history of the earth and
in my own personal history; now it's disappearing. I'd like to
think that when I die it will all still be here: the lush hills, the
creatures of the land, all of it, but it won't be."

"I think you're talking politics there," Coke said, attempting a smile. "Let's not talk politics, sir, if you don't mind. Not on this occasion."

Mr. Prebble's voice rose higher. "Good, let's don't. Because you are Mfifo on that subject, aren't you? On most subjects, I'd say."

"Please," Colly pleaded softly.

"Think of it this way," Mr. Prebble told Coke. "You want to use up everything in my life. You want the land, the animals, the history I live in, and, thank you, my only daughter as well!"

Coke blinked, struggling for a reply. Mrs. Prebble's mascara became black pools in the corners of her eyes.

"Well, ahem, I'll be back from safari in a month," Coke managed to say, carrying on bravely. "In the meantime, my brother—"

"No and no and no!" Mr. Prebble shouted in a strange off-key tenor. "If there's a ceremony I won't attend! If there's a house, I won't visit! If there's a marriage, I won't contribute a shilling!"

Coke gathered himself, then addressed him as if none of this had been uttered. "After I return," he said, "we'll, ahem, get together, sir, I really hope we do. Have lunch. That sort of thing. Talk over our views on animal conservation."

"My views? Talk over my views? Do you think so?"

"I'm afraid this isn't going too well," Colly whispered to Lucien. Her voice made him ache.

"Out!" Mr. Prebble shouted. "Please! Out! Leave us!"

"Call on me for anything," Lucien said to the women, getting to his feet and backing toward the door.

"Go home, Mfifo!" the father said, herding them out. "I can't take any more of this!"

Afterward, Coke and Lucien went down to the Thorn Tree Café and drank a few Tuskers. They took off their uncomfortable ties and draped their seersucker jackets over the backs of the wire chairs as they watched the boys hawking newspapers among the tourists. Coke allowed that in his opinion the meeting with the Prebbles had gone pretty well.

"How do you figure that?" Lucien asked.

"Oh, her old man didn't mean much of what he said. He'll be at the wedding and we'll get a nice sum from him."

"What makes you think so?"

"He doesn't disapprove of us all that much. I know for a fact that he goes on hunting safaris himself. He was out with Jambo Tiner once. So I figure he carries on about lots of things he doesn't mean."

"I think things went damned awful."

"Look, he didn't bar us from the house, did he? He threw us out, but he didn't say we couldn't come back."

"That seems like a technical point."

"Now here's what I want you to do," Coke said. "When I've gone on safari I want you to go back for visits. Take Colly riding, will you do that? She likes her ponies. And hang around Mrs. Prebble. They've got that piano in the little room off to the side, so if you get a chance sit down and play them a tune. Understand what I'm saying?"

"Soothe them with music."

"I've got rough edges, but you don't," Coke said. "If you can get to that piano, they'll like you."

"I didn't feel welcome up there."

"Tell them about all the damn books you read. I'll be out in the Selous ripping the guts out of a kudu, but they'll think we're nice civilized chaps. Audrey's sons. Do this for me, all right?"

"I'll try."

"And hands off Colly, mind you. I don't want her rutting around with you."

"She has a strange voice," Lucien admitted.

"Gets to you, doesn't it? Like a little girl's voice. Just think about it: waking up every morning to that sound. She drives me crazy."

Lucien thought about it.

It became a strategy of the hunt, like cutting the trophy animal out of the herd, moving it away from its cover, and capturing it.

Two days after Coke went off with his clients, Lucien phoned Colly. She seemed relieved and pleased to hear from him. As Coke had suggested, they arranged to ride together.

As they guided their mounts through the coffee groves and green lanes near the Prebble house, they made their first small talk. But by eye contact, by that subtle coo of her voice, by a shrug here or a bit of laughter there, Lucien began to know her. On the surface, she was this tiny, helpless thing, this little girl: tight jeans across her firm backside, her breasts loose in the white shirt, her hands like small flowers on the reins. Daddy's girl: educated, willful, and spoiled. But her charms were all weapons, Lucien noted, and she had undoubtedly used them successfully on her father, on men in general, and on brute society. Poor Coke. He was just a fool who shot straight. This was a truly decisive young woman, not what she seemed at all, with a cruel and useful sensuality.

As they rode along she mentioned the aunt in Cape Town.

"The one your father threatened to send you to?"

"That's right. Aunt Lee has a flat in the city and a nice house in the vineyards up in a wine valley. I could live in one place and she could stay at another if we didn't get along. But I think I'd like Aunt Lee. I've even thought of being especially naughty so I'd be sent there. She has a fast car. And there are a lot of men with money down there."

Lucien listened carefully. A question kept bothering him, but they had returned to the stables before he asked it.

"Why do you want to marry Coke?"

"Why do you think?" she asked in reply.

"Is it because all girls want to get married?"

She gave him a smile that was both coy and conniving. By this time they were inside the stables, dismounting next to a stall. The heavy odors of straw and horseflesh rode the air, but Colly's perfume excited him. There were naturally other associations— that stable long ago up at the racecourse, the lovely Tamu, the first time his fingers had touched female flesh. In those soft moments as they turned their horses over to a stable boy, he wanted to drag Colly into a mound of hay, unbutton that riding shirt, and succumb to all her little moves.

But somehow they strolled toward the house.

"I'm marrying your brother because we're both in love," she told him, but he felt this was a lie. There were better catches: men with more money, better looks, real prospects. He struggled to understand what was incomprehensible; he was young and believed in rational behavior. But he knew that if Colly loved Coke, then she loved all other males equally.

"Do you want to come inside and have tea?" she asked, turning and blocking his way into the house.

"Sure, that'll be fine," he said.

"Are you certain that's what you want?" she asked coyly. "Tell me the truth. Tell me what you really want."

She moved her shoulders and planted her feet apart, her body asking him to touch it; she stood there blocking his way as if she might be expecting his kiss. So he stepped back. All their words seemed to have double meanings; she addled him with every nuance and gesture until he was unable to calculate, unable to speak, melting with a fever low in his gut.

"I'll come play the piano for your mother," he blurted out.

"Ah, I was told you played the piano," she cooed, still blocking his path. The words seemed to say something more.

"Not tonight," he said. "Later. I'll come over some evening and give a performance."

"I'd like that. Do you mean it?"

"Sure, if you want me to."

"So you're a brave hunter who plays the piano?"

"I suppose that's right."

"And do you have a girl?"

"No, not at the moment."

"But you've had girls, haven't you?"

"Yes," he said, and she looked at him as if she scarcely believed him.

"Tomorrow night, then," she said. "After supper. Come and play. And what sort of music do you play? Mama likes Nat King Cole."

"Nocturnes and études," he told her. "Things like that."

"Ah, a real musician. Good. Come about eight o'clock."

Throughout the next day he had lewd visions of her, images he couldn't get out of his mind. She was his brother's dearest, yes, but he saw her little backside rolling in the saddle, her wanton breath close to his mouth, Colly in the stable, Colly with her shirt off, and his senses sank into delirium.

Finally, he got his thoughts straight and asked Audrey to go with him to the Prebble house. She agreed and phoned Colly's mother. Good: it would be an uneventful evening with no flirtations or betrayals—possibly even beneficial to Coke's prospects.

The old upright had two dead keys. Lucien played a few somber melodies, then Mr. Prebble excused himself, going off to the coffee warehouse, leaving Lucien to perform for the women, all of whom wrapped themselves in smiles for him. After the music they had wine, cheese, coffee, and dark chocolates. When Audrey fell into a conversation with Mrs. Prebble, Colly summoned Lucien to the kitchen.

"You play beautifully," she said. "I had no idea."

He assured her that he had no talent at all.

She gave him a bottle of wine and a corkscrew, their excuse for leaving the parlor.

"And I know why you brought your mother along tonight," she said, standing close while he popped the cork.

"Oh, why?"

"Because you were afraid of you and me."

His throat went dry and he wanted to manufacture some witty denial, but couldn't.

"I want to tell you about Coke and me," she went on. "And I want to tell you more about the question you asked me yesterday."

"You answered it. You said you were in love."

"I want to tell you more. And I want to tell you on Sunday. We can drive up to the lodge at Mount Kenya. All right? For lunch?"

When she drove them into the mountains that Sunday she wore a filmy dress that she pulled over her knees as she steered. Her hair was tied with a silk scarf and her moods alternated between light laughter and earnest confession. To his consternation, she talked about making love to his brother.

"Don't be embarrassed," she said as she drove. "That's what we have together. The main thing!"

He found nothing to say.

"Maybe the marriage won't last," she went on, a happy ring in her voice. "But I'll never find anyone else like him. He's marvelous. Any woman would want him!"

In his confusion, he wanted to ask, so, good, why are you here with me? Where is this going? What do you want?

They had Sunday brunch on the lawn at the rear of the lodge: white tablecloths, black waiters, a green lawn sloping toward formal gardens, a peacock moving through the distant hedges and flowers. Colly talked on and on about Coke as Lucien ate his roast beef.

"What am I to do?" she cooed. "I've thought of packing my gear and going off to find him in the Selous! Crawling into his tent! It's insane, I know it, but I can't help myself with him! And maybe he isn't right for me, but I can't think of anything else! That's why I'm marrying him! Isn't that why people get married?"

Uneasy and unsure of how to answer, he went to get another helping at the servery. He stood in line with the large Sunday crowd: older people in woolen suits and crepe dresses who talked about money and sports and crops. Audrey's people: landowners with accounts at Barclay's, fierce dogs, bungalows, and bits of Kikuyu or Kiswahili in their vocabularies. He could pass as one of them this noon, but he really wasn't. He was too much his father's son, an American, yet that only in the sense that Americans were a nomadic tribe now, a people spread all over the earth living lives that were curiously borrowed.

Waiting at the buffet, he realized he didn't know who he was and he was too young to say all that he felt, but he knew everybody was a foreigner here. All these good Sunday clothes, all these reassuring noises of the dining room, all this roast beef and sherry and British phlegm: it had all been imposed on this odd spot on the globe and there was a great wrongness to all of it. Who am I and who is she and who are we? He felt a loss of equilibrium. He was out of sorts with sexual desire, with all definitions, and with himself.

"More please," he told the chef who did the carving, and slices of rare roast beef were piled on his plate. He glanced outside. Colly sat watching the peacock.

Grave intuitions and uncertainties.

"You eat just like your brother," she said, laughing, when he had returned to the table and resumed his meal. "Coke eats one item at a time and never mixes the food on his plate."

"I could get you something else from the buffet, too. Would you like some nice berries and cream?"

"I'll bet your father eats that way, too."

"I've never noticed."

"I'll bet the three of you are very much the same."

He didn't dare return her gaze just now.

"You're all untamed, aren't you?" she went on. "Is that how you'd describe the three of you?"

He paid close attention to his food.

"I want to know, Lucien, do you like me?"

He couldn't answer.

"I've seen you study me," she told him. "You have clever eyes. You see and understand lots of things, don't you?"

"I think you're nice," he managed.

"Nice? Does that mean attractive?"

"Hm, very attractive. You know you are."

"Coke thinks I'm desirable. The most desirable woman, he says, he's ever met."

"I can see why," Lucien agreed, and for the moment she seemed satisfied. A kind of hopelessness grew in him.

As they drove back toward Nairobi they passed through two military roadblocks. The ongoing troubles. In the city there were men guarding the banks with machine guns. There was always something, and Lucien was trying to figure out what Kenya meant, who he was in this place, what marrying into it meant.

"Our mothers are planning the ceremony," she was telling him. "There'll be the traditional cake and champagne, but we can't decide if the reception should be at the club or not. What do you think?"

He had no opinion. He just knew this was a bad marriage, far worse than Chili's and Audrey's before it: the rough American element wedded to a false Brit civility, each equally alien and out of place here. Who cared if anyone's wedding reception was at the Muthiaga Club? Or if one eccentric group of whites fussed and finally married into another crazy group of whites? He wished he could see it all clearly, so that he could say what he felt; he wanted to see the silliness of it from a great height, as if he viewed it from up there in the pure, objective snow of Mount Kenya itself.

"Now kiss me goodnight," she commanded. They stood beside her father's car in the shady darkness of the eucalyptus trees, near the front door to her house.

Lucien took a breath. "Like a brother only," he protested, and he bent toward her cheek.

But she caught his mouth with hers and wrapped him in her arms. Her breasts flattened against him and he felt the beginnings of a humiliating arousal.

"There," she whispered, finally letting him go.

He coughed out a goodnight, turned away, hid himself in the purple shadow of those overhanging limbs, and walked away from the house along Ambassador Row. His jeep was parked out there, the old familiar jeep, and he drove away down a dark arcade of trees, passing all those fancy homes and terraces until at last he turned into the city streets. He began to get his breath back.

Before and after the wedding he avoided seeing Colly alone, but his fantasies sometimes waylaid him. He had a recurring dream of swimming with her in a jungle stream, stretching out on a mossy bank afterward, and kissing her as someone passed close by, just beyond their vision.

He did see her at the club, once, when Audrey and Mrs. Prebble were making wedding preparations. Colly wore shorts and her hair was tied in a ponytail; she looked fourteen years old. She barely acknowledged him, as if that wild kiss had never happened.

Chili served as best man at the wedding ceremony, but skipped the reception, leaving Lucien to raise the toast that represented the good wishes of the Cavenaughs.

"Long life and long love," Lucien managed, and that seemed enough. Everyone applauded except Mr. Prebble who tossed his champagne underneath a table adorned with white roses. Colly and Lucien exchanged a restrained but extended smile.

The marriage lasted one year.

Lucien was on safari in the Mara when Coke flew out to

confront him. It was the year Coke first qualified as a pilot, and he landed the little Cherokee on a crude clearing where he dodged brush piles and stumps once the wheels touched the ground.

Lucien's clients were a big red-faced Swiss policeman and his wife. The man had saved all his life for this hunting trip and Lucien was trying to make it perfect for him, borrowing both Watu and Bubba from Chili so that the camp was smoothly run. They had taken a trophy buffalo and now they were having lunch off white tablecloths underneath an acacia tree. The plane buzzed them twice, tipped its wings, then made its landing among the stumps.

"Nutty fellow," the policeman said, watching the plane swerve here and there as it landed.

Lucien excused himself from the meal and walked out to meet his brother. Halfway between the plane and the tents they began screaming at each other, and the policeman stood up, a potato on the end of his fork, wondering if he should do anything. Watu and Bubba became very busy.

"She's gone and she says it's because of you!" Coke yelled.

"Well, that's a damn lie!"

"You're calling her a liar?"

"When have I seen her? Tell me that! When have Colly and I ever seen each other alone?"

"It must've happened someplace!"

"Two times in the last year! At Audrey's dinner table! You were sitting right there with us!"

"Goddammit, Lucien, she said you kissed her and got her confused! She says she should've married you, not me!"

"I did kiss her! Before she married you! More than a year ago!"

"You made her kiss you, didn't you?"

"That's right, I forced myself on her," Lucien lied. "But she wouldn't have any of it!"

"Ah, you bastard! Behind my back!"

"I'm sorry I did it! But I couldn't resist it! I'm sorry!"

Lucien guided them toward the plane, hopefully out of earshot of his clients. Coke gave a nearby stump a mighty kick, hurting his foot more than he let on.

"If she left you, Coke, it was none of my fault."

"She caught me seeing someone else," Coke admitted. "That's part of it, too."

"There you are."

"But she said she'd forgive me. Then she said you did this to us!"

"She's just finding reasons for leaving you," Lucien said.

"She told me you were always on her mind. She wouldn't say a thing like that just out of the blue."

"Remember when you were in the Selous that month before the wedding?"

"You took her to bed, didn't you?"

"No, but I was crazy for her," Lucien said. "That's when I made her kiss me. It maybe flattered her, but she turned me down. She said she loved you. But now she wants to hurt you back. But nothing happened between us. Nothing."

Coke banged his fist into the side of the plane. "Who the hell are you hunting with?" he wanted to know.

Lucien told him and invited him for a drink.

"I hurt my damned foot," Coke complained, and he bent over and straightened up several times in agony.

"Sorry," Lucien said, and he almost laughed.

"You coveted your brother's wife," Coke finally said, and the accusation came out so stilted, so biblical, and so very much out of character that Lucien actually laughed. Another minute passed as they stood by the plane, Coke's foot still hurting.

"You're better than her," Lucien told him. "You'll be glad you're rid of her."

"She's going to Cape Town."

"She's not up to you, Coke, she really isn't."

"You mean it?"

"She's divisive. She uses a man."

"Well, she's a hot number, little brother, and you wanted her."

"Maybe I did. But I was loyal to you."

"So you didn't score with her?" Coke asked again, making sure. He watched Lucien, knowing one thing: Lucien would never lie to him. Whatever came between them, this was his certainty.

"Never came close. I tried to kiss her and she resisted."

They started walking toward the clients.

"She uses everybody," Coke agreed. "You're right about that. And maybe I'll be better off without her. I'm not like her or any of those people."

"True. You're reckless and stupid and better than any of them."

"Reckless and stupid? Is that what you think?" Coke asked, allowing himself to be led toward camp.

"Sure, everybody admires you for it," Lucien assured him.

SAFARI:
The Croc Feast

Early the next morning the refugees hurried to the shore with their knives and baskets. The noisy uproar woke everyone at the clinic except Coke, who had to have his sleep.

"What's going on?" Chili asked Abba.

"The croc man!" Abba replied. "He comes back!"

He had come out of the desert again: a nameless solitary figure who visited the lake annually to kill as many crocodiles as he could.

There is always a man, Chili once said, who is more than the best notion you have of yourself; when you think you're strong or wise or lucky or unafraid, he appears.

Trey avoided Lucien, so he went off with Chili and Abba to the shore.

The raw physical presence of the visitor was a measure of any man at the north end of the lake. Shiny black pectorals, biceps, sinew of neck, set of jaw: he made Coke look puny and made the poor refugees resemble cadavers. A great scar crossed his chest and stomach, a bandolier of raised flesh. One leg had been mutilated, yet it gave the appearance of strength, too, as if it were comprised of exposed tendons twisted into cable. Each finger was a talon of separate muscle. In his eyes there was a slant of cunning, and his black skin looked seared as if he had come out of a fire. He wore a loincloth and an old army utility belt into which he stuck his dagger and pistol. A coil of rope hung from his shoulder.

He spoke only to himself, in a language nobody knew.

"This man, he kills very much," Abba reported. "He kills making no more bullets in his pistol, then he travels far away and don't come back for one year."

"He's sure something," Chili said.

For the fishermen, the refugees and the wandering herdsmen around the lake the visit meant revenge, celebration, and fresh meat. All year long the crocs ruled the lake and shore. The fishermen's traps were always ravaged. Boats were harassed. Goats that wandered into the mud flats and got stuck were snatched away. Even low-flying waterbirds were sometimes taken right out of the air. During Trey's first weeks at the clinic a croc had seized the arm of a young girl as she bent in the shallows to wash away the sting of a bee. Her parents began a tug of war with the croc, losing ground, inching into deeper water, the mangled arm between them and the brute, until a second croc arrived, got the mother's and father's legs in one bite, and the whole family disappeared into the waves.

But now the croc man was back. Carcasses would be hacked up, skins would be stretched out along the shoreline, and everyone would feast.

"Where'd he get that pistol and ammo?" Chili wanted to know.

Old Abba could only shake his head.

There were rumors: the croc man was a fugitive from one of the army purges over in Uganda; he was a former mercenary; he was an escaped slave; he was a survivor of a lost tribe: But nobody really knew. He sat, Abba said, by no man's fire.

When Chili, Lucien, and Abba first saw the croc man that morning he was walking slowly along a stretch of sandy beach, bending over, and listening for baby crocs. It was the time of year for eggs to hatch and even before the shells broke open a trained ear could detect the soft muffled *chirrup* sound of the little reptiles buried in the sand.

As they watched, the croc man stooped, dug in the sand, and uncovered two eggs—one of them already cracked and in the process of hatching. He smashed the eggs with his fist, then gouged out the life of two slimy little creatures with his thumbs.

The ritual had begun. Abba told them the croc man would dig up as many croc eggs and kill as many babies as he could find. This indignity would bring dozens of angry crocs into the shallows of the bay and a war would follow.

The contents of the eggs—the first delicacies—were passed along to the bolder refugees who followed the croc man's progress. His every move was studied by an attentive audience as he continued his bent stroll along the beach, yet everyone also kept an occasional eye on the shallows in the event some monster might scurry forward.

More eggs were dug up. Lucien and Chili stopped for a closer look at the thin, curled, striped creatures that were exposed in death to the hot morning sunlight. Gripping the new ones he found, the croc man murdered them with his thumb—an economical exercise.

Around midmorning Chili and Lucien went back to the clinic and were having cups of coffee when Coke appeared, greeted

them with a yawn, and poured a cup for himself. Chili gave him
all the details on the arrival of the croc man.

"What's he got for weapons?" Coke asked.

"A dagger and an old Colt pistol."

"How much ammo?"

"Didn't see anything on him except that utility belt. He might
have a few rounds, but not much."

Intrigued, Coke turned his chair so that he could watch the
faraway crowd down at the shore.

Trey arrived at the clinic with a small boy whose sores needed
attention. She acknowledged no one as she led the child indoors
to her medicine cabinet. Lucien watched over the rim of his cup,
wanting to speak, saying nothing. He felt as though he had a
bullet in him; his insides were hot and leaking away.

Coke sat on the edge of his chair, watching.

Chili told him about the croc eggs.

"I don't want to hunt today," Coke said, wide awake now.
"I want to shoot crocs with this guy." Grinning and energetic,
he stood up and walked around.

"We've got to hunt," Lucien said. "We can hunt all day, then
you can join tonight's show."

"What happens tonight?"

"Abba says there'll be a hell of a fight by torchlight out there
in the shallows," Chili told him.

"That's for me," Coke said. "Let's get out the arsenal, Lucy."

"Let's tend to the leopard," Lucien insisted.

"C'mon, Pop, how about it?" Coke pleaded. He was the
spoiled boy, begging, and knowing very well that the parent
would relent. He walked over and plucked the big Korth pistol
out of its holster as Chili stood up from his chair. The matter
seemed settled: they were going to indulge.

"We'll look damn bad if the leopard comes and takes another refugee," Lucien said.

"Aw, I don't think that'll happen today," his father drawled.

"Goddammit, this is stupid." Lucien felt helpless. "I'm going to rig a bait up on the hillside. Somebody has to tend to business."

"Good idea, son. I'll give you a hand later."

Coke went inside the clinic looking for ammo, and Lucien heard a slightly stilted exchange between his brother and Trey. The formality seemed wrong, as if they hid behind the words. Lucien felt that hot leaking-away: a trickling wound inside him. And he could only pretend it wasn't happening.

Finally he went inside the clinic and watched Trey apply salve to the child's sores. She waited a long time before raising her eyes to him.

"When you came back to camp last night your jeans were wet," he said to her evenly.

She turned to the medicine cabinet, searching for more bandage. The antiseptic salve put a heavy odor between them.

"I saw a light in the plane, so I waded out," she finally said. "I thought it might be you."

He tried to respond, but let the alibi stand. As she went on wrapping the child's arm, he walked outside into the rising wind.

That afternoon he went to the old lorry and found its battery dead. So he walked over to the plane, borrowed Coke's spare, and installed it in the lorry. He cleaned the spark plugs, checked all the belts and hoses, then drove the lorry to the slope of the hill. He found a strip of tin and a piece of cardboard out of which he fashioned crude funnels for the headlights.

The wind became stronger as the day became hotter. Sad anger swam inside him as he worked.

It occurred to him that he didn't know this woman, not at all. Somehow he had miscalculated.

He aimed the headlights at a gnarled stump in the middle of a graveled clearing. Then he went to buy a goat. On the way across camp, Abba fell into stride with him.

"What's happening at the shore?" Lucien asked him.

"Mfifo, he shows all his many guns. The croc man digs for the eggs and says nothing."

"Ah, sure, my brother's bribing him with weapons and ammo. He wants to shoot crocs, too, so he's offering his firepower."

Abba nodded and grinned.

They crossed a low hill above the lake, a field of thorn grass and sage. Two naked shepherds tended nine scrawny goats on the far side. Lucien slowed his pace for old Abba, who walked with his arms folded across his chest.

They asked the shepherds about buying a goat, starting a long palaver. Abba attempted to act as interpreter and buying agent, but the shepherds—a Turkana boy and a man even more ancient than Abba—kept eyeing that double set of ears with apprehension.

"Hay! Hay!" the boy and old man kept repeating, as if someone had struck them a blow to their stomachs. It was the usual Turkana utterance for anger, disgust, excitement, fright, and general punctuation. Several times they walked away from the negotiations, too, so that Lucien and Abba had to follow.

A goat is needed to kill the evil leopard, Abba kept telling them, but this upset them, too. At last they admitted that the goats weren't theirs to sell or barter away. When he heard this, Abba started reviling them. You are just worthless shepherds with nothing to do, he told them. Who owns these miserable goats? And why are you not pleasant to this white man?

Lucien understood only a little of what was being said, but he knew that information was always difficult to come by among the Turkana. They were a loud, insolent people who would never divulge much without confrontation or outright threat. Abba went on scolding the old man and boy for taking everyone's time. Finally, the boy pointed to another hill, saying, that's the owner, go ask him, leave us, we are very busy here.

Lucien and Abba started walking again, leaning against the hot wind. When they reached that distant hill, they saw no one. Out of spirits, they trudged back toward camp.

Lucien said the leopard could possibly be baited with croc meat.

"Goat very much better," Abba stated.

Lucien agreed as they reached camp again. There were three scrawny goats among the refugees, so he made inquiries. He stopped two happy men who were rolling a heavy iron pot down to the shore. They were laughing as they worked, expectant and looking forward to feasting all night, but they said no one could purchase such a valuable animal in this camp—especially since Dr. Trey had ordered that all livestock should be kept alive.

In the afternoon Lucien carried a five-gallon can of petrol up to the lorry and filled its tank. Then Abba joined him in the shade of the lorry as Lucien took off his khaki shirt and shared a plastic bottle of water with the old man. Sweat ran off their bodies and they tried to arrange themselves so they would both sit in the breeze and out of the brutal glare of the sun.

"This leopard should not be in this place," Abba remarked, wrinkling up his face in thought. "This leopard loses himself. He belongs very much five days to the east."

"He's a loner," Lucien agreed. "And how did you happen to be up here? Isn't this a bit far north for you?"

"I was thinking to walk until I was very much dead," Abba said with an impish face. Lucien watched him, trying to gauge how serious he was. The old man continued, "Then I stop in this place because of very much voices here."

"Voices in your cousin's ears?"

"Oh, very much yes."

"And are these voices you hear always sad?"

Abba pondered this briefly. "In this place the leopard and all the people are very much lost and confused," he concluded.

"That's also true," Lucien told him, "in all the cities I've ever known."

They finished the bottle of water as a delegation of two women appeared, both fat, both wearing razored bracelets and decorative welts of raised flesh on their shoulders and faces. They belonged to no tribe Lucien knew, but spoke enough Swahili to convey that their husband and chief, the mighty Mussa, had a bait he would sell.

Mussa was well known to Lucien as the troublemaker in camp. But a live bait was needed, so Lucien and Abba followed the women toward a small peninsula of rock at the northern extremity of camp, a spot where Mussa had installed his little group as far from the authority of Trey's clinic as he could get. Mussa was the thief of thieves and often threatened with his knife those who made fun of his claim that he was chief over the whole settlement.

He was a tall, heavy specimen who spat with every sentence, leaving his saliva on the ground near each of his royal assertions. He wore a brass necklace with a hawk's wing stuck in it, the feathers fanning out over his chest.

The bait he offered was a small girl, perhaps four years old, who was tied to a stake at his feet. She was covered with flies, so that her thin arms and bony shoulders gave off a green glow with their movement.

This child belongs to no one, Mussa boomed out, spitting here and there as Abba interpreted. Besides, she is possessed by a demon. She will make a fine bait. She is for sale. Let the evil leopard devour this one who is possessed.

"What's the price?" Lucien asked with a smirk.

Mussa turned to his women, spitting and discussing terms.

Sisi ni kiu, they all said. *Biya*. They wanted beer. Mussa's fat tribe, comprised mostly of wives, were thirsty.

Then Mussa spat and relayed a last requirement: *mbuzi*. One goat as well.

Lucien knelt down, took out his Swiss army knife, and cut the leather thongs that bound the child. She stank of putrid bowel. He brushed away the flies, lifted her to her feet, and took her hand.

Mussa boomed out his disapproval, folding his arms over his chest, but Lucien told him, yes, all right, he would get some beer.

The goat, too, Mussa demanded, spitting and cursing.

If we had a goat, why would we want this child? Abba shouted. And why would we even bother talking to you?

Many beers, Mussa contended. A box filled with beers.

"Yes, yes," Lucien agreed, and he led the little girl away. Mussa and the two fat wives who had served as ambassadors followed and soon there was a procession traversing the camp toward the clinic. Demands and saliva continued, but Lucien was too angry to say anything.

At the clinic he turned the child over to Trey with a quick explanation. Then he went to the beer supply, plucked out two bottles, and thrust them into Mussa's hands. Mussa and the wives kicked up dirt outside the clinic, shouted, spat, protested, and seemed on the verge of an attack.

"Where's my pistol?" Lucien said, and went looking for it. "Damn! Coke's got every weapon down at the lake!"

Mussa's knife was drawn, but Abba conveyed to him that the white master was searching for a gun. The chief ran up to the door of the clinic, spat on it, then withdrew. His wives threw handfuls of dirt into the air and let the dust settle on their heads.

I am the chief here and I require more than two beers, Mussa argued, spitting on his knife.

This brought Trey out of the clinic.

"You're no chief!" she shouted at him, and Abba gladly put this sentiment into several trade languages. "You are a renegade who left your tribe! And you give us a pain here!" She slapped her backside.

I am the killer of my enemies, Mussa claimed, pointing at her with one of the two prize beers.

"You hang around this camp stealing food!" she went on. "You are a loud fool, not a great warrior chief!"

The child has a demon, Mussa argued.

"Goddammit, where's a weapon?" Lucien shouted from inside the clinic.

The wives continued to throw dirt into the air and to step underneath its descending cloud.

This child will enter the soul of the leopard and will kill these white men, Mussa asserted. He spat in Trey's direction.

Furious, Trey moved forward and spat squarely on the man's feet. Abba laughed out loud while the wives glared.

Then Lucien appeared with one more bottle of beer and tossed it in the dust, shouting *Ondoka!* Go on, get out of here!

The first wife scurried forward and picked up the beer bottle. Satisfied with another prize, they made their retreat.

For a moment Trey and Lucien were left to regard one another before she said, "What exactly were you doing with Mussa?"

"Taking that little girl away from him! And I'm busy as hell, so I'll talk to you later," he answered. "Tend to your patient!" His tone was angrier than he intended, but he turned and walked away.

"Very much good," Abba commented on the incident, giving Trey an indefinite shrug and smile as he followed Lucien.

By dusk the hot winds had died off. It was the time of day in Africa when the earth and its creatures settled into silence, when the evening fires begin and hushed voices become part of the descending quiet, but tonight the refugee camp would be different. More than one hundred refugees, fishermen, and tribesmen had gathered with torches along the shoreline where, earlier in the day, the croc man had found the eggs in the sand. Gourds of homemade *pombe* were passed around. The Turkana shouts of "Hah! Hey!" pierced the crowd and the laughter, and the storytelling had started.

The croc man stood waist-deep offshore, waiting for the first attackers. Coke stood unashamed in the shallows near the beach, naked except for his baggage of artillery: the Korth pistol, his Mauser, Lucien's misplaced .45 pistol, and several pounds of crisscrossed ammo belts. His mustache twitched with anticipation, for he had heard all the descriptions of the croc man's techniques and he knew they would go at the slaughter in suitable freestyle. Chili had perched atop an overturned fishing boat so he could get a good view of the melee. The refugees had gathered wood for fires and the pots sat waiting.

Lucien arrived, shaking his head with dismay. The black girls kept finding excuses to stroll near the water's edge, so they could get a peek at Coke's genitals. He made an elaborate show, in turn, of loading, checking, and displaying all his weapons, sending the girls off giggling with his every movement and gesture.

" 'Lo, Lucy!" Coke called out. "Come for a bit of sport?"

"As you depart this world," Lucien called back, "don't forget to wave good-bye."

Coke only laughed and reset his feet in the mud of the shallows. He was so full of himself that Lucien wished Trey could be here to witness the silliness.

Some forty yards away a shot was fired. The crowd on the beach sighed and groaned its approval. The croc man, who had been giving the water around him a lot of somber consideration, had put a bullet in the head of the first arrival.

Lucien climbed on the overturned boat with Chili. Propped against the sides of the boat was the remainder of the family arsenal.

Chili craned to see the action and uttered in admiration his old Arkansas line: "Scares me and I'm fearless."

"I'm surprised you're not out there," Lucien told him.

"Aw, not me, son. If I stand around in water for any length of time these days I get leg cramps."

Now the croc man had a noose on the croc and dragged it, bleeding, toward shore. It flailed around, but he muscled it forward as the cooks on the beach set up a howl.

"As I understand it," Chili observed, "they'll drag a few crocs almost to shore. The crocs kick and writhe around for a couple of hours even after they're shot dead, but the blood and splashing brings all the others."

"You've talked to the locals about this?"

"Yeah, they saw it last year. And for several years, I take it: this same damn method. Works out okay, they tell me."

"I came to get one of the rifles," Lucien said, after they had watched for a little longer.

"Need any help up on the hill?"

"No, Abba's volunteered. Maybe I'll send him back here for a slab of croc meat, so we can use it for bait. See that he gets some, can you do that?"

"Aw sure, but you don't have a goat?"

"It's a long story, but no."

By this time Coke had joined the croc man with his first kill. Its white belly flashed beneath Coke's torch and when Coke dodged its heavy tail everyone on shore laughed and applauded. The fires burned high now as women hurried back and forth filling pots with water.

Six young tribesmen arrived with drums. They wore coils of beads, bone necklaces, feathers, patches of old cotton bedding, and one of them even had a skirt made of discarded Polaroid negatives. They went into their frenzied drumming with cocky aloofness.

Coke and the croc man were so close to shore that their audience could see the glowing red eyes of the next attacker. As Coke pointed at it with the torch, the croc man allowed the beast to swim within four feet of him before pulling the trigger.

Loud gasps, drumming, and applause went up from the spectators as another croc splashed around in death.

Lucien picked up the Armsport rifle and left. On his climb uphill, he paused to glance back at the festivities. Drums, torches, boiling pots, blood and dirt: the good old basics of idiot ritual. A giddy carelessness of blood.

He stopped at the clinic, gathered up the needed rounds of ammo, and called Trey's name. No answer. In the back room he found the two children, the boy with the sores and the girl he had rescued from Mussa. They lay awake in facing beds, watching one another. At the outdoor kitchen he stopped to pick up some bean cakes. The cooks grinned toothless smiles, telling him, yes, *hizi ni zako*, please, this is for you, take it.

At the lorry he found Abba sleeping underneath the front axle. It was a strange, calm evening with scarcely a breeze, and as Lucien slipped into the lorry's front seat a few stars appeared above the ridge.

The leopard, if it came at all, would come long after the ruckus down at the shore was finished, and when a rich darkness arrived. For now, a caesura in a day of bad rhythms: he put his head back on the old vinyl and closed his eyes.

He was asleep when, later, Abba appeared beside him at the lorry's window, an old, thin, black creature sniffing food.

Lucien woke up slowly and blinked him into focus.

"Bean cake?" Abba asked, and Lucien passed him his portion while giving him instructions about the croc meat.

"It smells even worse when it's cooked, so wait until they boil a big chunk," Lucien said. Abba, his mouth full, nodded that he understood, folded his arms over his chest, and trudged off.

Lucien slouched in the seat, trying to get back to sleep. He tried to think about Trey, then tried not to. Half an hour later he heard footsteps on the gravel below. She had come to the lorry with a cup of coffee for him.

"You did very good work with Mussa today," she said, giving him the steaming mug. She stood beside him at the window of the lorry as he told her how they looked for a goat, how they found the child tied to the stake, and how they now had to settle for croc meat as bait.

"Do you invite me inside or do I stand out here?" she asked when he had finished all that.

"Come in."

She slipped in beside him, but didn't touch him in greeting. At first she told him about the two children at the clinic, their insect bites, their tribes, and the few phrases she had understood from them. Lucien tried to listen and, in turn, told her about the big show down at the lake.

She went on about how she liked his father. Then she told about the croc man's visit last year, how everyone ate the flatulent croc meat for days, and how all the alcohol in the clinic was stolen to make pot liquor.

She chatted on, he decided, in order to keep from saying anything. Once again, he was bleeding inside.

Then, curiously, she was talking about dating boys back in California. Football players. Swimming at Zuma Beach and Malibu, names he seemed to faintly recall. A jukebox in a favorite bar where she was too young to buy beer. And in college, the intellectuals: a boyfriend who was a music major, a composer, and another who got killed in a car wreck in Oregon, leaving a notebook in her possession with equations, doodles, and her name in block letters on a page by itself. She went on and on, telling him about her marriage again, how she wanted more, much more, and it became a kind of confessional out there in the darkness of the lorry, yet not exactly: she was, he decided, like one of the tourists, who suddenly tell you all about themselves in the act of saying good-bye. Med school: one of her professors wanted to leave his wife for her, then an intern came along. She wanted to get away to a place like this, she said, where work became purely itself.

The more she talked, the less he seemed to know her.

An hour passed. She was laughing about something she had said, a remark he had missed, when they heard Abba pulling a slab of croc meat uphill. The sound startled her, then they saw the old man with half a croc in tow, huffing and wheezing as he came toward them.

"Well," she said at last, sliding out of the lorry. "Maybe I'll stop down at the shore and see what's going on."

"Sure, you do that."

"I can't imagine your brother with the croc man," she said, with a curious, affected laughter.

Lucien gave her a tight smile, then went to help Abba with the bait.

"Can I have the cooks bring you supper?" she asked, pausing as she walked away.

"No, we'll be fine," he called to her, and he turned back to the smelly business at hand.

An awkward pause, then she was gone.

They dragged that slab of meat—perhaps eighty pounds— toward the gnarled stump in the middle of the clearing. After tying it securely, they came away with the odor all over them. Nothing smelled as foul as croc meat. At the lorry, Lucien poured petrol over their arms, then they rinsed off the petrol with half the remainder of their drinking water. After that he started the lorry's rattling motor and aimed the headlights at the stump. There: a stinking bait, bright orange and putrid in the glare of the lights, a noisy engine, two hunters reeking of petrol and croc meat, and the whole stupid night.

With the rifle between them, they sat in the lorry again.

Lucien tried to sleep first, but when he put his head back and closed his eyes he saw only Trey.

Faraway drumming down at the lake.

And that awful hemorrhage: he felt himself go weak, as if the best part of him was leaking away.

Torches surrounded the cove now as the croc man and Mfifo stood waist-deep waiting for and shooting the attacking crocs. Made bold by the success of the slaughter, torchbearers waded out up to their ankles, their flaming bundles above their heads, pulling the dying crocs to shore. The water had turned red.

On the long sandbank nine dead crocs lay bellies up waiting to be cut open, skinned, chopped into slabs, and thrown into the cooking pots. A team of fishermen and refugees hauled yet another croc toward the bank, heaving against the rope, and grunting in unison. The air was gray with smoke. In the shallows, dazzled by the torches, blinded and frenzied by all the blood and movement, more crocs swam forward out of the lake. Others flailed and twitched, shot in the head, fighting death, and occasionally a big tail sent up a geyser of water as it splashed down.

Mfifo and the croc man, side by side, became more daring, looking this way and that, trying to distinguish live crocs from those already shot, as they kicked up new targets. The croc man carried the big Korth pistol now, enjoying its loud reports.

Chili sat on the overturned boat as a bite of steaming meat was presented to him by one of the Turkana women. He took out his bottle of Worcestershire sauce, covered the meat with his favorite seasoning, and popped it in his mouth.

Mussa and his women edged the cooks away from one of the pots, claiming it for themselves.

Trey joined Chili. She stood up on the boat, stretching to see the action out in the cove.

"Damn," she said, admiringly.

Another croc, shot through the eye, broke water and arched high out of the shallows, his tail almost clearing the waves, peeling back, its white belly flashing, then splashing down to everyone's cheers. The drummers doubled their beat.

Toward morning, when everyone had glutted at the feast, when more than twenty skins hung on wooden racks, when the meat had been stripped from the carcasses, and when everyone had strolled back to the clinic and camp, six hyenas waited in the darkness. The thick odor brought them out of the desert, and slowly they made their way toward the shore. By the time the refugees and tribesmen had settled around the fires and curled themselves up to sleep, the hyenas started on the remains. Their strong jaws fastened on the croc skulls and the sounds of breaking bone became as loud as gunshots. Chili and Coke lay drunk outside the clinic—Coke sprawled on a table and Chili tucked into his ususal hip hole—and they slept on, although Trey stirred in her bed, raised herself, and listened to the hyenas do their work. The refugee children edged close to their mothers.

Lucien, restless and awake, sat in the lorry and stared along the beam of its headlights.

ZAMANI:
The Blue Hotel

For more than a year after their flight from Ambrose School, the boys witnessed a long argument between their parents. Audrey wanted her sons to attend school in either Europe or America, but Chili argued that foreign schools were no better than Ambrose. He actually favored the rough life for them until they were old enough to determine for themselves how much and what sort of education they wanted.

The typical low, brute, common view, Audrey contended: ask no discipline from them, teach them nothing, and let them swagger around with the other hunters.

It was flattering to hear their parents argue over them.

On one occasion Chili called their mother "artsy-tartsy."

She began pronouncing his name as if she were speaking of a vile, greasy, bean-filled Texas mush.

Her tactic with the boys that summer was to give them daily assignments. Coke was forced to become a writer of long letters.

He wrote to his grandfather's relatives, telling them about the less controversial family news, sending out Cavenaugh photographs, and inquiring about the possibility of future visits. He pushed and pulled that old Parker pen as if it were a plow. Audrey wouldn't let him come down to meals if he didn't do at least two pages a day. Lucien, meanwhile was set down at the piano—which he liked far more than he could let his mother know. He filled the house with missed notes and facsimiles of tunes by Schubert, Brahms, and Dvořák.

Much of the remainder of the boys' time that summer was spent walking into the city center, playing football on dusty patches of ground with the boys from various Indian families, and fondling themselves behind locked doors.

Audrey denied them two safaris with their father and toward August she convinced him—because it was too dangerous—not to take them with him on a hunt in the South Sudan. Their mother seemed satisfied that she was winning. Her upstairs desk bore a stack of catalogs and brochures from schools in which she planned to enroll them.

Then Chili came home from the Sudan. He took a long bath that afternoon, spent an hour upstairs with Audrey, and sat at his accustomed place at the head of the table for supper. An exciting thing occurred on the hunt, he began telling them as they ate their steak pies, but Audrey said no, none of that, after we've finished eating. So they made a conversation out of what Coke had been writing in his letters and what Lucien had attempted on the piano. Then, after supper, Chili took them off to the parlor.

"You're sure this is all right?" he asked Audrey. "Taking my sons into the parlor for some talk?"

"Don't get them too excited," she cautioned.

"No, we wouldn't want to do that," he drawled in his best sarcasm and closed the door quietly.

They loved it. And the stories were about John Dilly, a hunter who was known for his close calls.

"We waded into this marshy area," Chili told them, as the boys draped themselves across him on the sofa. "Dilly and I had these two Dutchmen, each one dumber than the other."

The boys laughed hard—filled with expectation—as Chili found his pipe and touched a match to the bowl.

"Dilly took his Dutchman around one edge of the marsh and I took mine the other way. We'd seen lots of antelope and waterfowl, but I tell you, I thought I heard a definite whistling snort—and I believe Dilly heard it, too."

"Rhino," the boys said in unison.

"I took the precaution of telling my Dutchman to shoot anything that moved, but I didn't tell him what I suspected. Then we walked up a little mound. I could see across the marsh. Dilly and his client were walking right up on a young bull rhino. Hidden by the reeds, see. They were maybe thirty yards from it, so I started hurrying back around to their side to help out. The wind was with 'em, boys, and they were going to creep right up its ass. And when I started running, my Dutchman thought something was chasing us and almost passed me."

Lucien hung onto the long hair at the base of his father's neck. Coke had his legs entwined with Chili's.

"Dilly and his Dutchman must've been no more than ninety feet from the brute when he turned and charged. I heard Dilly yell at his client to shoot, but he never did. By then there was only a second left. Dilly fired—and maybe his round hit the horn and glanced off. Run, goddammit, run, he shouted, and when his Dutchman went one way Dilly went the other. That's the thing you do, boys: don't ever'body run in the same direction. The odds get to fifty-fifty when you split up."

Coke breathed in the smoke from Chili's pipe while Lucien admired his father's profile.

"So the rhino came after Dilly. Naturally. I mean, the Dill never has all that much luck. Anyway, he dives into the muddy water of the marsh, rolls, and fires as the rhino comes thundering over him. The big brute stepped on his leg, but didn't break it because of the soft mud underneath. And when Dilly was ass-side up—right underneath the rhino—he fires straight up through its belly. It was a great shot, sons, all things considered. I saw it plain."

"Fucking Jesus," Coke said.

Lucien wanted to know if the shot killed it.

"Nope, didn't kill it, but hurt it bad. Dilly limped out of the water, leaving that rhino snorting and tossing. So by this time Dilly's client is back. So's mine. So I ask my Dutchman if he wants a shot and he says, sure, good, I shoot it, but where do I shoot? Dilly recommended the second wrinkle behind the eye. So my Dutchman wades forward over his shoe-tops, aims, fires, and misses. He was maybe twenty feet from this dying trophy. Then the other client says, no, wait, my shot. And he aims real careful and puts a slug square into the rhino's foot—at which point the two clients start arguing over who killed it. An interesting discussion, but I decided to put in a bullet of my own before the rhino got up and charged again. So I took out its heart and lungs, and that was that. Then I went over to see about Dilly's leg and to compliment him on his acrobatics. He was complaining that every time he really needed a smoke his cigarettes were wet."

Audrey entered the room. Coke quickly dropped his feet off the sofa and onto the floor where they belonged.

"If you've finished serving up the gore," she said, "we might have dessert and a couple of piano selections."

"No, c'mon, please," Lucien protested.

"It's too soon after dinner," Coke put in. "Lucien's playing gives me the nausea."

"I happen to make my living as a hunter," Chili said, offended. "And maybe we're not quite finished with our conversation."

"There's a tray of puddings in the fridge," Audrey told Lucien, ignoring this last remark. "Why don't you bring them in here?"

Lucien obediently stood up to go, but so did Chili. He was wildly angry.

"Gentlemen," he told the boys, "you're a good audience. A man likes sitting home telling tales."

"The pudding," Audrey said, urging Lucien to fetch dessert.

"Not for me," Chili said, and there was a hard edge on his voice. "I'll be going out. And, boys, I think we should dine out tomorrow night, so we can finish our stories in peace. Dinner and drinks, what do you say?"

Lucien didn't know what to do. As Chili moved to the door, Audrey raised her chin defiantly.

"Of course, boys, you don't have to join me," he said. "A man decides for himself. But, by god, I'll be out on the town."

"Me too," Coke added.

"And what about you, Lucien?" Chili asked, satisfied.

"Sounds fine," Lucien answered.

Chili gave Audrey a confident grin, turned, and walked out of the room, while Lucien was left to observe his mother's quivering chin, still held high but not behaving itself. He didn't know how matters could go so badly so quickly, but there they were:

Coke gone upstairs, Chili off with the gypsies, he and his mother in heavy silence.

She tried to say something bright, but the effort failed.

He went for the puddings, staying in the kitchen as long as possible, waiting for the kettle to boil. Then he brought tea and the little servings of pudding back to the parlor.

They spent the evening discussing movies and movie stars. She liked Alec Guinness and he liked Gary Cooper. As they finished all the puddings, he watched her talk: elegant, he thought, so completely elegant. She should have been a teacher, a doctor, or even a movie star herself, something on the order of Greer Garson, and he felt that her life was serene and composed with the exception of his father's presence. With Chili her composure was always in jeopardy and her chin was often unruly like that. Otherwise, who would she be? The thought amazed him.

The next night the men went out to the New Stanley Hotel for dinner. The boys saw little of their father at the meal, but enjoyed the buffet while he moved from one table to another around the dining room. He knew everybody. He touched the wives, joshed with the Anglican bishop, told Dilly's recent story to a table of businessmen, and sat down for a whiskey with a black politician. Lucien and Coke sat there stiffly in their neckties, gorging themselves and enjoying their father's popularity.

At last he stood between their chairs, his hands on their shoulders, and said, "Let's see the world, boys," and they abandoned their last course to follow him outside. He seemed in a bad mood, suddenly, and they got into the jeep with him and drove silently through the streets. He glowered at the night and they resisted asking him what was wrong.

The Blue Hotel stood inside a crumbling rock wall not far from Nairobi Center. There was a scruffy garden where the girls sat on benches beneath a mango tree while their children played with cigarette butts and empty bottles in the dust. Chickens pecked around the base of a dry, cracked fountain and often wandered inside the hotel itself. The garden: a sagging clothesline, three old wooden radios playing a cacophony of competing tunes, little charcoal braziers on which the cooks grilled strips of meat, a lame mongrel, the shell of an old Land Rover.

Wide doors opened into the hotel bar, Chili's favorite spot in the city. He and the boys occupied stools, crowded together, their knees bumping, and he ordered them Tusker beers while he knocked back two quick Johnnie Walkers and ordered a third.

His talk rambled, mostly the old stories, but Lucien felt he was somehow hearing them for the first time: the old days, narrow escapes, women, lucky shots.

"It's snow-covered up there, you know, and below the treeline it's all that giant heather and all those pines," their father drawled, speaking of Mount Kenya, and Lucien seemed to see it clearly. "Damn me, it filled me up the first time I saw it! I was up there to shoot a herd of elephants led by a big rogue who had caused them to trample hell out of two villages. I had this girl with me, boys, and this was my first native girl, long before your mother, see, and I've forgotten her name, but she gave me lanolin and whiskey rubs because the sun at that altitude—in spite of the cool air—gets pretty harsh."

Jambo Tiner entered the bar, nodded, made a move to join them, but saw that Chili concentrated on the boys, so moved on.

"It was rougher back then. When it rained, our old cars had to be pulled out of the mire by teams of oxen or gangs of men. The roads got to be this thick gumbo, not made for cars. You've seen the same black mud over around Ngorongoro. We went places on horseback if we wanted to make sure."

He told them the familiar story of how the male lion came to the open flap of his tent and roared: how he woke up scrambling for his rifle, flailing out of his cot, screaming with terror, and how the big cat quietly slipped away after announcing himself.

The glass of beer turned warm in Lucien's hands. Jambo Tiner was out in the garden, dancing with one of the girls.

"I made money as best I could," Chili went on. "Clients were scarce and fees were small, so I did control work—like that herd of elephants. Or I traded guns. Or tried to capture animals to sell. Or even collected a little ivory, but there were others much better at it, and, besides it usually involved sawing around on some carcass, so I never cared for it.

Coke had his face so close to Chili's that their breaths mingled. Chili was in an attack of nostalgia and his fourth whiskey.

"I hunted it all and learned it all: grass thicket, riverine forest, bamboo patch, lugger, open savannah. We followed trails we called shit-hot: new spoor and droppings. And we just ran the buggers down, whatever they were, wherever they went, no damn matter, we needed the kill and the money."

Lucien excused himself to visit the latrine. He took his warm beer with him and poured it into the urinal, so he could pretend he was keeping up with the drinking. When he returned, Chili was talking about women. Lucien hoped to hear something philosophical and useful, but only got more stories.

There was a long story about a female client who almost got Percy Spence killed because she wanted to copulate within sight of a pride of lions. Chili laughed as he went on with this— although the boys had heard it before. Then Coke interrupted with the news that he was no longer a virgin and offered the opinion that he'd prefer an hour upstairs to another round of drinks.

"What's that?" Chili asked, rocking back on his barstool.

Together, they told their father about their afternoon in the stable at Lake Nukuru.

"Let me get this straight? You paid money for this girl?"

"Yessir, and I paid her every day we were there," Coke admitted.

"And, Lucien, you did this, too?"

"Well, I touched her."

"Oh, touched her where?"

"On the shoulder."

Chili shook his head with wonder. Then he took their hands in his and pressed their palms to his cheeks.

"Lordy," he said. "Time gets away."

The narrow upstairs hallway of the hotel was filled with the night's traffic: drunks, girls, chickens, a police officer in a soiled uniform, the lame dog, cooks selling those grilled strips of meat, and the old crone herself in a halter and jeans.

Chili entered into negotiations with the madam, insisting on bargain rates. Lucien feared what he'd get. This was no time, he wanted to tell his father, to save money on cheaper goods. There was also one particularly pretty whore, a leggy Somali fifteen-year-old with obviously large breasts. But, sure enough, Coke grabbed her arm and held on throughout Chili's discussion.

Lucien's fate was a tall wiry specimen who looked like a Watusi and who grinned at him with buck teeth.

As money exchanged hands, Teddy Wickham staggered out of a nearby room. Red-faced, watery-eyed, fatigued, but sentimental as ever, he embraced Chili and produced a bottle of local brandy.

In parting, Chili instructed Lucien's partner. "Do him right and mind your manners," he said, then he turned to advise Coke, but his eldest had disappeared into the room Teddy had vacated.

His hand in hers, Lucien was led away. She was far less than desirable, but he tried to encourage himself as best he could.

The room was illumined by the pale glow from the garden below. As the bed separated Lucien and his date, he could hear his own breathing. She shrugged off her thin wrap, put one knee on the mattress, and waited.

"*Pole, pole*," he said softly. Slowly.

She smiled with bored impatience and as he fingered the buttons on his shirt he studied her: a dark tubular body, small knobs of breasts, a bush down there like a jungle. Not the girl of his dreams, not even comparable to the generous Tamu. His body made no response at all.

He thought of Coke, who was probably finished by now, and of Coke's girl down the hall. He preferred to be second in line with someone prettier. So he worked at a fantasy. He tried to think of this apparition before him as, say, Cleopatra: musky, exotic, eager, and just different from anyone he had ever expected. He tried to imagine himself as a young Roman soldier unbuckling his sword. Here she was: this slender black reed, this Nile creature.

She pivoted on that knee, slumped down, and sat on the side of the bed. As he took off his shoes, worries beset him: what position? wordless or with conversation? I have beer breath, but, sure, she's used to that, isn't she? My body isn't responding. Nothing there. Nobody home.

Someone in the garden switched stations on the radio. Lucien also heard the clink of glass and Chili's laughter from the distant bar.

Cleopatra, he tried to convince himself, but in the end he began putting his shoes back on. She lay back on the pillow for a nap and he eventually went to the window. Beyond the garden wall the city kept its late-night silence. A cave, Chili once called the city, maybe referring to all cities. A cave where madness is.

In the bar, later, Chili asked him if things went well.

"Well, she wasn't much my type," he began, meaning to explain, but both Teddy Wickham and Chili laughed and clapped him on the shoulders, assuming the best for him. Jambo Tiner had joined them and brought a new round of drinks.

In a half hour Coke appeared. His hair hung down in sweaty strands, his shirt was wrongly buttoned, and he wanted beer and specific discussion. The laughter started up again.

"Note your brother," Teddy Wickham belched. "See how cool the lad is? You look a sight!"

"Me, I'm in love," Coke told them. "And I've got to buy her out of this place because she loves me, too!"

"Spare us," Chili begged, exchanging laughs with Jambo and Teddy. But Coke was solemn.

"Either we get her out of here or I'll come here every night and buy her for myself!" Coke stated. "Pop, listen, stop laughing, this is serious! It could cost lots of money!"

"Cost who? Better get yourself a job, son!"

Lucien drank his beer and became sleepy through all this. When he suggested they might want to go home before morning, Jambo said, "Ah, kid, you're like your old man, who can always make love for eight solid hours: one minute of foreplay, one minute of furious fucking, and seven hours and fifty-eight minutes of snoring!" The men howled with laughter again.

Jambo eventually drove Lucien home while Chili, Coke, and Teddy stayed on.

Audrey sat at the kitchen table with a book and a cup of tea. Declining anything to eat or drink, Lucien stood in the doorway.

"You've been waiting for us?"

She nodded and closed her book. "He took you to the Blue Hotel, didn't he?" she asked with a heavy sigh.

"We had dinner at the New Stanley first. Pop talked with the bishop. Then, yeah, we talked in the bar at the Blue Hotel for a long time. Teddy and Jambo were there."

"I knew it," she said. "Get yourself a hot bath before you go to bed."

Lucien came to the table and slumped in a chair.

"Years ago," she said, her voice raspy with exhaustion, "I used to have a hiding place from which I watched the Blue Hotel. I spied on your father when he went there. I could see right into the bar—see him sitting on his favorite barstool. Drinking and talking for hours. I knew the name of the madam. Hannah. And the names of some of her girls. My secret hiding place."

"You did that, Mama? Why?"

"Because I was jealous. And angry."

"I wouldn't think you'd do a thing like that."

"It was humiliating, sure, but I did it," she said, finishing her tea.

Lucien felt awful and he didn't want to confirm for her that most of her battles were lost, but he said suddenly, "Mama, you'll never get Coke back in school."

"Oh? He told you this?"

"He wants to be with Pop. And be like Pop. And Pop never went to school, did he?"

"Not so it shows."

"Besides, school's always there. Like church. For later. When there's nothing else for a person to do."

"Are you speaking for yourself, too?"

"I'm not sure. I can't make up my mind."

"No, I think you already have. Tell the truth. You want what Coke wants, too, don't you?"

She cocked her head bravely. She was everything to him, and he wanted to be her ally even as he confirmed her losses. He hoped she knew that.

"I can't talk about it right now," he replied, knowing that too much had already been said. "I've got to get some sleep."

"Yes, all right, go to bed. Is Coke with your father?"

"They'll be home soon," he promised, moving to the door again.

"Lucien, remember," she said, rising and going to him. "I want you to remember the rhino: it shakes itself to drive away the tickbirds. You're going to have to do the same all your life."

She put her arms around him.

"The tickbirds?"

"You're not a common boy. Very uncommon, I believe, and you'll have to shake loose from certain people and things."

"Sure, all right," he said, and he patted her, comforting her.

She kissed his cheek and he went upstairs.

She was calm in her losses. Morally right and elegant and perfect. Somehow the fact that she used to spy on the Blue Hotel was part of her perfection. And, yes, it wasn't his sort of place, he'd shake loose from it tonight, he'd probably never go back.

After all, damn, that keen embarrassment with that lanky whore: it was too awful even to think about.

Yet he did think about it. Undressing, his fingers lingered on his body. The bedsheets were like a cool deep pond drawing him under.

His thoughts ran with the beasts.

The mammoths, extinct. The dogs, overbred. The cities, madness.

And he thought of that girl again, yet not as Cleopatra of the Nile anymore. The fantasy was the room itself: that radio music from the garden, the bed, her knee up on the mattress, those knobby breasts. And the night that didn't exactly happen was pressed forever in his imagination and memory.

SAFARI:
The Hunt Begins

A gale began with dawn and continued all morning, but they got ready. Ammo, a little food, several canteens of water this time.

Lucien drank coffee with Abba. Their bait was still in place, untouched, and the lorry sat idle, dusted with windblown volcanic ash, as the clouds hurried across a pale sun. The stench of camp had mostly blown away and everyone was thankful for that—although the high winds threatened the success of the day's hunt.

"Damn wind. We won't be able to hear anything up there this morning," Chili admitted to Trey. "And there'll be lots of movement: twigs blowing around, lots of dust and shadows."

"Then maybe you should wait," she said.

"Oh, no, hell, no need for that."

See, it's the way he likes it, Lucien wanted to explain.

Coke was all confidence. He came out of the clinic rubbing his hands together briskly, grinning, and ready to shoot some-

thing else. He stuck his nose up, sniffed the gale, and asked about
the croc man.

"Gone to desert," Abba informed him. "He takes your pistol."

"Gone with my Korth?"

"He say to leave you this," Abba said, and he handed Coke
the old Colt. There was a single bullet left in its cylinder. Coke
accepted it with a grunt, then shrugged and smiled.

Whitecaps dotted the lake. Down at the shore tribesmen
tended to their croc skins. The bones were scattered now, becoming perches for dozens of gulls.

"Let's walk," Chili said, fixing the sling of his rifle on his
shoulder.

"Hold on, this is dumb," Lucien said.

"Son, damn, it's time to hunt."

"In this wind?"

"By the time we get up there, the wind'll probably die down."

"Not likely."

"C'mon, Lucy, time to go," Coke said, knowing very well how
he sounded, grinning, and daring Lucien to complain about the
delay for the croc shoot yesterday.

They stood for a moment longer beside the cooking pots at
the rear of the clinic, Trey offering Coke the last of the coffee.
He said, no, thanks, it wasn't coffee he was in a mood for, and
his mustache slanted into a grin so that she laughed. Lucien could
only pretend to see and hear none of this, but when he spoke to
Chili again he was more petulant and sarcastic than he wanted
to be.

"Hell, let's just go up on the ridge one by one," he suggested.
"You go first. If you're not back by noon, I'll send Coke next."

"My plan will work," Chili told him.

"Your plan is always to have no plan."

Chili trudged off and Abba fell in behind, his cousin's ears twirling in the stiff breeze. Then Coke followed. Lucien gave Trey a last glance before he did the same.

Their intimidation, the weather, and his own foolishness amazed him, yet he walked after them, checking his gear as he went: his favorite Armsport, ammo, canteen, knife, food, binoculars, and a single bottle of beer. He clanked as he walked, mocking himself in his movements. Like a mobile hardware store, he told himself. Like an idiot.

Of course Chili hunted by intuition—meaning, Lucien felt, that guesswork and luck were much preferred over reason and intelligence. The reasonable male was no man in Chili's view— or, at best, a lesser specimen.

Walking against the wind was no easy chore. Rivulets of sweat were running under Lucien's clothes by the time he looked up the hill and saw that Abba had sat down on the path.

Chili was far ahead, as if the climb was the first of the day's competitions. Sadly, it was. And if Lucien had wanted the whole safari pitched to a higher level, gamesmanship would now prevail. Always and forever the same. Over the years Chili held an edge in rope tricks, walking on the hands, poker, bridge, canasta, horseshoe pitching, gunsmithing, whiskey drinking and excuses. Coke was the family champion at bird calls, dice, swimming, drumming, distance spitting, mechanics, beer drinking, and opening lines with women. (One standard: "Excuse me, miss, but could you possibly stay in my villa while I'm on holiday in Europe?") Lucien, finally, led the competition in arithmetic, photography, books, movies, music, history, facts, gin drinking, and diplomacy. An unsettled matter was who could skip a stone across a river with the greatest number of hops. Ridiculous and tiresome; yet there it was.

As he approached Abba, the path became even steeper. The old man sat squarely in the middle of it, clasping his cousin's ears against his own as if he were listening to a recorded message. His eyes were closed tight in concentration.

"You sick? What's the matter?"

Abba gave his head a slight shake, but made no reply. Further up the hillside Coke stopped to look back, then signaled to Chili.

Abba rocked back and forth, still holding his ears. "Talk to me," Lucien said. "You need help?"

Clouds raced from one horizon to the next: winds seemed to blow away the senses.

Both Coke and Chili came back down the path, kicking up tiny whirlwinds of dust.

The three of them eventually squatted around Abba, forming a tight circle so their voices could be heard against the gale. The old man just rocked back and forth, his lips tight, his eyes shut, his hands against his head.

"Maybe this is a trance," Chili suggested hopefully.

"He told me there are lots of voices up here at the lake," Lucien reported. "Maybe he's tuning in."

"Lordy, this is great," Chili said. He liked witch doctors and spiritual activities for their entertainment value.

"Jesus, Pop," Coke said, raising his eyes at such nonsense. He tried to touch a lighted match to the tip of his cigarette, but the wind prevented it.

"Now hold on," Chili said. "This interests me."

Abba seemed to grow smaller, folding in on himself, tightening his hands on his head and face as if he meant to disappear.

Coke tried more matches as Chili began to talk. His father preferred to sit in discomfort while telling stories, Lucien knew, so here they were: sitting on their heels, trying to keep the dust out of their eyes, watching Abba, as Chili began telling about the witch doctor at Lake Victoria—they'd heard this one before, too—who for a price put spells on gardens so that no thief and no animal would come and steal produce. "See, I always understood that the local tribesmen might be spooked by this guy's act," Chili said. "I mean, they were afraid of this guy's *juju*. But why did the animals stay out of the garden, too? That got to me. Now your mother's a Methodist, but I say, shit, John Wesley never got to Africa, did he? I was talking to this Dinka warrior who told me I couldn't know much because I wore shoes. A man who can't feel the earth with his bare feet, he told me, can't be much of a hunter and he certainly can't hear what the gods have to say."

Lucien could see beyond the dark shingles of the beach as the lake churned with foam. Better to sit here listening to Chili's confused mysticism, he concluded, than to go hunting in a windstorm.

Chili went on to tell how certain Zaire tribesmen put themselves into trances by distilling the essence of the candelabra tree. Or, wait, was it some other tree? He couldn't recall. He also knew of a tribe with a pet mamba, who reportedly told everybody what to do. They used to make human sacrifices to the snake in *zamani*, but gave that up as uncivilized. He knew of another tribe with a sorceress who provided sexual initiations to all the young males.

"You told us about it," Lucien shouted through the wind.

This sorceress was the only sanitary female in the tribe, Chili went on, because the others—wives and single girls alike—occupied themselves in building the tribal shelters out of cow dung.

Chili laughed hard at his own story. By this time Coke had a cigarette going.

Abba sat holding himself while Chili started another long tale. Lucien could only marvel at his father, who had this infuriating innocence: an elder statesman of the fuck, a hunter who had lived his life in gore, a master of white lies and massive deceptions, yet for all that he remained somehow innocent. Was it just an act? No, not really, because such an actor would have to be a monster: a psychotic, a liar down through whole layers of himself, a spy in the landscape of real human beings. No, Chili had this natural innocence that bordered on evil, Lucien decided, as if he hadn't heard anyone telling him to get out of Eden, as if he thought it was a perfectly fine garden, snakes and all, and as if he just wanted another good piece of fruit to eat.

This sorceress, Chili went on: she definitely wouldn't let outsiders become honorary members of the tribe. He had explained the whole concept of honorary status to her, he said, and had suggested arrangements. In eastern Zambia, all this. He insisted it had happened just as he'd said.

The better part of an hour went by.

And if the three of us met such a woman in the forest primeval, Lucien thought, as the wind lashed them in their little huddle, I'd somehow comprehend the improprieties of lying down with her and I'd refrain. And Coke would score with her and feel like a bad boy for doing it. And Chili would bang her, then want his supper and whiskey afterward.

Innocent devils, all of us.

Abba interrupted this reverie by getting to his feet. They stood around, holding his arms to steady him.

"Everything all right?"

The old man concocted a weak smile. "I go back," he told them.

"Going back down? Why?" Chili wanted to know.

"Ah, shit, let him go," Coke said. "Can't you see he's scared?"
A harsh judgment, Lucien felt, but maybe true.

"What's wrong? You been in a trance?" Chili asked, pulling
at his sleeve. But Abba moved off downhill, never looking back,
his feet sliding on the loose gravel as he left them.

"Let him go," Coke repeated, and they started off again toward
the ridge, with Lucien feeling an ominous retreat in his bones.

ZAMANI: Clients

In the beginning there were women, then more women, and always women.

Some were older, with broad rumps and heavy breasts and too much rouge. Some were old acquaintances of Chili's who had come out on safaris with their husbands or boyfriends, then had returned alone as repeat clients. They had loose flesh at their throats and both Lucien and Coke agreed that they looked awful compared to Audrey. They wore perfume during the hunts, came out of their tents for supper in off-the-shoulder blouses, and trilled the evenings away with false laughter. Then there were friends of friends, for the word got out: he shoots straight, this hunter stalks well, he possesses a fine weapon, trust him, go to him. Even some of the women who had never been to Kenya and who hadn't been told anything seemed to know about Chili—as if he advertised his specialty. They knew how he dug hip holes in the sand and how he went about his services. Or sometimes there were those who didn't know, but came to find out—even though carefully watched over and guarded by the men in their party. Things just got arranged. Watu, Bubba, Coke or Lucien took the men off in one direction while Chili and the woman went another. Or the woman had a headache and remained in camp. Or she was just loaned out, all very civilized. Then sometimes there were young ones, daughters of the family or university students or secretaries, and the strategies seemed infinite. You go there, I go here, meet you over yonder. The sleeping tents got properly spaced apart, everything worked out, see you at breakfast. Yet it all happened without much talk or overt movement, and with such discretion that even the boys in those early years seldom understood the intrigues. Conversations tended toward cups of tea, insect repellent, the quarry, nips of whiskey and the African night.

The boys learned, at last, by watching their father. The guide pays elaborate attention, Chili showed them, at first to the man who pays. Ask about the business back home, all that. Tell stories. Then the women. Let the small tasks and courtesies in camp turn into familiarities, everything progressing naturally.

Remember, Chili might have said, we are in nature, sex is nature itself, you don't give them a meaningful glance, go slow, let them feel your presence, be attentive, slow, stay natural.

Chili's oldest friends—the orginal gypsies—were Deidre, Sammie, and Cat. They came almost every year. Both Sammie and Cat had husbands, virtually new ones every season and one poor man they had even shared between them, but they always got away for their safaris. Deidre was a clothing buyer in London and the best shot of the three. She had that low, hoarse laughter. Sammie was the talker, going on about this or that even when Chili took her to the edge of the camp in the late moonlight and scooped out their hole in the sand, lining it with his khaki shirt and fitting her into it. Cat said very little, just purred and mur-

mured, making all those sounds in her throat as if she might be talking to the lions in the darkness. Cat also liked younger men and had an eye on both Coke and Lucien, but Chili remained possessive.

The younger women interested them most, anyway, and later when they had their own clients—and the Cavenaughs were conducting three safaris simultaneously—the brothers created opportunities for themselves.

Lucien's first real conquest came late that first season he was on his own. They were out in the Mara just before the monsoon rains. A Portuguese widower, soft and white and apprehensive, and his daughter: full breasts and a sly mouth. The widower didn't really want to be out there in the bush, but kept his bearing as best as he could. He had promised his daughter the trip so they could recover from their recent grief. Yet he seemed afraid and uncomfortable with everything: thorns, insects, possible snakes, and any movement on the periphery of camp. Lucien attempted to make him comfortable with pillows, gin coolers and Bubba's cooking. On the second day the girl, Dena, made a move. They were within sight of camp, moving along a dry nullah and hoping to flank a dozen gazelle who fed among some spike grass. Lucien and the girl were several paces behind the widower and Bubba.

"You a virgin?" she suddenly asked him.

"No, how about you?" he asked in return.

She just gave him her sly half smile.

That night the wind blew up cool. As they sat around a big fire, they smelled the distant rain. Lucien introduced the subject of malaria.

"You have it around here?" the widower asked, startled. "It's cool here. I didn't think of malaria in weather so cold."

"We've had a wet season," Lucien said. "Lots of mosquitoes breeding. Actually, we've got a small epidemic."

"But, no, I didn't prepare!" the widower said.

"Not taking your quinine?"

"No, not at all! This is terrible! We should leave!"

"Never mind," Lucien assured him. "I have malaria pills for all of us." He went to his kit and brought the widower an oversized white pill, then ordered Bubba to fetch another glass of gin. "Take one of these larger ones just before supper every evening," Lucien instructed him. "I'll get Dena smaller ones— she's small and needs a smaller dose."

Her skin glowed orange as she gazed at him from across the campfire. She looked resolute, as if that treasure there in the folds of her safari skirt was the thing she would fiercely protect and fiercely give away. Seventeen years old and glowing. Lucien felt older, wiser and superior.

The father got drowsy and only finished that last gin cooler in the midst of yawns and complaints. He soon kissed his daughter and shuffled off to bed in his tent. When he was gone, Dena avoided Lucien's eyes and quickly said goodnight, too.

It was an hour later that he went to her.

"May I come in?" he asked, outside the flap of her tent.

"If you wish," she answered. Her English was formal and beautifully accented.

He tried to adjust his eyes in the dark tent. She lay covered up in the wide cot, and there were no chairs or stools for him.

"What did you give Papa?" she asked.

"A sleeping pill," he admitted. "He won't wake up until noon."

"It won't hurt him, will it?"

"He'll feel wonderful tomorrow. If he complains about sleeping so much, I'll say he might have a touch of the fever already. Anyway, your father needs the rest, not all the tracking we've been doing."

"I knew it was a sleeping pill," she said. "I suppose you expect to get in my bed, don't you?"

"You're the one who started talking about sex."

"I certainly didn't!"

"You asked me if I was a virgin," he reminded her, sitting down on the thin frame of the cot beside her.

"I was curious," she said. "But you won't sleep with me, if that's what you're thinking."

He took off his shoes.

"I am Roman Catholic," she announced.

He took off his shirt and folded it atop the shoes.

"And it's almost my time of month."

He pulled the thin blanket away from her naked shoulder.

"You won't touch me," she said sharply, yet she failed to restore the blanket to its place.

Her deep perfume reeled through his head.

"And I cannot get pregnant," she went on.

"You won't," he said, assuring her with total recklessness. They could hear each other's breathing as he unbuttoned himself. The warmth from their bodies seemed to illumine the close confines of the tent now, so their features became recognizable.

He exposed himself to her, knowing she could see that well enough, too.

"And you won't look at me," she argued. "I'm getting fat and you won't look at me. Not tonight and not at anytime during this next week on safari. You won't put your eyes on me, no matter how many times we do this."

He pulled the blanket aside and inspected her as best as he could.

"Also, I am not good at making love," she went on. "I am clumsy and do not get it right. I will not satisfy you. And you will not satisfy me."

He eased in beside her.

"Also, you must hold me awhile," she said more softly. "You must not begin too quickly. We must kiss for a very long time." This was her last command and protest as her voice became a whisper. He pulled her close, happy to obey.

Those first years: all sorts of arrangements and combinations. Watu and Bubba enjoyed the constant farce, and Bubba got into the habit of giggling nervously and running off to hide his face in his hands when the activities became obvious. On one safari Chili had to go up to Mount Elgon on government business, so Lucien and Coke were left with three women between them. Every day and night there would be an odd woman out.

"Now we have the extra woman," Bubba proposed in his broken Swahili, laughing. "And we must entertain this woman. Me, I have the solution."

The brothers thought he was suggesting his own participation every evening. He was a wiry, ugly, happy specimen, clearly male and capable. Yet he had always been so discreet, even embarrassed by arrangements.

"Bubba," Coke said, trying not to hurt any feelings, "I don't think you can help us in this."

"Oh, truly, Mfifo, yes. I will take the extra lady to hunt every day! She will learn to shoot! This can be much fun on safari, also, I will tell her!" He laughed and hid his face.

On another occasion there was an American husband, wife,

and older daughter, so the game of keeping Daddy occupied became essential. He was an accountant with a pencil mustache who smoked a corncob pipe filled with awful tabacco, and called his women Dooley and Tootie, but the brothers never understood which was which. On the third day he complained that he wasn't seeing much of either of them and hoped to share a hunt with them.

"Ah, but you're looking for rhino or lion," Chili assured him. "We figured you wouldn't want to put the girls at that much risk."

"No, I suppose not," the accountant agreed, and that settled matters.

As it turned out his best shot was on a giraffe that happened to stroll by camp: a shotgun slug at thirty feet. The beast went down like a gangling puppet with its strings cut.

Tootie—the daughter, if that was her name—was a noisy partner who wanted to play in the cot. In the evenings her sharp cries and moans became cause for concern. Coke suggested placing a hand over her mouth during the act, but even Chili considered that crude. Chili himself would have nothing to do with her after sundown because of all her alarms, and in turn she accused him of getting old. Lucien suggested oral sex as a solution, but Coke said, no, that works only half the time at best, and in Chili's opinion no man should ever stoop to such entertainments.

They constantly worried about the accountant being woken up in the middle of the night by his noisy daughter, so poured more and more whiskey down the poor man trying to ensure that he slept soundly. Besides, Chili offered, he was a pipe smoker. Smoking a pipe was a full-time business that exhausted a man. So let the lion's distant roar be answered by the girl's wails. As for the mother, she was content with someone's attentions once a day—and never mind the daughter's energies.

At the Long Bar in Nairobi the Cavenaugh notoriety received both good-natured derision and sniffing admiration. The jokes might have been stronger except that the hunter and his sons continued to bag dozens of trophies and their skills in the bush were still admirable.

Lucien also made his contribution. He confided one afternoon how they actually accomplished their seductions.

"We try to arrange to save the lady's life," he said, sipping his drink in the middle of his story. The pause was Chili's affectation: very effective, if managed rightly. "It all goes pretty well after a lady's had her life saved. She becomes grateful."

The men laughed and asked the three of them for particulars. The bar was crowded that Friday afternoon, Montagu and Percy Spence among the others.

"First off, we get her out in the bush with an unloaded weapon," Lucien went on. Both Chili and Coke nodded solemn agreement with all this. "When the quarry charges, she tries to shoot, but we later tell her that the gun misfired. Just before she's pounced on, we pick off the beast. Drop it right at her feet, if possible. If it grazes or scratches her, all the better. She's breathless. She might even scream or cry or carry on a bit. But, gentlemen, she's filled with gratitude. There are times—vouch for me here, Coke—when she lies down right there on the carcass."

Those afternoons, long ago: lots of ribald exaggeration. And certain clients and stories—the accountant and his noisy daughter, for instance—were talked about and elaborated upon and made their contributions to the Cavenaugh reputations. Other hunters had their little intrigues, too. It was part of the business— like any other—and the stuff of male boasting. And looking back, Lucien reckoned, there weren't that many sexual safaris if one totaled them up. Yet Chili and his sons were always at the center of the talk.

For a long time, Lucien enjoyed it, then it all began to change.

It began with a safari down at Mount Kilimanjaro with a stuffy Brit and his young wife. The monsoon rains came on early and stayed for days until the client suggested that they pack up camp and check into the old mountain hotel down at Arusha.

They slogged into town and reached the hotel on the muddy slopes of the western side—an old building with a massive stone hearth in the lobby and all those tiny rooms. They drank glasses of straight gin while they registered, standing there with Lucien's guns and gear, puddles of muddy water under their boots. The client wore tweedy stuff, but he was the one shivering, the gin glass trembling in his fingers. He was a professor of something and the wife had been a student of his someplace. She had those pursed lips and a permanent scowl of disapproval, but she was pretty enough, with an excellent figure. Lucien considered it as they registered while she walked across the lobby in search of the powder room. A tight little butt.

"Cozy spot, this," the professor admitted with a shiver. "I can't say I'm unhappy being here."

"The rain this time of year can be damned chilly," Lucien agreed. "But there's not much to do here at the hotel. We might get a hike up the mountain, if you're up to it tomorrow."

"There's an idea. I don't much think Leah would take to it, but I might give it a go."

There was a pause as the professor worked his mouth into a speech. "My wife, she, well, both of us, actually, would like your close personal service these next few evenings."

Lucien gave him an uncomprehending stare. "Yes?" he managed.

"Not that I require your services, not me personally, no," the professor went on with a hapless laugh. "But just for my wife, you see. An intimate service for her."

"For Leah?" Lucien asked, making sure.

"An intimate arrangement, ah, every night," the professor repeated, and Lucien felt a little tremor of revulsion. It was all he could do to smile.

"That will cost extra," he said, surprised at himself and at his cruel tone.

"Ah, I see, yes, how much more?"

"A hundred pounds."

"Yes, I see, so much? Very well. What shall be the arrangements?"

"How do you mean?"

"Room arrangements. You and Leah can take one room, if you prefer, and I'll take the other. Whatever suits you."

"I'll want my own private room," Lucien said evenly, his voice more and more cruel as he went on. "And I don't want anyone lying around in it. I'll come over to your room when you're out— or after supper in the evenings. I don't suppose you want to stay there and watch, do you?"

"She won't allow it," the professor said softly. "No, I'll just come to the lounge. Will that be all right? I'll read magazines in the lounge."

Lucien picked up his gear and turned away. He followed a boy up a creaking flight of stairs toward his room.

Supper was a long, ghastly business: a crowded dining room, thin soup, tough slices of roast beef, overcooked vegetables the way the Brit liked them. The wine had gone to vinegar, so they drank beer. And they had nothing to say to one another.

The little hotel creaked and moaned around them, lashed by rain. There were too many guests and the constant footfall on the uneven boards of the hallways set up a hollow echo. Voices traveled from room to room, and around the hearth in the lounge the residents were a marooned, lonely, desperate bunch. Everyone soon knew, Lucien supposed, everyone else's arrangements.

She went to the room ahead of him to prepare herself. When he went to her she wore a flannel shirt and knelt down in the center of the bed. As he undressed, she sneered at him, saying, "Just who do you think you are?" She said it several times and he had no idea what she meant. She might have been angry about his asking extra money for this duty. But it sounded like a line from a bad movie and he laughed at her, making her even more furious.

He got on the bed with her, opened her roughly, mounted her, entered her, and moved like an engine. He surprised himself because he felt nothing except disgust, yet he had this hard lust for her, and he drove at her until she went into a seizure: clawing at the sheets, twisting under him, and drooling. She raised her head again and again, then slammed it back into the pillow. Insane, he told himself. She hates this. She loves it. She's going crazy. It was her orgasm: an ugly thing to cause and to watch.

She cursed him as he dressed himself afterward. "If women were stronger than men, know what they'd do? They'd rape the same as men rape! I'd like to bash you and rape you, goddammit, and make you sick with it!"

"You do make me sick," he assured her, and he went downstairs for a drink. The professor seemed pleased that everything had gone so quickly and wanted to stand at the bar and chat, but Lucien wouldn't talk to him.

The next morning Lucien drove into Arusha, a sad little safari town in those days: banana vendors, lottery tickets at a forlorn kiosk on the main square, dozens of shoeshine boys, beer bottles on the window sills. The day grew dark before each rain, then light and muggy, then dark again before the next downpour. He walked around getting angry with Chili, but mostly at himself because he had inherited the urge: muscles and nerves tightening every day of his life. He hated this professor and his bitch, yet they knew he would do this. They knew him well enough, never mind the money. And he thought, well, the old boy's impotent, and this is his way of trying to keep her. Maybe that's it, but who cares? He wanted no psychologies. And in spite of everything he wanted to get back to that grim little hotel on the slopes; he wanted supper finished and the whole tawdry business over again.

A long wet day. The mountain wore its gray shroud and said nothing at all.

There were oversized gun closets with shuttered doors in each little room of the hotel and the one in Leah's room smelled as if an army of hunters had used it. It smelled of leather, bluing, gunpowder and wax.

"In there," she said. "Let's do it in there."

He dragged the big overstuffed chair into the darkness of the closet and shoved her down on its cushion. He spread her legs over the arms of the chair and went at her. A window was forgotten and left open in all this, so rain drenched the bed. Thunder sounded as her body contorted underneath him, and afterward he felt tense, maimed, and broken apart.

Was sex going to be like this? Maybe only Chili and a few like him had it uncomplicated.

The Germans flew their sex clubs in by private plane, landing out there on the Masai Plains where they bought and bargained for willing girls. Everyone watching everyone else: fat business-men with stubby pink pricks and the slender black *yangus*. Lucien had seen a photo—every Deutschland tourist had his little Has-selblad—with all the men at the edge of a camp table, their penises hard and lying on the tabletop for inspection, compar-ison, and measurement: tourists and natives together, pink sau-sages and black rods, smiles on their faces, brothers in prickhood.

And maybe the Brits, he knew, had this corner of the world so they could have their colonial housegirls, pliant houseboys, and the Blue Hotel. And the beasts in the field lie down with each other, the beasts being somehow more noble and less frantic in their copulations than anyone Lucien knew.

In another day the rain slackened, but the professor said he was happy enough to stay on at the hotel. They were finishing that third evening when he said it.

"Didn't you originally say you wanted to do some shooting on this safari?" Lucien asked.

"Originally, he lied," Leah answered.

The professor scratched his tweeds, coughed, twitched, and placed a hand over Leah's. "I think we're doing perfectly fine here, don't you?" he asked her.

"Well, I'm going hunting in the morning," Lucien said.

"You're being paid your rate all the same," the professor noted. "Does it matter where we are?"

"I'm paid to hunt."

"Apparently you can be paid for anything," the bitch added.

Thinking of no quick reply, Lucien placed his fork on his plate, got up, and went to his room. His strides took him back and forth at the foot of his bed, but the pacing reminded him of his father so he sat down. He heard their laughter from the next room. He hated being young and without all the practiced rudeness that could hurt them. He'd never touch her again, that he knew. Bitch. Perverts. He tried to think of other girls, of Dena especially with her Portuguese accent and her magnificent breasts. Night sounds entered his room from the open window along with the cool air off the mountain.

Leah knocked at his door, asking to come in.

No, he said, and go away.

So she came in and stood with her back to the wall. She had a hard little smile, a remnant of having been laughing at him.

Then she came over and began unbuttoning him. She unbuttoned all his senses.

His disappointment in himself became profound and he swore he'd never have a women like that again. He knew it was probably impossible, but he wanted to love somebody, and years later he could pinpoint when this change in him began, in the rooms with the big gun closets on that rainy mountainside.

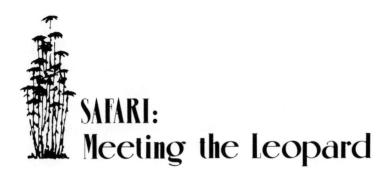

SAFARI:
Meeting the Leopard

The wind kept on.

Chili, meanwhile, arugued his cockeyed plan: they would spread out, see, and move across the top of the ridge. He proposed this as if they might all stroll across a lush meadow, as if they were going bird hunting, say, in Devon or Nebraska. It was a senile and deadly idea, Lucien knew, yet funny, too, because Coke was assigned the middle of that pile of sawtoothed boulders. As the old man somehow reasoned it, Lucien was just too intelligent to climb over all those obstacles and Chili himself was exempt because of seniority. And, besides, the crocs didn't get you, so no damn leopard's going to, Chili shouted in the wind, and Coke could only answer, wait now, hold it, we should trade off, we should take turns, I'm going to bust my butt out there.

They stood for half an hour in the middle of the windstorm arguing all this. Lucien pretended to get dust in his eye and turned away so he could laugh.

Then off they went, saying how important it was to keep each other in view, although, of course, they couldn't. Coke jumped and climbed and clawed his way from boulder to boulder, dropping out of sight then reappearing, more disheveled each time he bobbed back up. Lucien couldn't see his father at all.

Ludicrous and stupid, but they trudged forward.

Lucien went along the western edge of the ridge, in full view of the lake. The furnace of the wind burned his eyes whenever he turned toward Coke. Should trouble come, he knew he'd be no help. The gale would carry away his brother's last cry. Or Chili would simply disappear, making a mockery and a waste of everything. Didn't the old sonofabitch know? Something awful could happen here: the heavens could reel out of control, the Southern Cross could tip on its side, and in the swirling clouds and shadows the years could become surreal and lost.

Yet Lucien went on, the safety off his rifle.

There was always the possibility that they'd flush the leopard in a classic maneuver. It might bolt between them or just ahead, presenting itself in sudden profile, leaping away so that one of them could lead it with a quick swing of the rifle barrel, and so at the arc of a graceful leap there would be the perfect shot. Not likely, but what if? If that occurred, the competition would confirm itself again and Chili would be right in his wrongness. Whoever made the shot and got the kill would be the hero. If Chili himself made it, he'd get some of his fading patriarchy back and his sons would crawl back into his shadow. If Coke shot the man-eater, the domain of the lake would be his: hills, water, crocs, refugees, and pretty Trey. If Lucien got the kill, he'd surface from the merchant class for a moment. Having failed to communicate with his father as they sat around the fire the other evening, he'd make mere talk unnecessary and trivial. He'd see his father's eyes and glass raised toward him again. And all the constellations would be set straight in the sky.

A pair of ring-necked doves broke cover and flew off on the

wind like blades of light. Startled, Lucien recovered and moved on. He took a circular path into the boulders themselves: rooms of rock in there, small clearings with floors of that same volcanic powder glistening with flecks of glass, remnants of a molten heat eons ago. The sheer stone walls gave him a wave of claustrophobia, so he hurried back to the outside path.

Girls, women, clients. There was a woman named Angela who worked in the USIA library in Nairobi, a perfectly good woman, he recalled, plain and gentle. She wore oversized glasses. Tinted. He took her to dinners for perhaps three years of his life. Occasionally they played three-sided bridge with Audrey. And cooked for each other in her flat and made love on her waterbed. Yet he couldn't summon Angela's face to mind. She eventually moved on to another assignment with the American government—took a battery of tests and improved her job rating, he remembered—and not long after she left town he discovered that he just couldn't recall what she looked like. And so many others. The bitch, Leah: he could see her pursed lips, ready with insults. Or Colly's childish whine of a voice. Or Kira. But certain faces blinked in and out of his memory now. And he wondered if Trey would become a lost face.

He stopped and opened his canteen. Coke, standing high on a boulder, pushed his palms down, signaling that they should stop. Lucien realized that on the far side of the ridge Chili obeyed the same gesture. For the moment, they were all still safe.

Lucien propped his rifle against a boulder as he drank from the canteen. Those thoughts and memories were still with him: all the women in their lives, what happened down in Arusha that time, how his mother had put up with so much. He thought about playing bridge with their friends Emilene and Terence: lost, everything lost. The people in their lives.

Then, curiously, Lucien began to feel a small knife-prick of fear. That strange sense: the tingle at the base of the neck, the wind hissing in the ears, the iron taste of water from the canteen, and beyond all this the certainty that he was in a presence, being watched. He turned slowly, looking over his left shoulder.

Scarcely ten meters away the leopard sat on a boulder beside the path. The glare of the lake behind it made it seem like a hallucination, but there it was: unmoving, sitting in idle repose, curious and waiting.

They watched each other without moving as Lucien forgot to breathe.

His rifle, propped against that rock perhaps three meters away, was uselessly out of reach. If he made a quick movement for it, he knew the leopard would coil and spring.

In that odd glare from the lake the creature wore a nimbus of light. Its eyes did seem white and blank, without mercy, and it stared as if to study him and as if to pose, too, so it could be studied in return. Both its pelt and rosettes were pale, and the wind fanned out a tuft of long blond hair on its chest. Its paws were heavy pads, the claws retracted, and its ears pitched forward as if it waited for Lucien to speak his name. The set of the jaw seemed relaxed as if it announced, there now, this is my territory, I'm perfectly at ease here, watch me, no hurry, and you're all nervous and sweating. Its legs and hindquarters were supple and frightening. It was surely the largest male leopard Lucien had ever seen.

His knife was in his belt, but he dared not move his hand to it.

The eyes again: the cat's vertical slit, yes, but all gray and milky white, eyes that narrowed in a quiet, private, peaceful display of power and seemed to say, yes, I can kill you now, but it won't be so bad, you'll be finished in just a moment, then you'll pass over into another light beyond our light.

Lucien began to know that he was going to die. It could quickly get his neck and his brittle spine; it could have him suddenly and easily, whenever it wanted, and he might get his knife out and bury it into the leopard's gut, but probably not.

For a moment Lucien could feel it: snap of bone, gush of blood, then the numb indifference of the wind.

Then—just as quickly—the feeling began to pass. The leopard's calm moved over into Lucien and he passed beyond the raw anxiety of getting killed and eaten. A sudden, unexplainable tranquility.

Then his rifle toppled over.

Perhaps the wind had made it slip off the rock and rattle to the ground. He turned to look at it—to see that it had actually fallen further from his grasp, beyond any hope of reaching it in time. Yet the calmness stayed with him and grew and expanded. Fear drained into a curious serenity he couldn't comprehend. It was as if all his life he had waited for this feeling—which was both less than knowledge and more. Concerns melted away. Who slept with whom, who loved well and who didn't, what mistakes had been made: none of that mattered much. He was in perfect solitude, alone, at the edge of the lake of voices. Death was no great thing. His breath and being were with the cat now, he felt, and their rhythms out here had become one: they paused in this momentary seclusion among the boulders, in a dream beyond place or species, in a terrible shared loneliness.

The wind seemed to be dying all around him.

He looked back toward the boulder beside the path. The leopard was gone.

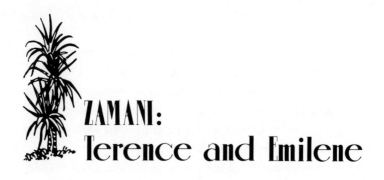

ZAMANI:
Terence and Emilene

They were best friends with his parents.

This was long after the boys worked on safaris with Chili, after Coke's divorce from Colly, and in the first days of the outfitting business. Terence, who was a government advisor of some sort, and his short, dark wife, Emilene, who was bright and happy and who made everyone laugh when she drank a little too much, used to come over for card games and dinners.

Emilene was the sort who said, "Ah, I know what let's do!" and everybody wanted to do it. She liked her Kentucky bourbon. She also had a pet bird, Wapi, and a small jewel case that went everywhere with her. She spoke in shorthand. And she was a bridge expert who had easily been champion at the club, though her partner's husband got transferred out of the country, forcing Emilene to play with Terence. She liked moving the card table around, playing out beside the pool or beside the jacaranda tree on the side lawn, and she liked picnics rather than formal meals, so everybody was always on the back porch or on rubber floats in the pool itself. Often Lucien's parents went out to Terence's place on Langata Road, where Emilene spread tables under Chinese lanterns outdoors.

She and Audrey became special friends with a black woman named Dura, who taught them ceramics. They learned to throw at the wheel and both Audrey and Emilene bought small electric kilns. After they had made dozens of pots they turned to jewelry making, and Lucien would often find them sitting in the shade rolling little balls of clay into beads, punching holes through these with wire instruments, and glazing them with dazzling colors. Dura came to the house a great deal in the late mornings and the threee women drank strong coffee, a little bourbon occasionally, and laughed over their gossip. Dura had a low dirty laughter, as if something naughty had been said, which it often had been. She employed nine workers at her little pottery shop on Government Road. In her day, Audrey said, she had been a real beauty, but now Dura was a single businesswoman, making her way as a potter and a shopkeeper, and the necklaces and bracelets fashioned by Audrey and Emilene were contributed to the displays of costume jewelry at Dura's shop. Dura's beauty had faded into a refined ugliness: she was gaunt and skeletal, yet wise in the eyes, a dear old crone, Lucien thought, and the sort of woman other women tell their secrets to.

Inside Emilene's case were strands of pearls, a few diamond rings, an emerald drop, and a number of gold items. She carried the case, she said, because she didn't trust leaving it at home, and, besides, this was her getaway money if she ever got tired of Terence. So it was the jewelry case, Wapi the bird, a deck of cards and a bottle of bourbon wherever Emilene went.

Audrey taught both women to cook. They did desserts mostly, devouring them as the day progressed, moving from cookstove to kiln, from porch to kitchen, from sitting room to pool. They were like young girls, getting messy with clay or flour, then washing off with a dip in the pool, then eating or drinking a while, then starting all over again with their clay or their cakes.

It was a happy year. Lucien often came home from the outfitting store at the noon hour for lunch, to be enlisted as a bridge partner while Dura received her first instructions in the game. She was never a particularly good player, but Lucien admired and enjoyed this Kikuyu lady of undetermined age, who had managed to transcend time and tribe and who dearly loved Audrey. Later on, Dura was often at the house for dinners or parties, but more often it was Terence, Emilene, Audrey and Chili night after night.

Couples. Audrey took pride that Chili stayed home, conversed, played cards and dined in an acceptable social atmosphere instead of circulating through the bars of the city.

Terence: lanky, stoop-shouldered, a thin clown of a man with his plastic cigarette holder and his old Buick convertible. He never had any cash. And never hunted. But he and Chili had an unshakeable political faith in America.

"Trust the Yanks to be as impatient as the Moslems in the Middle East, as the Irish in Belfast, as the gooks in Asia, and the Jews in Israel," Terence offered. "Makes for balance of power. Count on the Yanks, I say, to bully the right people."

"God bless America," Chili added, raising a glass which gave Emilene the opportunity to raise one with them.

"Yanks. Balance. Impatience," she announced in her shorthand.

So they played cards, with Wapi up in the jacaranda tree. Or they went to the movies—on which occasions Lucien sometimes joined them. And eventually there were two tables for bridge, with Lucien, Dura, and others invited. It was during this period that Chili had the pool patched and cleaned, making it sanitary for swimming. There were occasional loud suggestions that all clothes should be discarded, but nobody ever did it. Cakes, souf- flés, and puddings came out of the kitchen. The booze flowed, but only Emilene got tipsy and everyone enjoyed how she did it. Lucien sometimes went to the piano and Terence sang in his fautly tenor. Coke sometimes dropped by with a girlfriend. And Dura had a way of saying goodnight, taking a long time to do it, pressing her cheek against Audrey's or Lucien's as if to say, there, I trust you, this is love, we are holding each other briefly at this little distance, it is better and truer like this, see, this is how it's done, good-bye dears until tomorrow.

A year of Cavenaugh social life. Only a year before Lucien had been down in Arusha, disgusted with the professor, the bitch, and himself. He was cynical and easily annoyed in this period, but the times at the house lifted his spirits.

"Nairobi's getting terrible," he sometimes complained. "There are all those damned grasshoppers everywhere. The beggars are eating them, cooking them over open fires in the gutters down- town. And all those tiny children are running around the streets until dawn, chewing their stalks of sugarcane. I'll tell you what it's like: a human game reserve. The savannahs are clean by comparison, and Mother Nature has arranged for all of us to be locked in the cities."

"You sound like your father," Audrey would answer.

"It's the damned store," he'd say. "I'm stuck in the middle of it all. In the middle of a sewer."

"Come on, don't be a bore," she'd say. "Have some cake and let's play bridge."

A petulant, uneasy time for him, but in the end he always did play cards or go to movies or drive someone here or there on errands. He was skeptical of all the newfound domestic activities, but his mother seemed so happy that he let himself be persuaded. Chili as host and husband? No, it wasn't much right, and the gypsies would probably come get him. And Lucien was proud of Audrey's friendship with Dura, but concerned about that, too, because when a white and a black really became friends there were always wicked volunteers pleased to make trouble for them. He also fretted over Emilene's drunkenness. And Chili's curious friendship with Terence: they had only their political assertions in common, and his father was neglecting his cronies at the Long Bar and the Blue Hotel. Yet, all right: the house had some music and laughter in it.

One evening Chili was off on safari down in Tsavo. Emilene was also absent, staying home with a cold, nursing herself, as she put it, with "Toddies, bad novels, and beddie-bye." So Lucien and Dura agreed to play cards, failing to do much that evening, with Audrey and Terence opposing them. They stopped playing around nine o'clock, ate some ice cream, then got into heavy talk. They had all recently gone to see the movie *On the Beach* and the film got them started on nuclear war. Terence approved the idea that both Russia and America had a nuclear force.

"Because mankind requires a champion," he stated. "A sort of aristocratic warrior elite. Keeps everyone in line, you see. Or else every jack dictator would begin something against his neighbor—some nice holy war—and would get us all buggered in the middle of it."

"Come on, who in his right mind can be pro-nuke?" Lucien asked.

"Ah, listen, my boy, and hear me. The world consists of brutal little kingdoms. So we very much need our international policemen with very big weapons who can say, here now, you've gone too far, keep in line. And in our lifetimes it's going to be America and the Reds, isn't it?"

"But they can't get along with each other," Audrey said.

"And the little wars crop up anyway," Lucien, argued. "And if anything works against them it's economic retaliation, not the threat of big bombs."

Terence argued his line of thought, Lucien objected, and Audrey added her comments until they turned to Dura for an opinion. She was reluctant, buy they urged her on.

"This movie I didn't like," she said, "because it makes us think of a future that hasn't happened. And the big disaster. But it takes our minds off the real problems."

"Meaning what?" Terence asked.

"Meaning the sore that festers under our skin. You like to speak of politics far away. You like to think on these politics, never at home. Never the injustice or hunger. Never anything here."

"We were discussing the film," Terence objected. "We weren't gearing up for another fuss about Kenya."

"Kenya and Africa, yes, here is the wickedness."

"Well, things are much more settled around here, I'd say," Terence replied. "The Mau Mau are gone. We have black rule and accommodation for the white businessman. There are sticky matters, but I'd say we're a model nation at the moment."

Dura gave him a straight look.

"This is parlor chitchat," she said coldly. "But there is much wrong and we all know it. The people are hungry. One movie ticket can feed one family. There are guns in the street."

"You are living at a very high standard," Terence told her. "With your own shop. How can you complain?"

Dura was on her feet, looking for her wrap.

"Oh, Dura," Audrey said, hurting for her.

Dura asked Lucien to please drive her home.

"Of course," he said. "But don't be angry."

"Who is angry? I am having card games with ice cream and chitchat. I am owning my little shop. My people suffer, but my politics should be atom bombs that are far away from all this."

"Black power is a very old subject," Terence put in. "There are other conversations of an evening besides that one."

Audrey crossed to Dura and embraced her. And Dura, in turn, melted into the hug, pressing her cheek on Audrey's and saying, fine, all right, yes, I'm perfectly fine.

"Don't ever let us upset you," Audrey whispered in her ear.

"No, please, I am just tired. I need my rest. And tomorrow I have some new clay to show you. Porcelain clay. We can get muddy together in the morning and have lunch, yes?"

"I look forward to it," Audrey said, and she kissed Dura's bony cheek as Terence stood, bowed slightly, and wished her good evening.

Lucien drove across town. A clear, crystalline evening: the stars bright over the boulevards. Dura lived in rooms above her shop. She was still grumpy when they arrived.

"I don't like that Terence. No one needs bombs," she said.

"People are insane. It's the nuclear age."

"And I don't like his wife either, if you want to know."

"Emilene? She's harmless enough."

"You don't know her." Dura sat as rigid as a totem in the car beside him. "I tell you, I love your mother. Everything else at her house I don't always love so much. Too many sweets and too many games. I prefer *pombe*. And your father is unhappy. And his friend is much a fool. And the chitchat is like so much cobweb getting in the way."

"You think my father's unhappy?"

"He likes his house, but it is also his cage. And you don't understand, do you?"

Lucien assured her he did, but perhaps he didn't.

"In my neighborhood people come to me for advice," she went on. They were sitting in the car outside her shop, the motor still running. "I have the intuition. But at your house Audrey is much the wise one with me. I tell her about all my husbands. I show her my fears. She talks to me very clear and straight."

"She loves you, Dura, she really does."

"Friends," Dura replied with a sigh. "Ah me, tomorrow I show her the porcelain clay. Very smooth under the hand like silk. She will love this very much. But I wish I could say to her my intuition."

"What? Tell me."

"What good is it? And you should see for yourself."

"What's wrong?"

"Your father and that woman. You don't see it?"

"Emilene? Oh, no, I don't think so, Dura. It's Terence and Chili that are friends."

"Your father likes to play cards with Terence?"

Lucien fell into silence, thinking, sure, that's certainly not it. Clearly, Dura was right.

"Do you think so?" he asked weakly.

"I hate what I know," she said, trying a laugh. "In my neighborhood I don't prefer to know. Or in your house. But there is your mother: I know very much her heart. And how can I say anything?"

"If you're a friend, you must," he advised her.

"But I would lose the friendship, I think. This I cannot say."

Lucien walked her to her door, his hand draped on her shoulder.

"Say to my mother what you can," he advised her. "And be her friend. That's all you can be."

Dura kissed his cheek. This was a valuable woman and friend: a warm black pain in the center of her, the dark wisdom of bad years, yet a treasure for his family. He kissed her cheek in return and said goodnight.

Driving back toward the Muthiaga district, the night and stars were the only things on his mind until something occurred to him. He turned at a crossroads and went out toward Langata. His nerves tingled. It was only half-past ten, so Audrey and Terence would be having a nightcap and talking, giving him time for this intrigue.

Even at this late hour both sides of the road were crowded with blacks making their last trudge home from the local bars and dukas. There was an old woman carrying on her shoulder what seemed to be half a tree: tomorrow's firewood. Two boys in oversized men's white shirts yelled and raised their middle fingers as he drove by. There was a cemetery out this way, he remembered, where the hyenas constantly dug up the new graves, so that Nairobi's best families no longer buried their dead there.

The last two miles were on a red dirt road: eroded ruts, cactus and acacia trees, a lone baboon sitting on a fencepost and shielding its eyes from the glare of the headlights.

Terence had been given this estate rent-free as partial payment for whatever he did in the government. He usually talked in vague terms about his job, but when he became specific he sounded like an accountant. Even so, he reported to the Parliament buildings every morning and often had hotel lunches with ministers and military types. The house was near the road, with a circular drive leading up to a stone archway and the front door.

Lucien stopped in the driveway, the car's headlights flooding the house and driveway for perhaps twenty seconds. Then he backed up, turned around, and drove back toward the city.

Chili's old Jeep was parked there.

It all fell into place, painfully and completely: Chili was supposed to get back from Tsavo tomorrow, but of course he had arranged to return early and to visit Emilene.

They're also playing it close to the minute, Lucien thought, or do they even care if Terence comes back to find them together? The notion made him think of what happened at Arusha and sickened him.

He drove back to find Audrey and Terence leaning against the old Buick, having more chitchat as Terence prepared to leave. He stayed in his car as he drove up beside them.

"You took a long time," Audrey said.

"Dura had lots to say."

"Is she very upset?"

"No, not at all. She's excited about showing you how to work with porcelain tomorrow."

"Afraid I hurt her feelings," Terence said. "But there's more in the world than underpaid blacks and all that."

"She's all right now. And I just came back to say I'm going off for a late drink with a friend. I'll be in late."

"I'll keep a light on," his mother said, and she reached through the window of the car to touch his arm before he drove away.

He went to the bar at the Blue Hotel, ordered a gin and tonic, and waited. He sat beside the staircase at the end of the bar, the stairs that led up to the girls' rooms, and he could hear their voices up there. The stairway railing had been covered with tinfoil: a sad, sad decoration.

He was here on a hunch. If he proved right, he'd have something to say to his father, but exactly what he didn't know.

Sure enough, he hadn't finished that first drink when Chili ambled into the bar, looking around for the regulars. When he finally spotted Lucien, he came over and sat down on the next stool.

"What's this? You becoming a solitary drinker?"

"No, there's always company here," Lucien replied.

Chili tried to get the bartender's attention and when his initial effort failed he became agitated without a glass to fondle. He rubbed his hands together and put on his inquisitive smile.

"So, really, what're you doing here?"

"We were playing cards at the house: Dura, Terence, and Mother. When the game broke up, I drove Dura home."

"Well, as you see, I'm back early from Tsavo. And tell the truth, I'm worn thin."

"After I drove Dura home, I drove out to Emilene's. I saw your Jeep there."

Chili finally got the bartender's attention and ordered a double. In the silence between them, Lucien could hear the upstairs voices again. When the drink was served, the bartender picked up a flyswatter and concentrated on a wasp buzzing among the bottles lined up before the mirror.

"I once told your mother that I'd never lie to her except about sex," Chili began.

"Was that supposed to be funny?"

"She didn't laugh at it. But I've said it places where it was considered amusing."

"It's not funny to me, either."

"No, I can see that." Chili tilted his glass, drained it, and tried to get a refill from the preoccupied bartender. A working girl came in from the garden and went upstairs, making eye contact with Lucien as she passed.

"You're a prick," Lucien said.

"Call me whatever you want."

"And now you've brought your prick business right into the house. Into Mother's house, with her best friend. With the wife of a friend of yours."

"Say whatever you have to say."

Lucien thought of lots more to say, but the words hung in his throat. He wanted to throw his gin in Chili's face, to hit him, to bang his nose on the ebony bar.

"You've compromised me for years," he finally went on. "I wish I didn't know so damn much. I know too much I'm not supposed to mention or think about. I know all your prick secrets."

Chili got another double and stared down into the glass, nodding his head in agreement.

"Prick brain," Lucien said.

The wasp flew outdoors. Chili sipped his whiskey.

"The business with Emilene shouldn't have started and I promise you it'll be finished," his father drawled with full deliberation. "And you're right. I shouldn't have got ole Terence mixed up in it. And I shouldn't be playing that card game because I don't know point count from grand slam. And you're right: it's your mother's house and that's shit."

"If Dura knows about it, Mother probably knows, too."

"Your mother doesn't know."

"It's just such prick behavior."

"Agreed, it is."

Lucien felt dizzy: the gin and the anger swimming together in him.

Chili worked his mouth toward another statement.

"The reason a man has to lie," he began, then he stopped. He cleared his throat and studied the tinfoil for a moment. "The reason I always lie is the goddamned embarrassment. When I married Audrey we were always in bed, always, except when I was out on safari. But even then I always had at least one other woman. Then as time went on the old girlfriends came back: Sammie and all that bunch. And besides that I abused myself."

"I'm impressed. You're a virile prick."

"This isn't to impress you and maybe you don't have this drive, all right, but usually, say, you eat three times a day. If that was considered obscene, then, damn, just imagine how we'd have to conceal it. Imagine how there's this one restaurant you're supposed to get your one meal every day, but you're hungrier than that. You want three meals and it's damned embarrassing. So you go to other restaurants for more food. And you start keeping secrets—and telling lies, if you have to."

"But sex and hunger aren't the same. Nobody starves to death from lack of physical affection."

"For me they're equal drives."

"Maybe for me, too," Lucien admitted.

"Sure, for a lot of people, it's an awful thing. I talked this over with Cat. You remember her, don't you?"

"Sure, Cat's a real philosopher."

"Listen, a lot of women have the same problem. There's a name for it with them: nymphomania."

"We're just pricks."

"I was a prick about Emilene. I admit."

"No one has an uncontrollable physical need. It's just ego. It's just prick ego."

"It was a definite mistake, but I'll quit. Promise."

"I suppose she was a snack you just couldn't refuse?"

"Exactly like that, yes."

The bartender brought fresh drinks they hadn't ordered, but they accepted them and as they raised their glasses, they exchanged an unintentional glance. Chili did look weary: a stubble of beard and one bloodshot eye.

Lucien heaved a long sigh. "Who'd you take on safari?" he asked, trying to return them to normalcy. He realized that they must have raised their voices.

"Oh, you know Cat," Chili admitted.

"The philosopher, oh sure," Lucien answered, and he watched his father, chastised, with his head down, and thought, god, he must be exhausted, he must have left Tsavo at midday for the long drive to Emilene's. A busy lover: hungry in the heart, the glutton of the bed and hip hole. Lucien felt pity for him and tried to take solace in the promise that the affair would end.

But Chili had lied again, as he warned he would. At the next Fourth of July party Audrey caught him with Emilene in one of the upstairs bathrooms, the one with the two doors, one of which they had neglected to lock. Screams, accusations, excuses, threats, tears, more lies, and all the embarrassments Chili feared then followed. Everyone at the party soon knew the exact details: Emilene was sitting on the toilet and Chili was standing to receive her favors, so there were few ambiguities. The party quickly broke up, although some firecrackers and rockets were set off—and jokes, of course, about those.

During the remainder of July, Chili hurried off to another safari. When he returned, Audrey went up to Naivasha to visit friends, taking Dura as her companion.

Lucien kept the store and busied himself with leasing adjacent property for an expansion. He had lunch with Coke during this

period and heard his brother place the full blame on that hussy
Emilene.

"She forced him," he contended. "She's a damn tart and I
intend to prove it!"

"Prove it how?"

He refused to be specific. But by the time Audrey came back
from Naivasha, Coke had managed to successfully finish off the
marriage between Emilene and Terence. He went out to the estate
one morning, somehow got Emilene into bed before noon, and
arranged to have Terence appear unannounced for lunch. According to the houseboys—and, later, everyone at the club knew
the story—Terence sat down on the lawn and wept, while Emilene went into hysterics. The bird Wapi was mixed up in it.
Versions of the story had it that the pet got tangled in the bedsheets during the lovemaking or that Terence killed it or that it
simply died of excitement in the lunch-hour chaos.

Then Coke bragged about his conquest to Audrey. It was all
by way of proving what a bad girl Emilene was. Lucien was
upstairs when Coke entered the house with the assertion that
she was a loose woman who chased after everyone, that he had
just been to bed with her himself, and that Chili ought to be
forgiven as her victim.

Lucien stood in the upstairs hallway listening.

Audrey was appalled. She told Coke that he was as stupid as
his father and that Emilene had twice the character and integrity
of any man she knew.

Coke was dismayed.

"She's a hot pants!" he cried out. "A nympho! She seduced
us!"

"Get out!" Audrey shouted back. "I don't want to see you in
this house for ten years! Out! Give me some peace!"

Coke retreated to Lucien. They drove downtown together.

"Now I've done it," he moaned. "She never wants to see me again."

"She said ten years," Lucien said, consoling him. "Just give her the decade she asked for."

"Don't kid around! What do I do?"

"You could try an apology."

"But she won't let me in the house to do that!"

"Call out from the lawn. Call out that you're a prick, like Chili, and never understand what the hell's going on."

Buffoonery and anguish: the Cavenaugh sexual follies. At times, legendary farce. At other times the tall tale fucked up, overdone, and stretched toward the ridiculous. One could visit the bars of the city years after an event and hear the story of how one of the Cavenaughs slipped some husband or chaperone a sleeping pill, saying it was malaria medicine, or hear about Emilene and her bird, or hear about copulating with a hand over the girl's mouth so she wouldn't disturb the countryside. Elaborations. Added vulgarities. A few more lies each time the tales got told.

Yet Lucien felt the erosion in the burlesque, an erosion into pure pain. He often wondered if he alone felt it and he could only guess at Audrey's desperations. He didn't ask. But his mother's pain clearly hurt him most.

He tried not to think about Terence or Emilene: splinters from a wreckage. Refuse washed up on a tide of bad jokes and laughter.

Sometimes he saw Terence passing on the street: still a lanky clown of a man, gangling, slightly lost. When they acknowledged each other, Terence was always in an understandable hurry.

Once, months later in Mombasa where he had gone to buy

cotton goods for the store, Lucien saw Emilene again. He was having supper at a little table café beside the old fort when she stopped at his table.

"How're you doing?" he asked her.

She wore her emerald drop—a gold chain with a stone at the end of it weighing perhaps eight carats. The cleavage at her blouse drew his eyes. A yellow skirt. A tired smile, but a smile still.

"Oh, my jewel case. Stolen. Otherwise, good. I play bridge with this new partner. The son of a rajah. Perhaps. Something. We make a bit of money every week."

The old shorthand speech. She asked about his mother.

"She's fine. Sorry to hear about your jewelry."

"Carried that case for years. Poof. Gone. Except for this. Still on my throat. Had it on that night or it would be gone, too. Wear it all the time now. Even to bed."

She retained the smile and some of the old enthusiasm, looking as though she might say, come on, let's go swimming, hurry, and if she did say it, he knew he might run headlong toward the surf with her, stripping off his clothes as he went. She was one of those people.

"And I have this mongoose," she went on. "Lovely. Here in the hotel. Carry it with me everywhere. Nuzzles. A good pet and handy if you happen to run into cobras."

"You look tanned and healthy," he said. "Can you sit down for a glass of wine?"

"Thanks, but no wine. Getting chubby. But tell me. Your mother. Say something."

"She still does clay with Dura."

"Ah, the ceramics! Costume jewelry. Odd, isn't it? My real stuff gone. Audrey doing clay necklaces. Mud to her elbows. Ah me, I'd like to be there. You know that, I hope?"

"Sit down and have one drink while I finish my supper," he urged her.

"No, nothing now. Chubby. You eat. I have to go."

"Please don't hurry off."

She stood there, pulling back a strand of graying hair and letting the evening breeze caress her face and tanned throat. A woman of perhaps fifty, small and brown and not particularly pretty, yet he could see what both his parents had seen in her.

"Coffee and mud to our elbows," she said to the terrace, to the breeze, and to him. "Stringing beads. Some BBC music on the radio. Lots of desserts. I'd like to be there again. Very much. Just a gaggle of woman-talk. Even though Dura didn't care for me."

"Emilene," he began, not knowing what he might say next.

"Late for the evening game," she said suddenly. "See you. Tell her you ran into me, will you? Tell her hello and love. Will you?"

"Yes, I'll tell her," he lied, and he watched her wave over her shoulder as she walked away.

SAFARI:
The Attack

In a short time the wind settled, became a stiff breeze, then a soothing zephyr, then stopped altogether.

Fortunate, yet the calm became a deadly thing itself.

Lucien climbed into Coke's view, pointed, and shouted.

"There! Between us! Over there!"

His best sense of where the leopard could have gone was between them and ahead of them, but there was no hard evidence that it hadn't gone down the ridge toward the lake or retreated along the narrow path. Its tracks gave only one clear indication: back into those boulders.

"You saw it?" Coke pulled out, in obvious disbelief.

Lucien pointed again and Coke relayed the signal to Chili.

They went on, making the same slow progress because of Coke's continuing barriers. Each time he reappeared at the top of a new rock, Lucien sighed with relief.

Seeing the leopard—it had occurred not more than five minutes ago—had already become so unreal that Lucien thought of it as a mystic visitation. His arms and shoulders still tingled as he edged along a narrow part of the path. Sounds invaded his consciousness: the chirping of birds, a distant hyrax call, the dull echo of human voices far below in camp, and Coke's rattling around out there. It was as if the leopard had stopped the wind and had given him these live noises as a reminder of his physical existence after that odd calm that had come to him. He was also so unafraid that he had to urge himself to pay close attention to the hunt.

"Goddamnit, where?" Coke called out.

Chili's voice was raised in windless tranquillity: sharp, indistinct, and questioning. He and his father were now less than sixty meters apart, Lucien guessed, as the ridge narrowed.

Lucien pointed again. An educated guess, nothing more.

Gradually they moved within sight of each other as the boulders flattened out at the north end of the ridge.

"You didn't see a damn thing," Coke accused him.

"But I did. He's a big one. Tuft of blond hair on his chest. White eyes like milk. And he's big."

"All that and you didn't get a shot?" Chili drawled.

"Believe it or not, I didn't have my rifle in hand. I was drinking from my canteen."

"Believe it or not? Okay, I don't believe it," Coke said.

"That's a damned specific description," Chili allowed. "But, lordy, son, you didn't have your rifle?"

"The other night he says he heard the damn leopard and now he says he sees it!"

"I did see it," Lucien contended.

Their old competition again. Coke walked off and stopped to light a cigarette. Lucien told his father exactly where and how the meeting took place and how he reckoned the leopard's whereabouts afterward.

"So there were tracks, too?" Coke asked, turning back to him. "Or did he stay on the rocks, so he didn't make any tracks?"

"We can go back and you can see for yourself," Lucien said sharply.

Chili studied the boulders. "He must've slipped by us right back there," he mused.

Coke returned to Chili, jabbing the air with his cigarette. "All right," he argued. "Maybe he saw some tracks. But damned if I think he saw the goddamned leopard itself and didn't shoot it."

"I sure as hell did see it!"

"Boys, shut up," Chili told them.

They went back along Lucien's path, making their way single file. Coke dropped back, sulking and watching the rocks, while Chili speculated out loud.

"Damned odd it didn't jump you. What'd it do exactly?"

"Just sat and watched me. Seemed at ease. Just cocked its head and studied me."

"Acted like a curious tabby, didn't it? I've seen that before. But, damn, it must be feeding time for the brute. And we're in his territory—which is enough reason to go after anybody. Strange he didn't pounce."

"Maybe I just wasn't his kind of meat," Lucien said.

"Big fellow, was he?"

"Huge paws. You should see the prints."

They returned and inspected the prints, sweating through their clothes now. Coke's knees were bloody from his efforts out there among the boulders.

"Well, Lucien, what now?" Chili asked.

The deference to Lucien annoyed Coke even more.

"This won't get us anywhere," Lucien replied, giving him the same views again. "We need at least another dozen drivers up here—and luck then. Or a good bait and some real patience."

"Sure, we could hang around up here for weeks," Coke said.

"That should suit you," Lucien told him.

"What the fuck does that mean?"

"You know what it means!"

"C'mon, boys. Christ, it's too hot to raise a fuss. Give us some water."

"Mine's gone," Coke admitted.

Lucien passed his canteen to his father as they trudged back toward the powdery ash where the hunt had started. Disgusted with their bickering, Chili increased his pace and walked ahead.

Falling in beside Coke as the path widened, an accusation gushed out of Lucien. "You made a move on Trey and don't deny it," he blurted out.

"That's a lie," Coke replied. "I never!"

"She was out in the plane with you!"

"Fancy you saying anything after all you did with Colly and Kira and—for all I know—lots of others!"

"Admit it! She was with you in the plane!"

"She was! And it was her business!"

"You made a move on her. Or did she make one toward you? Which?"

"She's a grown woman and does what she pleases!"

"The two of you, betrayed me, goddammit!"

"You're not her damn husband!"

Their angry strides brought them near Chili, and he turned and glared at them. Lucien faced his brother, a fool from a family of fools: there was no love or caring in them, they were just pricks.

As Chili walked on, Lucien's anger became a hoarse rasp. "I asked Trey to come to Nairobi and marry me."

"So what? You came between me and two wives!"

"Rot! Pure damned rot! One kiss between Colly and me before you were married! And with Kira there was nothing! You knew it, too, that night you raised a ruckus at her flat!"

"I knew nothing of the sort! I saw you cozying up in the kitchen—that's all I knew!"

"You wanted to fight, so I gave it to you! You remember that?"

"You hit me when I was dead drunk!"

"And you know how much Trey means to me! You've known! I'm over forty years old, never married, never wanted anyone so much, and you fucking knew! That's why you made your move!"

"I can't take what isn't yours!"

"You're a bastard to the bone."

"She came wading out to me. I didn't drag her out there!"

"True prick bastard!"

Chili reached that field of dark volcanic ash where days ago the leopard's prints had been erased in those thousands of insect prints. He turned to watch his sons coming toward him, Lucien out front, both of them taking long angry strides, their voices still raised, both of them gesturing dangerously with their weapons.

"Will the two of you watch your guns?" he called to them. "And can we hold off the family business until—"

He stopped. They paid him no attention anyway. But something had caught his eye.

A peripheral movement: just the shadow of a shadow, so quick and faint and out of his immediate awareness that he didn't fully turn toward it.

The leopard went by him. A streak of white.

It found a boulder between him and Lucien, where it landed in a pounce before changing directions in the same graceful movement.

It seemed to be choosing among them.

Springing from that boulder, it went to another. A long arc.

Coke had just entered the field of ash when the leopard hit him.

It had covered perhaps thirty meters in three quick bounds, giving none of them a chance to raise a weapon.

As it knocked Coke down, both Chili and Lucien brought their rifles around. But too late. Coke and his attacker were engulfed in a cloud of ashen powder and nothing could be seen of them.

"Don't fire!" Chili yelled, but Lucien knew already.

Among the snarls and deep grunts, they heard the sound of breaking bone.

Where was the wind now that they needed it to blow the cloud of ash away? Nature still conspired with the leopard.

A curtain of ash and dust that gave them only glimpses: a swish of the cat's tail, the tilt of Coke's arm, then nothing more.

Chili darted left and right looking for an opening, but a shot was impossible.

The mauling could be quick and over in seconds.

With no time, Lucien went in with his knife.

Inside the cloud, his eyes and mouth quickly filled with ash. His nostrils flared with warm dust. But he groped toward the noise, his hands stretched out, searching blindly. The three of them rolled and tumbled, coming down hard to the ground again and again, churning in quick flashes of energy. Lost in there, Lucien's equilibrium vanished, but he found the leopard's heaving fur. The cat's head seemed buried inside his brother's torso, gone, buried, eating away in there. Lost and eating away in there, he said to himself: eating him from inside. Where are you? Come to me! And his fingers found a soft place under a foreleg to put the knife in.

A paw knocked him down.

He drew the knife out for another strike, but the cat broke free and was gone.

Chili saw it fly out on a stream of ash and blood. It gave him only the worst of shots, a keyhole shot, as he called it: the departing flanks and a curve of tail. The cat flashed away from him, heading for the nearest boulders; one more leap and it would be gone, off in the rocks where they'd never find it. But Chili's momentary glimpse was enough. The old hunter expects nothing in perfect profile for his sights; he expects that awkward, fleeting target.

Chili fired, putting a bullet through its anus and blowing its heart out its mouth.

He watched for only a second before he said, "There, you sonofabitch, you're blind now!" Then he turned to the boys.

Lucien dragged Coke into clear air. They both choked and gasped for breath.

Coke's shoulder was bloody gristle. The leopard had missed its mark slightly—Coke had turned at the last instant—so had bitten into the shoulder rather than the neck, snapping the collarbone and pulling away a mouthful of flesh. It had held Coke's upper arms in its grip, but somehow Coke's rifle had stayed over his stomach so the cat couldn't rake with its hind paws and disembowel him.

Coke choked, spat, and finally got his breath. After that he tried not to make a sound.

Chili let out a string of curses when he saw the wound.

Lucien tore off his shirt and used it to bind the shoulder and neck, stuffing and wrapping as best as he could.

Blood everywhere. They all knew what was happening, but it was Coke who said it for them. "Hurry," he whispered. "I don't have too many quarts of this stuff."

In seconds they had him straddling Lucien's back, but blood quickly soaked them both and there was a brief argument about whether to hurry toward the clinic or to try and wrap the wound more tightly.

"We can't do any better here!" Lucien finally said, and he grunted under Coke's weight as he began to move.

Still cursing, Chili ran alongside them, trying to hold the gory shirt in place. "You won't make it, goddammit! Let's wrap that better!" he shouted, but Lucien was off, leaving his father behind, trotting over the powdery field and starting down the path. As he ran, Coke's cheek bumped against his and he felt his backside soggy with blood.

Chili picked up the scattered weapons and gear, then ran to the dead leopard. He got a firm grip on its tail and with an effort managed to pull it after him. They weren't going back to camp with Coke in that shape, he decided, and without their kill; he wanted those superstitious refugees and tribesmen to see they had won.

ZAMANI:
A Grand Piano

Coming off the ridge with Coke on his back, Lucien concentrated with each step, but stray thoughts bounced into his head: his old Ambrose blanket, Coke's prized crescent-shaped Arab dagger, the store, the house. But most of all Audrey.

What would they say to her about this?

Grunting under his brother's hot weight, struggling to keep his balance, and watching the loose gravel on the path ahead, he recalled her worst fear—that she'd outlive one of her children. And here was her eldest, his life leaking away: the hunter home from the hill. But what could be said?

Less than a month ago Lucien and his mother had gone on a round of errands together, doing the market, going by a little hardware store off Kimathi Street, and ending the morning at the Mini-Super grocery near the roundabout at Westlands. They had talked about Trey.

"Faults? She doesn't have any," Lucien insisted.

"Not one bad habit? Not one little tick that annoys you?"

They moved along the aisles filling two shopping baskets. Chili's brand of Worcestershire sauce had reappeared on the shelves after an absence, and Audrey placed four bottles among her items. Lucien was reciting Trey's virtues.

"Professional woman. Loves classical music. Has a nice touch with the refugees. Looks damn fine in camp clothes."

"I'll bet she smokes and has a touch of smoker's breath."

"Doesn't smoke. Breath like honey."

"A bit frigid, then?"

"None of your business. But, no, anything but that."

"And you say she's over thirty, so, all right, she's had a few bumps. Disappointments or worse. She's got to have her little problems, we all do."

"Don't be overprotective."

"I'm not. I just want you to marry and give me grandchildren. That's what you want yourself, isn't it?"

"Sure, I admit it. And I think Trey's the one."

"But, Lucien, why did she come to Africa? Think about it."

"What's that supposed to mean?"

"Africa means—well, she must be restless. And she wants to peek over the edge of the abyss, I'd say. I mean, she certainly didn't come here to marry a storekeeper and to have children. No, she wants a bit of danger. A bit of a scream. And one comes to Africa to let it out."

He respected Audrey's wisdom, and ignored it.

Audrey had the gift of the long view. In politics she had her opinions, but for the most part she kept above the turbulence. She had predicted that white rule would end in Kenya and she contended it would disappear even in those fierce bastions of South Africa and elsewhere. In the arts, she was a classicist: only the things that last, if you please, and let the passing fads pass on. In friendship, only true friends: as the last years came along,

Dura outlasted all the others. In matters of love, give to those around you. In matters of charity, give locally as well: the black orphanage out in Barton Valley would get her volunteer work while she lived and her money when she was gone. Her great quality was serene patience, as if she knew how all the frail fights would resolve themselves, as if she regarded history as more of a temporal annoyance than a spiritual enemy. She could be quiet and wait in the midst of monstrous foolishness. Chili had given her lots of practice.

Patience and the long view.

But what if Coke didn't make it? Could she take refuge in her usual calm reassurance that life goes on?

That bloody run toward the clinic.

The Darkness beyond. The shadowy water.

Audrey had learned this serenity, of course, and there were those years she hadn't mastered it. The grand piano and how they came by it was a story from those years. Lucien remembered learning his scales, those first carefully simple songs and melodies, and finally the Opus 55 she loved so much. A good book, a Chopin nocturne, a late-evening dessert: these made a perfect night at home for Audrey. But that corner of their main room got its elegant Steinway in the usual Cavenaugh manner.

The soprano had it shipped in. She came to the city with the orchestra Audrey always worked to help sponsor, and that season Chili took an interest in the occasion. The singer wasn't a Lily Pons or a Risë Stevens, but just as beautiful, and the conductor had her on his arm as often as he could, marching her around with her accompanist, a fellow with a leering interest in all the black waiters at the club.

They were at somebody's house on a patio lighted with hurricane lamps, and Lucien was very young, wearing a bow tie and tight black shoes as he kept his vigil beside a silver tray of pastries. He was standing there sampling the sweets when he heard his father saying to the soprano, "Now then, I have an instrument you might like to sing to." And Lucien thought, odd, what instrument? Is he musical, after all?

The soprano gave his father a curious smile.

The next afternoon Lucien went with his mother to the old Norfolk Hotel. In those days the hotel had a wide veranda with wicker furniture, but Lucien was given a dish of sherbet and told to remain in the garden where there was a monkey chained to a tree. A private matter, his mother told him, and I won't be long, and if you want more sherbet just ask one of the waiters. But Lucien felt insulted and neither he nor the monkey wanted the sherbet, so he crept around the side of the hotel and found the crawlspace beneath the veranda. He found a spot directly below his mother and soprano. They were at a small wicker table, having tea and what seemed to be a musical argument.

I'm glad you like it here, it is beautiful, Audrey was saying, and I'm just sorry that neither you nor your voice behaved all that well. And the soprano wanted to know whatever was meant by that, so his mother said, well, Puccini is never all that easy for sopranos who don't give themselves proper rest. There was considerable salt in his mother's voice—which was his father's term for that particular tone.

"So, then, you're the wife? The wife of exactly whom?" The soprano's voice had a bit of a hard melody in it.

Lucien sat in the crawlspace hugging his knees against his chest, listening carefully, although sometimes their voices became mere whispers as they poured tea. A clink of glass and a rattle of spoons accompanied their whispering, then the singer's notes rose slightly higher—and Audrey answered in counterpoint as the duet went on.

"Yes, then, all right," the soprano finally said, "so what?"

"So my servant will call on you," Audrey replied, and the singer asked with a laugh why she would ever want to meet Audrey's servant. Lucien wondered if he had heard this correctly. Perhaps his mother meant gunbearer, since, in fact, they didn't have a real servant at the house. But Audrey said, "Oh, you actually don't want to meet him, but you will indeed." Then she told the soprano what was done with women such as herself in this wild country, and Lucien heard it with great surprise: the bad women were taken by force, their throats sliced open, then stuffed headfirst down one of the giant antholes out on the savannah. "My servant is perfectly capable of taking care of such duties," she said, "and that is that."

The soprano began a few lilting denials.

"I know everything and so does everyone else," Audrey argued. "Everyone in the city knows exactly what sort of notes you sang last night and in what bed and at what precise hour."

More high notes of denial. The soprano walked around the little wicker table, her heels clicking above Lucien's head.

"You can hire yourself guards, but everyone here understands our justice, so no one will actually prevent this. You'll not leave the city until justice is served, believe me, you are going down an anthole, or, if you wish, I'll accept your Steinway."

"What? My piano?" The soprano banged one of her high heels beside the table. "That's not for giving away."

"Then my servant calls on you and I'll hate it because there's sure to be an inquiry. Or you can pay this *honga*, this tribute, in this particular instance the Steinway, but rest assured you'll never simply get on your plane and fly away from all of it."

"That piano is custom-made. It has flown all over the world with me," the soprano complained, "and I need it, it really belongs to my accompanist as well as to me, we couldn't give it up, we're going to Cairo next on the tour, this is robbery, one of the world's most expensive, you're out of your mind, impossible."

"But it's our unwritten law," Audrey said with a sigh, as if she couldn't help circumstances. "It's either the piano or the ants. And the ants will eat out your eyes and your inadequate larynx."

The soprano walked away and his mother followed her down the veranda, and it might not have been exactly like that, but six men delivered the Steinway: unloaded it from a rickety lorry, tilted it through the front door with its legs off, carefully screwed the legs back on, wheeled it slowly down the hallway, and sat it beside the window in the main room. The last worker touched a key, sending a single note echoing through the house.

It wasn't a serene time for Audrey. The serenity would come later, after years of gypsies, after Chili's hundreds of nights at the Blue Hotel, and after Emilene. In the year the Steinway became theirs she just said, there, sit down and play, let some good come out of this. And Chopin's Opus 55 eventually came out of the piano—Lucien practiced hard and saw to it—but she was always the good that came out of everything else in their lives, their highest incarnation as Cavenaughs, the steady presence as they went along making their cruel and noisy shots, blundering and bleeding and boasting along.

SAFARI: Flying Out

Halfway between the ridge and the clinic Coke began to cry out and curse.

"Dammit, Lucy, you're shaking my guts out!"

Lucien put him down, then watched his brother try to steady himself. He staggered left, then right, and grabbed an outstretched hand as he looked down at himself. "Jesus," he moaned. "I'm a sight!" From beneath that clumsy knot of shirt rivulets of blood spread down his arm. Deep scratches covered his back and there was a hole near his hairline, a little window directly into his head. But he mustered a grin, and his mustache, clotted and stiff, slanted across his face.

"Better let me carry you," Lucien offered, but Coke moaned and tottered off downhill.

"Where's Pop?" he asked, and Lucien could only follow.

By the time they reached the clinic Coke seemed genuinely alarmed at how everyone behaved toward him. Trey circled him, screaming, then ran after morphine. Abba covered his face with his hands, as if one of the lake's ghostly voices had taken form.

Refugees and fishermen hurried to the clinic for a look at this bloody apparition, then went to tell others what mischief had come out of that foolish leopard hunt.

"Sit down, for Christ's sake!" Lucien urged him, but there was no having it. Coke seemed invigorated by that gaping wound. For a while he staggered around, enjoying his own display, disoriented, but oddly pleased with it all. He finally sat down on the wobbly card table, propping his bloodstained boots on a camp chair. When Trey gave him the contents of a syringe of morphine he put on a goofy grin and tried to hug her. He also began to explain what had happened—not that he had anything straight—but everyone was too impressed with all the blood to do much listening.

"Damn," Trey said, untying the wet folds of the shirt and looking at the wound. She wrinkled up her face, then hurried into the clinic for bandages.

"We were choking, see, that was the main thing," Coke told whoever would listen. "And I might've won the tussle, but just couldn't get a breath in all that ash and dust! Then Lucy comes charging in! Gets the cat off me and drags me out! I had this ash up my nose and in the back of my throat, and I think I got dizzy and passed out because I couldn't breathe!"

Abba looked at Mfifo through the cracks in his fingers, still covering his face. Mussa and his fat wives came over a hill, running toward the clinic with loud cries and laughter. Coke asked for beer and Trey was there with her kit.

Then Chili appeared, dragging the leopard, waving like a victorious general. The leopard was in poor shape from its journey down the rocky path, but this pleased the loud gathering and they danced around, pointed, and spat on it.

Trey examined the bite wound. "Collarbone bitten in half,"

she said, wincing. "And the brachial artery may be severed and all those muscles and nerves might be gone. Can you use the arm?"

"Not a bit, but it doesn't hurt all that much," Coke said.

Lucien leaned in for a look.

"That could be bad," she said, preparing bandages. "Or you'll feel it later. I only gave you a small dose of morphine, so you may need more soon." She soaked a large gauze pad in antiseptic formula, pressed the pad directly into the wound, then began wrapping his upper body. He winced, but forced a smile.

"We've got to get him out of here," she told Lucien.

"Hey, you're good at this," Coke said, watching her twist the wrapping under the arm.

Abba placed a cigarette in Coke's mouth.

Meanwhile, Chili displayed the remains of the leopard, showing Mussa and the others the hole underneath its foreleg where Lucien had put the knife in. An old woman in the crowd requested one of the cat's paws. She was related to one of the victims, Abba explained, so Chili agreed. As she began hacking off the paw with a piece of sharpened stone, Chili went over to watch the bandaging.

"Okay, okay, you look fit enough to me," he said to Coke, who tried to look nonchalant, sipping a beer and blowing out a column of cigarette smoke. But Chili's face was creased with concern in spite of his teasing.

"He could lose the arm and go into shock from blood loss," Trey said. "We've got to fly him out of here."

The bite wound was tightly wrapped when a small bubble of blood formed in that hole on Coke's forehead, then trickled into his eye. It was an alarming thing to watch, stopping Chili in whatever he meant to say next.

Lucien summoned two refugees, instructed them to gather up the weapons and gear, and told them to get everything into the plane.

"Right you are. This is serious," Chili declared, watching the blood trickle into Coke's eye and trying to take charge. "Load up and I'll fly us out of here."

"Pop, I can fly the plane. I'll do it one-handed," Coke said.

"Then I'll fly co-pilot."

"No," Coke said. "I want Lucien as co-pilot."

Chili objected, beginning an argument in his own behalf, and Lucien, surprised to hear his father rejected, turned to listen. Trey announced that she'd go along, too, and since she spoke with a doctor's authority no one quarreled with her.

"Now, listen, son, I know the feel of that plane. You let me practice takeoffs, remember? I should sit up front."

"I want Lucien," Coke said, adamant. "He saved my life once today and he might do it again."

In spite of himself, Lucien grinned.

Trey arranged for Coke to be placed in a straight-backed chair and for two burly fishermen to carry the chair and its occupant to the plane. The two men nodded and started off with their load, but Coke was too heavy for them, so every few paces they stopped to rest. He offered them a bribe and payment: a cigarette each if they didn't drop him. As they staggered on with their burden, he crossed his legs and sipped at his beer.

Clothing, gear, and medicine were gathered from the clinic and during all the activity the little girl—the one who had been taken from Mussa—began to cry. Trey picked up the Colt pistol that had belonged to the croc man, held it above her head, and shouted instructions at the crowd standing and kneeling around the dead leopard. She spoke in rough Turkana. This weapon I am giving to Abba, she said, and he is chief of this clinic until I return. This is a powerful and magic weapon as all of you know. With it, this *mzee* will guard the medicine and beer—and give it to anyone who needs or earns it. He also possesses two sets of ears, so he is very wise. He will tell you what to do with the dead leopard and settle all your disputes.

Mussa stepped forward to protest that he was the rightful chief of this place and that Abba was merely an old fool.

Chili came forward in long strides and pointed a finger at Mussa's nose. If you don't behave, he said loudly, I'll set you loose on the ridge when I come back. His Turkana was better than Trey's and he spat for emphasis and shouted, Hey! I will hunt you on that ridge the same as I hunted and killed the evil leopard.

Faced with this threat, Mussa edged back into the crowd.

Abba accepted the pistol from Trey and put a protective arm around the crying child.

After gear was stored in the plane, Chili and Trey climbed into the rear seats. Coke placed himslf in the co-pilot's seat, giving Lucien the pilot's chair. Then they went through preflight checks: the fuel, the prime, the power, flaps, and rudder.

"And do we have a bit more morphine?" Coke asked Trey.

She nodded and fumbled in her kit. Blood had soaked through his thick bandage now and his smile was an effort.

"Takeoffs are a bit dicey on water, so I'll take her up myself," Coke explained to Lucien. "We'll want to keep her nose well up. Then I'll set a course for you and we'll kick her into automatic. Shouldn't be any trouble."

"It'll be a party," Chili assured them, and he opened his vest to reveal four bottles of beer tucked in the pockets.

The two burly fishermen pushed the plane out of the shallows as Coke, pale but efficient, started the engine and taxied out.

A windless, perfect lake. Across the mud flats perched on a rock there was a bird that caught Lucien's attention: an ibis, the ancient holy bird, and he pointed to it, wishing to himself that it could be a good omen.

Then Coke revved the engine and they moved out. Plumes of spray shot up, then the horizon fell beneath them and they could see the whole serpentine length of the lake. The Darkness: Ngiza. Lucien felt glad to leave it, never mind the perils ahead.

Trey gave their pilot another shot of morphine and as her fingers lingered on Coke's shoulder afterward he reached up and touched her hand with his. She leaned forward and brushed caked blood out of his mustache: an intimate little moment of grooming.

"Damn me, know what I want?" Chili asked, opening a beer. "Some hot curry! What's the name of that restaurant down in Mombasa?"

"The Splendid View Café," Lucien said, remembering.

"Best curry around. Good ribs, too."

They talked about food for a while. Trey wanted a hamburger with dill pickles. Coke said curry was fine, anything was fine, so long as they all went out to eat in the city tonight. As they gained altitude and leveled out, they named everything they were hungry for.

"There, automatic pilot," Coke finally said. "You flip these little paddles here when you want off automatic. See them, Lucy?"

"I see them."

"Don't forget that part."

"I won't."

"In less than two hours we'll be in Nairobi airspace, so we'll

kick off automatic, find Wilson Airport, and circle in. You remember how to coordinate the steering and foot pedals?"

"It's been a while since I did this."

"You remember how to turn?"

"I'll practice some, if I have to. And I can do it."

"Sure, you can handle it. Here's your flaps. Put 'em down to
twenty degrees when you're a mile from the end of the runway.
Then you'll bring this throttle back, so you'll be doing, oh, say,
eighty knots."

"Slow to eighty, then put the flaps down to twenty degrees,"
Lucien repeated.

"That's it. If you come in too slow, just add power. Try to
keep the plane level and hit the fucking runway."

"Simple," Lucien said, trying to sound confident.

They opened the rest of the beers and started talking about
food again. Camp food they liked best. Good caterers they knew.
Bubba's famous stews. Lucien's breakfast omelets.

Lucien glanced at Trey, giving her a smile. Her fingers were
interlaced around her beer, her knuckles white, and he knew she
was afraid. By this time the blood had oozed out of the bandage
and was dripping on the floor between Coke and Lucien, but
nobody mentioned it. Chili began telling how he shot the leopard,
but Coke interrupted.

"Wait a minute. Didn't Lucien kill it with his knife?"

"We all had a hand in it," Chili allowed. Then he began
recounting every move, addressing Trey, giving Lucien his due,
but taking credit himself for a nice snap shot at the end. Coke
wouldn't have any of this, either.

"What about me? I held him still. I held him until you two
got yourselves ready to do something."

"And you did a good job," Chili told him. "You got a grip on his jaws with your shoulder."

They looked westward at the dying sun. Toward the south end of the lake the volcano appeared and, beyond, there was Maralal, the Rift Escarpment, then the green highlands down to Nairobi. The minutes inched along.

"A few more things," Coke said, getting weaker. "This is for your wheels. They're still retracted, you know, up inside the pontoons. Put them down before you put down the flaps. Now go over everything with me again."

Lucien checked off landing procedure: the approach speed, wheels, flaps, balance.

"And when you touch down there's the toe brakes," Coke went on. "Put your feet on the pedals. There. Feel the toe brakes just above?"

"Yeah, I feel them."

"You're a hell of a good brother," Coke said.

Lucien looked at him, surprised. There was none of the usual sarcasm and a finality in the tone.

"But you know, Lucy, I think my arm's gone. It's paralyzed sure as hell."

"Don't think about it now," Lucien told him.

"I can't help thinking about it," Coke said, biting his lip for control. "Even if we get out of this, I'm a one-armed man sure as hell." He bit hard on his lower lip and looked down at the lake they were leaving behind.

Chili attempted to revive the subject of food, but it didn't work, so they all sat in silence for a few minutes. Lucien knew well enough what each of them thought: Coke would bleed to death, they'd go in without an experienced pilot, crash, and that would be the fitting damned end. And what had been accomplished? Less than nothing. Chili was still Chili, nothing patched up between them. Trey was gone: another lost love. Coke's arm. Unless luck rode with them now, they were probably all gone. Everything obliterated except for their legendary stupidity, which Trey in her brave ignorance had decided to share. She shouldn't be in this plane, Lucien told himself.

Trey asked Coke to tell the story about how his father-in-law came to throw him through a window.

"How'd you hear a thing like that?"

"From Abba the other day. The father of your wife, he said, called you Mfifo and made you fly through a glass window." She put her head back, brushed a strand of hair from her face, and tried a laugh. "Go on, let's hear it."

Getting tired, Coke slowly told how Mr. Prebble, who weighed only one hundred and forty pounds or so, used some form of jujitsu on him. A strong combination, he said: jujitsu and a daddy's wrath. He couldn't even recall what the argument was, but maybe Colly had accused him of something. And it wasn't a window. It was French doors.

Coke got tired, closed his eyes, and put his head back.

Chili finished the story.

"Old man Prebble got rich being mean to the coffee workers as a foreman, then he got to be the owner. He was always mean-spirited. The way I heard it, Coke was just standing there arguing a point and the next second he was sailing through a window or a door, whichever. There was a hell of a lot of broken glass, right, son?"

Coke tried to answer, but made only a sound. His tongue lolled in his mouth.

"He's going into shock," Trey said, bending forward to attend to him. "Here, does this seat fold back? Let's stretch him out."

With difficulty they dropped the back of the seat, turned Coke around, and placed his feet high. Trey, now without a seat of her own wedged herself beside him, made sure his throat was clear, and smoothed back his hair.

The automatic pilot carried them at 3,300 feet over a land of scrub brush and harsh savannah, but in the distance Lucien could see the green highlands: black earth with lush fields, trees, a quilted canopy of farms on rolling hills stretching off toward Mount Kenya.

"So what happens now?" Chili asked. "How long has he got?"

"This may be best," she told them. "Now that he's in shock, the bleeding will slow down or stop. He's all right just now."

"Then no worse than the rest of us," Lucien added.

Trey took a tube of salve from her kit and treated the deep scratches on Coke's arms. As Lucien watched, she also closed the hole above the eye with an adhesive patch, then took Coke's pulse.

And smoothed his hair, Lucien told himself. And brushed the dried blood from his mustache, too. He conceded again that he had lost her and there lay his rival: pot-bellied, rough, self-centered, half-dead Mfifo. So the last irony had arrived: the bastard was out cold when he was needed most, so they would all go down together. He longed to ask Audrey the big question he had never asked: Why didn't you leave Chili years ago? Why didn't you divorce yourself from this idiocy? And why didn't I?

Lucien flipped the controls off automatic and took charge of the plane: pedals underfoot, wheel in hand, throttle set, eyes on those meters and gauges as well as the horizon.

"I'm going to make some turns, so I can get the feel of this," he announced.

"Good idea, son. What can I do?"

"Try the radio here beside me. It's a tight squeeze, but we're still probably on the Nairobi frequency. We need to get on Nairobi or the emergency frequency numbers."

"Right," Chili said, and he edged by Trey so he could reach the radio dials.

"Look up the Nairobi frequency and the emergency frequency in that logbook there," Lucien told him. "See how that dial works?"

"Sure, I got it."

"And hold on. I'm going to make some standard turns."

Lucien took the plane right, then left, then back right. He lost altitude, then climbed, then made more turns. After a few minutes he set the controls on automatic again, so their course resumed.

"You're okay," Trey said.

He didn't respond, but he wanted to add, yes, I am okay, I've picked up after these two all their lives, I'm the salvage man, and if we go down and turn into cinders, they'll both expect me to pick up their charred pieces out of the wreckage and rebuild them again.

In another half hour Nairobi came into view. Chili was able to tell the tower operator that they were coming in with Coke unconscious and with an inexperienced pilot at the controls. The operator suggested one or two passes at the field, practice runs, but Lucien said, no, I'll bring it straight in down the runway first time. They talked checkpoints. Keep your airspeed, so you won't stall early. Check. Keep your nose up. Check. You can cut your power and just fall into the runway. Check. Just drop down, making sure of your flaps and airspeed. The field's clear and there's an ambulance. Check.

His hands and underarms were wet.

Worse, he felt busted up inside, hemorrhaging again, unlike Coke but bleeding into shock just the same. But now, forget that, piss on all losses, he had to salvage himself.

Wait and wait and wait. It was like keeping his finger on the trigger during a charge. Keep waiting.

The runway was there. The tower operator kept talking, but he no longer listened. Chili and Trey strapped themselves in, and she held onto Coke.

They went in hard, bounced, struck a field light that sent them off the runway, bounced once more, bumped across a dusty patch of ground, swerved, turned sharply, braked, skidded, and nudged to a stop against a barbed-wire fence.

Trey leaned over and touched his arm.

ZAMANI:
A Visit to Juba

Sitting around in the hospital waiting to hear about Coke's condition, Lucien thought of the time he went up to Juba in the Sudan to meet clients who didn't show up.

They were going to kill off a pride of scruffy lions that had moved into a spot near the river not far from town, but Lucien heard by radio that his clients had to change plans. It would be the next day before a plane could be sent to pick him up. He went into Juba and didn't want to stay at one of the brothels—a mistake—and ended up at a small hotel with mud walls, a café and bar illumined by a single neon tube that proclaimed an American beer, and no other residents except himself. They did give him a choice room: a cubicle on the roof, large open windows covered with bamboo shades, a hard mat draped with mosquito netting for a bed, and the roof itself as his private terrace. He accepted a plate of lamb stew from the kitchen and drank four beers—not the American brand, not Tusker, not anything bottled in a real brewery. Flies swarmed everywhere. It was about nine in the evening when he went upstairs to bed with his paperback novel.

A man on the roof next door was spraying his house with a garden hose, standing there in the desert night wetting down his mud house as if it needed soothing and cooling for getting through another hot day. Lucien could also see the Nile: men talking at a quay, a river barge, lights flickering on the water.

He read a few pages, then fell asleep.

Toward morning he woke out of his sickness. He had pulled the netting off its hooks and had tangled himself in it; everything was fouled, and his cubicle smelled like the sewer inside him had ruptured; the mat, his clothing, book, netting, everything was soiled, and his bowels were emptying again. He couldn't move. He was too weak to unwrap himself, so he just lay there, drowsy with fever, trying to get his thoughts together.

Cholera often kills quickly. Children usually die suddenly with it, often in five or six hours, and the dehydration sometimes takes the life of an adult in less than ten hours. A listless weakness comes on: the body's fluids leave the system, a swoon of fever arrives, then the last sleep. Toward the end, a horrible sight: pieces of the intestines themselves come out like small grains of rice.

He worked in long, slow-motion efforts, perhaps falling asleep from time to time as he fought the tangled netting. Sometimes, he decided, he just dreamed he was getting free. But he managed to crawl onto the roof, the netting clinging to him like a shroud as he made his way toward the open stairwell. He called downstairs in a weak voice—or thought he remembered calling out—but no one came. Eventually he launched himself onto the stairs and let himself fall. After daybreak an Arab boy found him, but seemed afraid of what he saw.

"Doctor," Lucien whispered, and the boy hurried off to summon the hotel owner.

Afterward Lucien stayed a month in the hospital in Nairobi. A year passed before he fully recovered.

And what do you die of in Africa?

You die of the things you die of everywhere: you die of microscopic germs; of accident and murder; of politics and poverty; of rooms in hotels and hospitals; of love and lack of love; of madness and silly obsessions; of the spirit that leaves you; of bad habits and time; but most of all you die of yourself and the private poison of loneliness.

That month he spent recovering in his hospital bed, he was mostly alone. Audrey was his only visitor. Both Chili and Coke were off on safaris or when they came to town failed to drop by. And he swore to himself that he'd see more people when he got out. He'd find his own circle of cronies, he decided. Maybe he'd check on some of the old timers, who were lonely enough themselves. But most of all he'd find a mate: somebody to hold his hand, so that he could somehow touch the center when the dizziness of things came on.

For years after Juba—and it was after all those camp romances, of course, and after what happened with that bitch and her professor down in Arusha—Lucien wanted a great love. It didn't seem too much to ask. He had some assets, after all: an uncombed if not exactly handsome look, a little money, and a good family on his mother's side. But it became a nagging irony that he didn't find the right woman. Dozens came and went—the librarian stayed for quite a length of time—but until Trey they all seemed to lose their faces and names.

He wanted children. He wanted to build a house. He wanted

to travel and to hold the hand of his companion when he faced the new geographies.

And just someone to share the tiny signals: she wears reading glasses, say, and she pushes them down on her nose and looks across the breakfast table at him and rattles her newspaper in a wordless morning hello. That sort of thing.

He sat in the hospital corridor, waiting for some word on Coke, thinking of it all, knowing that Trey had somehow been lost in the darkness of that bleak damned lake.

The waters, the deserts, Juba, the darkness: the great dreams of the lesser Cavenaugh.

Audrey came toward him and he got up to greet her.

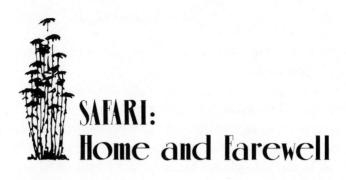

SAFARI:
Home and Farewell

"You have a devil of a bump on your head," his mother told him, tracing it with her thumb.

"Where?"

"Here. Half the size of your fist."

"Oh, I got a backhand swat from the leopard."

"Your father told me how you're twice the hero."

"Did he say that?"

"Not exactly, but he told me what you did."

"Tell me how he described it."

"Oh, not much elaboration. But he gave me a long description, of course, of how he made a particularly good shot, killing the leopard himself."

Smiling together about this, they strolled along the corridor. Chili had gone home for a quick shower and whiskey, and had told Audrey about everything before she started out. It would be one of those familiar family evenings at the hospital: everyone going here and there in shifts. Trey assisted the surgeon at the operating table, where the torn nerves in Coke's shoulder were the big concern.

Lucien told his mother about Buster getting killed and she said, yes, Chili even mentioned that.

"But about the operation," she said. "Chili says it's serious, but thinks surgery will do it."

"Chili's seen a lot of nasty wounds on safari and he never thinks *anything's* particularly serious, but this one is."

"How serious? Tell me anything you know."

"We'll just have to wait and see. The shoulder's badly torn up. Who knows how good the surgeon is? Look, when's Chili coming back?"

"He should be back soon. But now I'm here. Find yourself some supper. You look exhausted. And I want somebody to have a look at that bump on your head. Didn't your doctor notice it?"

"I might go home for a short rest," Lucien conceded. "And a lot happened at the lake. I want to talk to you later."

"What else went wrong?"

"Let's talk when the surgery's finished," he said.

He gave his mother a kiss, took the keys to her car, and started out of the hospital, but as he passed another corridor he saw Trey and a cluster of doctors. Clearly, the surgery was over, so he waited until their conversation was finished and she walked his way. She still wore the surgical gown and held the mask in her hand.

"How'd it go?" he asked.

"He's all right, but the arm is really pretty hopeless," she told him, and her voice broke slightly. "Now we just have to worry about infection."

Lucien took her hand in his.

"I'm getting out of the hospital for an hour or so," he said. "Take a break and come with me, all right?"

"No, I'll stay here," she managed, and she withdrew her hand from his. "And, Lucien, I'm sorry, I really am, so sorry." She covered her mouth, turned, and left him there, and he knew too well what she meant.

He went back and told Audrey the news. She sat down on a bench, but lifted her chin bravely.

"Maybe we should've flown him to London or New York," Lucien speculated. "There would've been better specialists. But the surgery had to be done quickly. We didn't really have the choice."

"I'll talk to other doctors," Audrey said. "Nothing's final. There also might be some sort of therapy."

There was nothing else to do, so he drove home. In the kitchen were the remnants of Chili's meal: half a small sausage, Worcestershire sauce everywhere, a bottle of whiskey half gone. In the shower, Lucien tried to clear his thoughts. This was probably the last big cat his father would ever shoot, he decided. Time lost and gone. *Zamani*.

The house was depressing, so he changed clothes and went back to the hospital. At the reception desk he learned the number of Coke's room and went directly there.

It was midnight now, the corridors silent. A faint odor of alcohol and cabbage.

He edged inside room 117, stood there, and let his eyes adjust to the darkness. The bed was in silhouette over by the window.

He heard a hoarse whisper.

Trey was lying beside Coke, a leg thrown over him. They spoke in low soft breaths with their faces pressed together.

He left quietly. The waiting room was empty and he strolled

through a maze of corridors until he found Audrey in an alcove. She was buying a cup of coffee from a palsied old vendor with his brass urn. The man looked as though he should be on the streets of Zanzibar instead of in these sterile surroundings as he filled the little metal cups with trembling hands.

"Seen your father?" she asked.

"No, he wasn't home."

She smirked, paid the vendor, and sipped the black coffee.

"I went by Coke's room and he's sleeping," he lied. "Maybe we should leave now and come back in the morning. There's nothing to do."

She agreed, finished the contents of the little cup, and took Lucien's arm as they walked toward a nearby exit.

"And where's your Dr. Trey Nichols?" she asked.

"With Coke."

"Ah, I see."

They drove home beneath the dark shade of the trees in the Muthiaga district, and his mother reached across the seat of the car and patted his knee.

"Poor Lucien," she said with a sigh.

In the middle of the night they made omelets and opened a bottle of wine. For Lucien, the kitchen and the whole house seemed sad: the cabinets white, the pots hanging neatly in a row, everything gleaming as if out of their hectic lives Audrey had brought about this polished order. Madness and muffins. The sad housewives: making the nests while the husbands bang and philander and bully their way along. Lucien ate his eggs, feeling awful for Audrey and for himself.

She told him he just cared too much.

He agreed.

"All those clients you took care of," she said. "The ones you tended—with beds and booze and comfort. They never liked you any better for what you did. They really just wanted to hunt with a team of idiot killers."

"Come on, let's not talk about me."

"Oh, we don't do too much of that. All your life you've been caring. But the pay's rotten. I know this as well: you hoped for a new start with your father up at the lake. But I'll bet it didn't work out."

"Who knows? Maybe we made some progress."

"I'll tell you what happened: you attacked a leopard with your knife and probably managed to get a tiny bit of Chili's grudging respect for it."

This struck Lucien as accurate and funny as he drank off his wine. They both laughed.

"I'm still hungry," he said. "Is there more?"

"I'll do more eggs and toast," she said, and went back to the stove. As she cooked for him, he told her about seeing the leopard alone: that strange moment among the boulders along the path. As he described it, she nodded thoughtfully. He told her how he was afraid, then how he got beyond fear.

She folded her hands as he ate more.

"There are rare moments when we sometimes put aside our physical needs and fears," she said. "Maybe we never find the proper language for such odd moments, but we usually refer to them as spiritual experiences."

This occurrence might fall into that category, he allowed, and she talked about how she occasionally had theological conversations with Dura, how they sometimes got embarrassed using certain words, but how we all have strange feelings and experiences and usually struggle to find ways to talk about them.

"Maybe the leopard was having a spiritual experience," Lucien mused, grinning.

"How do you mean?"

"Well, he was hungry and on the prowl. But he put aside his need. He just studied me and let me study him. It was quite a moment."

"Dura would probably attribute it all to reincarnation."

For a while they talked about Dura and Audrey's friendship: it was getting to be an old friendship now, several years old, and moving into that time when old friends sometimes think about the other's death.

"Dura's a great friend," Audrey agreed. Then she looked hard at Lucien and said, "But I hold back. It seems to me that a person has to hold back even in the great friendships."

"Or get hurt? Or make a fool of himself?"

"We have to keep our defenses up. You surely can't believe if you love hard enough that things will work out—anymore than you can believe that hard work alone will make you rich."

"Up at the lake," he said, taking a deep breath and letting it out again, "I knew I was an idiot. I knew because it hurt so damned bad."

"Your brother has a lot of charm."

"Hm, none I can detect."

"It's charm that says to a woman, there, I play rough and I don't owe you anything for what's happening here and you don't owe me anything, either."

"But I thought Trey and I had something a little better. How could she fall for that sort of thing?"

"You're old-fashioned. Think of all the recent movies we've seen together. No strings. Everybody walks away. Love is tough. You just haven't caught up."

"Maybe not," he said, opening a second bottle of wine. In his weariness he felt drunk already.

"I've just ached for you, Lucien, I really have. You've wanted to find somebody for a long time now—just as you've always wanted to do the right thing and take care of everybody around you. It's painful watching you."

"Funny," he said. "It's been painful for me watching you."

"Because of Chili?"

"Sure, what else?"

She measured herself another glass of wine. "I'm not cynical or indifferent to love, but if it's too serious it can break us. You can absolutely break your bones trying to win Chili's notice and affection—as you just did. But it won't work. Or you can break your heart over a woman like your doctor—who came to Africa, just as I told you once, to see the savages—not the storekeepers."

"That hurts."

"You can break yourself or you can hold back a bit. And I'll tell you the most amazing thing that can happen if you hold back, Lucien, although you might not believe me. You become more attractive, holding back. Others come to you. If you can manage to be just slightly aloof—even slightly—you might get a pinch of what you've been looking for."

"You've never said this to me before."

"No, never. I thought you might figure it out."

"I don't figure much out."

They walked to the porch to look at the stars.

Audrey, gazing at the sky, talked about Dura and her theory of reincarnation. But Lucien was only half listening. He was wondering if Coke would ever fly a plane again, if he would ever shoot again, and how he would adjust. Slightly tipsy and queasy, he heard his mother's philosophical voice and watched the African sky with its millions of unknown stars and its Southern Cross and its cold blackness: the *ngiza*, the great darkness, the rim of eternity.

"Ah, and look at this," Audrey called from the far end of the veranda. Lucien moved toward her and saw the sprawling form in the wicker lounge: Chili. He reeked of whiskey and a happy delirium of sleep.

"Dead or alive?" Lucien asked.

"He's totally potted. And just feel him. He's chilled to the bone out here. I'll go get a blanket."

The screen door slapped behind her as she went in to take a blanket kept especially for this purpose out of the hallway closet. She came back to the veranda, folded the blanket for extra warmth, and covered him. Lucien could only shake his head.

"In bad times," she said, "he's never worth a damn."

"I'm going to bed," Lucien told her.

"Yes, you do that. Sleep well."

She held his face and kissed him, keeping him for so long that he complained.

"Let go now," he said. "I'm drooping."

He went back to the kitchen, rattled through a cupboard, and found some bicarbonate of soda. After taking a dose, he decided to see if he should put away the dirty dishes and turn off the lights before going upstairs. He went back to the porch to ask Audrey.

She had curled onto the narrow wicker lounge beside Chili, covering herself with the edge of the blanket.

Without saying anything, he went through the house, clicking off the lights.

ZAMANI AND SAFARI: The Fourth of July

It was Chili's most successful celebration. Percy Spence and his Greek wife were in town, so the drinking that started in late June was now culminating in loud stories and louder laughter throughout the Cavenaugh house and around the pool. Dozens of tables with white tablecloths and flowers adorned the lawn. Waiters and bartenders had been brought over from the club to help. Among the three hundred guests there were perhaps fifty Americans, many of whom were new to the city, including a young banker and his beautiful wife who was as thin and cold as a model. The clerks from the store had prepared a fireworks display. Bubba served barbecued chickens, ribs, hot dogs, stew, beans, and slaw, and kegs of beer sat beneath the old ceiling fans on the veranda. Audrey had decorated the pool with floats bearing little candles and American flags. Dura was bringing a special friend. Coke was in the company of a new woman, a stewardess for British Airways. A few of the old regiment were close beside Chili, clapping him on the shoulder and urging him into nostalgia attacks. A good New Orleans jazz band wandered the premises, and Lucien had promised to join them at the piano later.

Months had passed since Lake Turkana. Coke carried his useless left arm in a handsome sling made of leather and brown linen. He still traveled around Kenya in his plane and had twice or three times flown up to the refugee camp to visit Trey, but that was finished.

" 'Lo, Lucien," he said when they met early that afternoon, and he introduced the stewardess, who had a professional smile. Coke was curious about how the party happened to be so big. Past affairs had often attracted fewer than a dozen celebrants—most of whom didn't know all the words to "The Star-Spangled Banner."

"By the way," he said, "I saw one of the original gypsies here. Can't recall her name. Not Cat, one of those other ones."

"I hope to hell you're mistaken," Lucien said, looking over the crowd on the lawn.

"Yeah, it's bad taste, I realize, but I'm pretty sure it was her," Coke said.

The piano, moved out on the veranda at the opposite end from the kegs, was surrounded by the jazz group now, and they were playing "Midnight in Moscow," one of Lucien's favorites. He paused to listen to the work of the trombonist, then scanned the crowd again. Audrey laughed with somebody.

Coke and the girl with the fixed smile edged away.

Everyone was inebriated with patriotism. This was one of Ronald Reagan's years, after all, and the movies showed rough American types winning victories for brawn and right all over the world, although in truth everyone agreed that much of the old prestige had worn away. That was part of the festive mood and reason enough for a large gathering: a false insistence. But there were other factors: Percy's homecoming, the absence of the usually dismal monsoon weather this time of year, the jazz band, and the presence of so many young women in bright clothes.

Odd, Chili's Americanism. He brought it out annually for show, but his old British Colonial regiment inspired much greater devotion. Or the open savannah. Or, for that matter, the Blue Hotel. We imagine ourselves, Lucien decided, in strange and wonderful tribes.

He drew a beer out of the keg and strolled down the length of the veranda, listening to the music.

A mysteriously good feeling this afternoon. The last weeks had gone well. He was enjoying the party for the first time in years. Trey had written him a short letter inviting him to come see her again, but he hadn't answered it. In April he had gone on a real holiday: Cairo, the pyramids, and one of those hotel boats that travel from Aswan to Luxor on the Nile. A lonely trip, but okay. He took a lot of photos he never bothered getting developed. After coming back, he went to movies with Audrey and Dura. He put in a small garden beyond the pool. He became a member of the board of directors of Ambrose School. He dated the daughter of an Australian businessman, but she smelled like Wrigley's gum and pumped rock 'n' roll into her head with a Walkman. This afternoon Dura was supposed to bring someone else for him to meet, another possibility in the gentle lineup his mother and her friend provided, but this one would be girlish, too, and would draw a blank look when he tried to explain why he went to Egypt to stare at those crumbling monuments.

When he stopped at the grill, Bubba sliced him a piece of chicken. Chili hailed him.

"C'mere! Hey, this is Percy's bride!"

They stood in a small circle talking about the Coptic religion. Then the band took a break, so the hum of conversation and laughter echoed around him. The Greek wife wore earrings of about two carats each and Percy, red-faced and overweight these days, nestled at her side like an oversized pet. She was saying over and over that hers was an intellectual Christianity.

Lucien looked across her shoulder and saw Dura with a familiar face. For a moment there was only surprise, then a greater surprise: they were here together, Dura and Kira.

He made his excuses to Percy when he could.

As he gently pushed his way into their presence, Dura said, "I believe you two know each other?"

Kira had changed, but not for the worse. Her beauty had aged some, yet softened, and her smile was more relaxed and warm. She reached out, grabbed him in a hug, kissed his cheek, and laughed.

"I must eat a hot dog," Dura said with resolution, going off toward Bubba at the grill. "Year after year I come to these occasions, and this year I will definitely do this American thing."

"Where in the world did you come from?" Lucien asked Kira.

She had taken his hand, moving them over by the jacaranda tree.

"I will tell you everything," she said, and her voice was the same: a nice English, tinted with a warmth right out of the Somali desert. She wore a fancy yellow dress, maybe something by Chanel for afternoon lawn parties. Black pearls at her slender throat. "But first I have the speech for you. And before the speech I want to ask if you remember when we saw each other last? All that cloth in my place? And we were going to have a cup of coffee? You probably don't remember."

Lucien smiled.

"So now I am giving you the speech: that one thousand pounds you gave me. This was the finest thing anyone had ever done for me. Generous. I never expected so much. And ever since no one gives me this generosity, not anyone."

"Kira, don't. I was glad to help."

"No, wait, I am saying this, all of it. Then you sold the cloth and sent more money. When this amount came I needed it very much. You can never know. I said to myself, there, I will be all right because of this honest man. You were not even my brother-in-law anymore. You owed me nothing."

"Coke's somewhere around," he said, looking away in embarrassment.

"I came back to see you, not your brother," she said, smiling. "But wait, please, there is more speech."

They were jostled by a group moving toward the pool. Chili was on the porch now in the company of the banker's pretty wife, and she touched his sleeve and laughed as they talked.

"I thought about you many times," Kira went on, and they had been pushed together now so that her breath—clove, perhaps, and the fragrance of strawberry lipstick—reached him. "I was in London, then Canada, then Houston, Texas. I worked in jobs. But I was never the whore, never once, and it was because of you. Not only because of the money, but because of the things you said. There was a man in my life for a time, but he had no kindness in him. Because of this—I don't know why—I compared him to you. For a long time now I have been alone, by myself with no one else, and for many months I began thinking of coming back here. I wrote a letter to Dura. And it was fortunate. She is a great friend of yours. She wrote back that you were unmarried and that I should come."

"You must have come to see your family," he suggested.

"No, this is to see you."

"I don't believe it," he said, flattered and uneasy with her straight gaze.

"But true. My father is dead for so long. Dura is a friend, but I didn't come to see her. I came for you. To finish that cup of coffee."

They were both laughing as Audrey appeared. She and Kira nodded and smiled, then something was said about Coke.

"I believe he left the party," Audrey said. "I think he has better plans for himself than all this." She tugged at Lucien's arm. "And you promised you'd play, so come on. The band's starting up again. Play some tunes they can join you in."

"Kira's back in town," he said dumbly.

"Yes, I see that. But please, some music. You two can finish everything later."

"Do it," Kira urged him. "Play the piano. I did not know this thing about you."

He went to the veranda, sat down at the piano, and went into a rendition of "New York, New York." The drummer picked up behind him and the trumpet player sent up a nice descant. Then he played more tunes about American cities: "I Left My Heart in San Francisco" and "Chicago" and "Way Down Yonder in New Orleans." On this last number the trombonist got going and sounded good.

A crowd gathered around the veranda, calling out names of other places. He did "Chattanooga Choo Choo"—missing a few notes and laughing. Everyone called for songs about other towns. He didn't know "San Antonio Rose," so glided back into "New York, New York" again.

Across the lawn Kira stood with Dura and Audrey, their faces happy and conspiratorial. She waved as he played on. The things she said to him, the look of her—he felt puzzled and excited and said to himself, all right, we'd be a real pair, none of this false Brit or false American thing. Our children would be a blend. And he watched her put those long fingers of hers to her mouth as she smiled: a gesture that he seemed to recall very clearly from a hundred years ago.

He tried the song "Wichita Lineman," but muffed it, and the band members helped out by leading him into "St. Louis Blues." They began to do so well that he slipped off the piano bench, leaving them to their enthusiasms. As the crowd gave him its applause, Chili waved and went on dancing with Percy Spence's wife.

Lucien moved slowly back toward the women. So they've conspired and arranged it all, he said to himself, but so what? As he moved through the crowd toward Kira he felt that he was making a great journey, another long safari down the whole length of the world, but he kept going.

WILLIAM HARRISON *is founder and director of the Creative Writing Program at the University of Arkansas. Since 1976 he has traveled extensively in Africa, the setting of four of his novels. He was a Guggenheim Fellow in Fiction in 1971. He lives in Fayetteville, Arkansas.*